D1523838

Master Me Softly

Club Subspace
Book 1

Encanta

Alexis Rey

Chapter One

It was inevitable, considering my emotional state. Driving wasn't a good idea, and I knew I wouldn't make it through the yellow light. Yet, caught in an odd stupor from the emotional overload, I gunned the engine, only to slam on the brakes at the last moment, resulting in a not-so-gentle rear-end collision.

"Shhiiit..." I blurted.

Almost instantly, a knock sounded on the driver's side window, and an assertive voice sounded as though from a distance.

"Hey! Are you alright in there?" The car door swung open, introducing a rush of cold air and damp autumn. "Miss, answer me. Are you hurt?"

"I'm... okay," I said slowly, as if testing it out.

This was my first ever accident, and apparently, it left me in a state of mild shock. I tended to panic in tricky traffic situations, and thus, tried not to create any. Plus, I hadn't been prepared for surprises, especially of this type. Tonight was meant for a pleasant girls' night, not unexpected adventures.

1

The night before, one of my friends had sent out a distress call to her fellow lonely hearts. The plan was simple: get dressed up, go out, and lend each other emotional support.

The outing turned out to be a blast. We got together at Don't Call Us, the one on Novokuznetsky, the trendiest bar we could think of, dressed up to the nines, hair and make-up done to perfection, and spent all night sharing war stories and talking about guys. We had a no-sad-stories agreement to keep the vibe positive, and it became a night of genuine female bonding.

But by the time I got in my car—by myself—to go home —by myself— I had this nasty niggling feeling gnawing its way right to my heart.

How did it happen that this was the first time in a whole year that I'd made the effort to dress up and go out? Suddenly restless, I simmered with frustration at my own negligence. How had I allowed myself to slip into such a stagnant routine, oblivious to the passing of time, trapped by my own apathy? The result? I was rocking this flirty skirt, and no one was around to appreciate it.

The situation was dire and needed to be fixed. Without delay. Immediately. Right this second. The restlessness was killing me.

Except even if all I wanted was to find a warm body for the night, it would take time and effort—and it was late, there was no one out, and I was on my way home anyway.

Cue the jitters, and voila! A collision. *Great.*

I unbuckled my seatbelt and got out to face the unfortunate soul who'd hit my car.

On the other hand, maybe the soul wasn't all that unfortunate—he smelled pretty good and didn't look terrible, either. Tall, well-built, wearing dark pants and a leather jacket, around my age—early thirties. Also, I liked his calm demeanor, especially considering the circumstances, and the kind, attentive look in his intelligent brown eyes.

Maybe, that warm body for the night had just found me.

I could use a warm body—I was shivering pretty violently. My legs, exposed to the cold in my stupid little skirt, were covered in goosebumps, plus the extra stress was positively giving me the shakes.

"Sure you're okay?" The man asked doubtfully, lowering his voice slightly.

"I'm fine."

"Alright..."

Glancing behind me, I had to chuckle — we stood right at an intersection with Warsaw Highway, busy main road, but our side street was deserted. It was around midnight, and we were alone. What an unfortunate confluence of events—he was tailgating me in the right lane while the left was wide open, just as I decided, at the last moment, to be good and not run a red light.

"Looks like this was meant to be," he remarked, following my gaze. "It's completely my fault, I'm very sorry."

What was the point of harboring a grudge after such a heartfelt apology?

"Accidents happen."

I circled my car, and my breath caught for an instant when I saw his. So pretty—a black, shiny BMW. I don't know cars, but clearly, it was several stations above my little Ford.

"Nice car," I said out loud.

"It's new." His voice carried a hint of regret.

Seized by a sudden burst of magnanimity, I admitted, "I'm at fault too. I braked too fast. Spaced out."

"Accidents do happen."

We both regarded my poor little car. At least, the damage didn't seem too severe: slight dents in our bumpers, his front and my back.

"Listen," he said hopefully. "Let's skip calling the police. I'll cover the repair, and we can go?"

After a moment's hesitation, I said, "I guess."

"I'll just need some kind of promissory note that we did this, and I'll pay you...ten thousand rubles?" he suggested, after a glance at my bumper.

I glanced at it too. By my calculations, a repair like this could be done cheaper, but then again, what did I know? There could be hidden damage. I was no good at this kind of thing, and it would be so easy to pull one over on me. On the other hand, standing here in the middle of the street and waiting for the police didn't sound fun at all, not even in the company of a cute guy.

"I have pen and paper in my car. Wanna come with me?" he suggested, suddenly changing his tone to something noticeably more casual. He probably got a good look at my face, clocked the flirty little skirt—this outfit made me look like a college girl. No one would guess I was thirty. Barely twenty five.

"How old are you?" he asked, reading my mind, as I slid into the passenger side of his car.

The seat was spacious, outfitted in soft leather–very luxe. I looked around as I opened my mouth to answer him, and my eyes fell on—

"Holy shit!"

On the dashboard lay a huge, coiled, black serpent.

No, wait. Why would he have a serpent in his car? That's

4

insane. And why would a "serpent" have several tails made of leather?

No, what I was looking at was...

A whip?

Yes! An enormous black leather whip. And on its imposing handle, stenciled in red, were the telling insignia: "Club Subspace."

Chapter Two

The sudden tickle of excitement made my breathing jagged. A whip in a car wasn't something you saw every day.

"What is that?" I exhaled, pointing.

"Uh..." the whip's owner mumbled something indistinctly, as my eyes darted back and forth from the instrument to his face.

I realized he was looking me over, as if trying to decide whether I had reached the age of consent, or whatever age he figured was appropriate to be feasting my eyes upon apparent BDSM equipment. Then, he must have remembered that I was out late at night and drove a car, which meant, yes, I had reached that age, and relaxed slightly.

Meanwhile, I couldn't stop looking at the massive, vaguely threatening hunk of braided black leather.

"Paper. Pen." His demanding voice sounded right in my ear, jostling me to attention, as he proffered the named objects.

I accepted the pen but ignored the paper, and voiced

the obvious, unable to keep the thrill out of my voice. "Are you like a… Dominant?"

He let out a small growl of annoyance before looking at me, clearly about to tell me to mind my own business. My curiosity and wonder must have been genuine, however, because his face, brightly illuminated by the cabin lights, suddenly softened into a patronizing expression, as if he were speaking to a child.

"Listen, sweetheart," he said.

I cocked a sardonic eyebrow at *sweetheart*, but he kept talking, unbothered.

"Whatever you're thinking, stop. This is not Fifty Shades. I'm not a billionaire and I don't have a jet. It's really not that interesting, trust me. Now, would you please sign?"

"Hm… And if I don't?" I asked slowly, smiling and deliberately infusing my voice with a flirtatious note.

He was impervious. "Then, we gotta call the cops, and we'll have to hang out here for at least an hour, then we'll be filling out papers for at least another hour, and then you'll spend two weeks on the phone making a claim with the insurance company, trying to get an estimate, another two trying to find someone to do your repair, and pay a deductible anyway. Now. Is that really what you want?"

By the end of the tirade, his tone became almost tender, and it made me want to giggle like a girl. Definitely a Dom. And most likely, an experienced one, and one who was getting annoyed with me, if his manner was anything to go by.

A man of passionate nature—my favorite kind.

The longer I gazed at his calm, confident face, the less I wanted to go home and the more curious I became about that bullwhip. Though, of course, not at the expense of my own skin.

"You're going to that club, right? Club Subspace?" I asked. "I've heard of it."

"Great, I'm so glad," he deadpanned.

"What if you take me with you, and in return, you don't have to give me any money?"

"Here we go," he lilted, rolling his eyes. Then he sighed and fixed me with another condescending look. "Sunshine, that is not possible. It's not the movies, and you don't look like you belong in BDSM."

"And what does that look like?" I insisted, looking at his skeptically pursed lips, which, incidentally, I found increasingly appealing. They were beautifully shaped, expressive, visually enticing.

"I don't know. Not you."

"Rude! And anyway, I don't care about the jets, and I think I want to try BDSM."

His tone dripped acid. "Having an epiphany, are you?"

"No! I've been thinking about it for a while!"

"So, when you stop thinking about it and make up your mind to do it, come on down, say hello, and apply for a membership. If I take you with me now, then you end up being my responsibility all night, and I honestly cannot be bothered."

"I promise I'll behave."

I batted my eyelashes like a school-girl, and he scoffed, rolling his eyes again.

"No, absolutely not."

"Fine," I said with a challenge in my voice, and folded my arms across my chest. "If you're that sure that you know everything, call the cops. We all know how helpful they are."

I knew I sounded petulant, but something had come over me at that moment. Suddenly, I was brave and reckless.

I was going to that club with him, and nothing could stop me—not even the sudden shift in his demeanor from a pleasant gentleman to a man who seemed capable of bending me over and giving me a thorough spanking right then and there.

In fact, it was possible I was aiming to provoke him to do just that.

After a minute-long, unsuccessful attempt to incinerate me with his eyes, he repeated his question. "How old are you again?"

"Thirty one—owww!" a sudden sharp pain in my scalp made me cry out.

He had seized a fistful of my hair and tilted my head back to examine my face under the light. "Bullshit."

I grabbed on to his wrist to get him literally out of my hair, but he had me in an iron grip, his gaze direct and icy.

He said, "I thought you said you wanted to play."

"Yeah, but..."

"Yeah but nothing."

Now I was confused. I did just demand to tag along to a kink club, but on the other hand, he no longer looked nearly as patient and friendly as he did five minutes ago, and his hand in my hair was hurting me. Did that mean he was right? BDSM wasn't my thing, and I shouldn't bother trying?

Well, I disagreed. "I—"

"Shut your mouth."

Stunned, I complied.

Meanwhile, as if it was the most normal thing in the world, he continued to scrutinize my face.

By now, my make-up probably didn't look so good... The thought made me fidget. I was betting I'd eaten all the lipstick, and my mascara had smudged all over my face, not to mention the dumb expression I must have been wearing, plus the unattractive grimace of pain, because his hand was still gripping my hair... Not the best first impression, to say the least.

I didn't know how to react to being grabbed by the hair and told to shut my mouth, but he'd apparently made a decision. He let go of me and proceeded to announce, "Fine. You can come with me as my bottom. I'll teach you some things, show you around the club, and we can try a session. But low threshold of sending you home, got it?"

"Uh..." Still a little stunned and a lot incredulous that my ploy had actually worked, I couldn't quite grasp what he was saying.

"I asked if you got it?" he repeated louder, and something inside me lurched with a very genuine fear.

"Yes," I answered quickly.

"Do you live far?"

"Not far." I gave him the address.

"Fantastic. We'll drop off your car and I'll drive to the club. You can follow me."

As I started my engine, I was still half-convinced that he'd just drive off and leave me. But the BMW pulled away from the curb, and slowly crossed the intersection with the next green light, inviting me to follow.

And I did.

Chapter Three

Wow. My new friend had undergone a transformation.

Slipping back into his car after leaving mine behind, I was met with a whole different vibe. He had ditched his jacket, revealing the definition of his muscular arms beneath that black T-shirt. Even without the interior light, I could still make out his face, too, now wearing a serious and almost severe expression. Gone was the warm, friendly, occasionally condescending stranger. Before me sat an intense, stern man.

"Take your coat off," he ordered.

I paused for a beat, but obeyed, swiftly untying the belt and undoing the buttons.

After examining what he could see of my body under my thin top and short skirt, he traced the neckline of my blouse with his fingertips and popped those buttons, too.

"Stockings?" he inquired, sliding a palm over my knee.

"Pantyhose," I mumbled, feeling ridiculous.

"Off."

I flushed all the way to the tips of my ears, my breath hitching. "Right here?"

"Right here. Right now. And right quick." Growing impatient, he directed his intense gaze onto my face, showing no inclination to turn around and afford me any privacy.

"Okay," I whispered, kicked off my shoes, and squirmed in my seat, maneuvering to remove the pantyhose without lifting my skirt.

The bastard waited until I was finished, and only then, flashed me a sadistic grin and said, "And now, your panties."

"But..."

"Panties. Right now."

The hard look in his eyes made it abundantly clear he wasn't joking.

His voice and his eyes... Something warm and wet spilled over my lower belly and the proverbial shiver ran down my spine. I couldn't believe how swiftly my body was responding to this stranger.

The panties were coming off.

When I was done, I stuffed my pantyhose and black lace underwear in my purse and looked up at him expectantly.

"Eyes!"

Jumping in surprise, I hastily dropped my gaze.

"What, I can't look at you?" I asked my lap.

"Like that? Definitely not," he said.

We sat in silence for a few moments, then, unexpectedly, he leaned forward.

All of a sudden, he was just inches away from me, and I could feel his body heat, my nostrils flaring as I drew in his scent. Instinctively, my knees knocked together, and everything inside me squeezed in anticipation. I had no idea what he was about to do.

As it happened, he was just reaching over to shut the car door—no big deal—though, I was almost sure he knew exactly what sort of embarrassing frisson he'd just caused.

Only when he settled back in his seat, turning slightly in my direction, was I finally able to release a breath.

"The rules are pretty simple," he began casually. "I say it and you do it. I don't repeat myself. You get one warning, and the next time, you're getting a consequence. Do you understand?"

Despite the rather stern words, he sounded mild and almost friendly—and it made me want to do just as he said. "Yes."

"The safe words are yellow, and red," he went on. "If you say yellow, it means you're approaching your limit, as far as pain or emotional distress. I will pause, and we'll address the issue. If you say red, everything stops and you go home."

"Got it."

"At the club, stay quiet and mind your manners. By protocol, you must be respectful toward all the Dominants, but no one should touch you unless you agree. Tonight, no one will bother you. You'll be with me."

"Okay."

"Now, let's talk about your limits for tonight. Since you're a total newbie, I'm not planning any hard play, but I should have some idea of your interests." He let a beat pass, then added, "You may look at me now."

I raised my eyes, working to make my gaze as docile as possible, but he still shook his head. "If you're a sub, I'm a fucking ballerina."

A sudden movement caught me off guard, making me

flinch in fear—I saw him raise his hand and, for some reason, braced for a possible slap. Instead, he gently brushed a warm palm against my cheek. Apparently, pleased, he said, "There you go. That was a nice submissive face. Frightened or pleading, and always deferential."

"Okay."

"Okay?" he teased, looking into my eyes. "It's 'Yes, Sir.'"

"Yes, Sir," I repeated obediently.

"Very nice. Now, how do you feel about spanking?"

"Yes." I barely whispered my agreement, licking my suddenly chapped lips. An accidental glimpse of the whip made my belly clench.

"No-no," he smirked. "I think my hand and maybe a paddle will be plenty for tonight. Probably enough to make you scream, actually."

The visual he just painted gave me a heady, dizzy feeling, and even my surroundings felt like they were shifting. The darkness inside the car's cabin thickened and intensified. His scent was pervasive and intoxicating; it surrounded me, tangy and fresh, with a bitter note. I breathed it like air. When he spoke, his velvety voice, laced with irrepressible seduction, vibrated through my body.

Struggling to take a full breath, I squeezed my legs together. The arousal was so strong I felt like I was about to soak right through my skirt.

"This getting you wet?" he asked suddenly, reading my thoughts again, and I glanced up, amazed.

How is he doing that?

"It's obvious, malysh," he answered my unspoken question, with a faintly condescending smile. "Anyway. That's a good start. How do you feel about public play?"

"Doing a scene in public?" I clarified, my eyes opening wide.

"*There's* that submissive face." He patted me on the cheek again, as if he was rewarding a good puppy for fetching the frisbee, and I lowered my eyes to hide my embarrassment. "So, you'd prefer to play in private."

"I think so," I squeezed out. "I don't know."

"How about bondage? Getting tied up or strapped down? A lot of people are scared to do that in private."

"I... don't know."

"All right. We'll figure it out. Buckle up."

As we drove, I covertly checked him out, taking in his muscular arms, the way he handled the car—mostly smooth, except for the occasional careless rush that might explain have explained our earlier collision. Looking at his face was awkward now—I wasn't eager for another reprimand—but I managed a few sneaky sideways glances. He had well-defined cheekbones, though overall his face was rather broad. Distinctive dark eyes glinted from beneath thick eyebrows, complemented by full lips and a firm mouth line.

Yes, this guy was definitely my type.

I wondered what he thought of my appearance. Were my clothes appropriate for this club? We'd already discovered that pantyhose were a definite no-go. What about the rest of my outfit?

He turned off Varshavka into the backstreets, and then into a courtyard of what looked like a residential building. It was a typical square Moscow courtyard, cluttered with cars in a way that made it a navigational nightmare. I usually avoided such places at all costs, since I would be the most likely to cause damage while trying to get into a parking spot. However, my new friend maneuvered confidently, boldly pulling up to the entrance.

He stepped out of the car, and pulled aside a metallic chain stretched between two posts that apparently guarded his own personal parking space, before backing into it and shutting off the engine.

I looked at him in surprise.

He said, "We're here. You can get out of the car."

Already? I had no idea there were any clubs in my neighborhood.

Stupidly, as I got out, I left my coat inside. Even though I rushed back to grab it and bundle up as fast as I could, the chill penetrated me to the bone, and my body was suddenly wracked with violent shivers.

"Hey," the stranger called out, coming around the car. "Come here."

I took a step in his direction and suddenly found myself enclosed in an unexpectedly warm and calming embrace. As he rocked us side to side, the shivers slowly abated.

"If you've changed your mind, it's no big deal," he said into the crown of my head. "Just say so."

"I haven't," I muttered somewhere in the vicinity of his T-shirt-clad chest.

"Sure?" This time, he held my face in his hands and peered into my eyes.

"Yes."

I caught a hint of a smile before he admonished, "'Yes, Sir.' That is your warning, sub."

"Yes, Sir," I rushed to correct myself. My mouth went dry again under his gaze, and a sweet, pulling sensation tugged at my stomach.

"Come on."

He took me by the hand, and we briskly crossed the courtyard. I followed him down a few steps into some sort of cellar. The unmarked door opened after one ring, and we found ourselves in a dimly-lit ante-chamber of sorts. Inside, languished two imposing guards, their stature and size reminiscent of body-building champions, plucked straight from the winner's circle.

"Good evening, master," they chimed, practically in unison, and suddenly, I shuddered with unease— I'd landed myself in a weird, other-dimension bizarro-world.

While I found myself in the throes of discomfort, looking at the two almost identical guards and wondering if they were actually identical or if it was an optical illusion, my companion was perfectly at ease. Casually, without looking, he handed his jacket off to one of the guards, then turned his attention to me. He tugged at my belt, easily undoing the loose knot, throwing my coat open, and eyed me up and down critically.

"Mish... why don't you bring the lady a dress?" he said, barely turning his head, and one of the hulking young men immediately vanished.

That answered my earlier question about the propriety of my attire, and the knowledge did nothing for my growing unease. Ironically, I looked to my stranger for comfort and with a start, realized I still didn't know his name. He didn't know mine either, and had not asked.

"What's your name?" I asked softly.

He shook his head, peering at me from above.

"What is your name... Sir?" I corrected, unable to suppress a smile.

"Max. And that's just for reference. You're not allowed to call me by my name, only Sir or master. Your name?"

"Liza," I replied, following the hulk Misha with my eyes as he returned carrying what looked like a diminutive red handkerchief.

"Well, Liza, go ahead and put this dress on," ordered my freshly-baked master, handing me the swath of red silk. "The changing room is over there."

"That's a dress?" I asked, astonished, shaking it out. It looked like something a little girl would wear, size-wise. Once I got a better look, however, I realized there was nothing little-girl about this "dress" at all.

"Sub, if you don't go to the locker room right this second, you'll be changing right here."

"All right, all right. Can't even ask a single question," I grumbled, hoping to hide my growing apprehension and embarrassment behind a facade of feigned insolence, and hurried to obey the command.

The dressing room turned out to be quite spacious with lockers and mirrors lining the walls. I found an open spot and began to remove my clothes. The club-issued dress was made of a lightweight, stretchy fabric and hugged my curves like a glove. It was immediately clear that a bra would be impossible. The neckline was so low that I was seriously worried—one wrong move, and I'd be giving the whole club a peepshow.

The good news was, I looked pretty shapely in that dress, if I said so myself. Also, my hairstyle had held up through all the adventures, and my make up hadn't smudged all that much. All I needed was to touch up my lipstick before stashing my bag in the locker.

The bad news: the damn dress barely covered my ass, and that was disconcerting. I couldn't bend over or sit down without flashing everyone my entire business. Thankfully, I'd just gotten a thorough bikini wax—but there was still a little bit of hair left, and that was one hairstyle I wasn't about to show off.

Max had mandated off with the panties, but given current circumstances, could I put my underwear back on or not?

Glancing in the mirror one more time, I decided I was

incapable of showing myself in this excuse of a dress without at least some coverage, and decisively reached into my purse. What was the worst that could happen? My panties were cute—black and lacy—and in principle, went well with the dress; maybe they could be part of the allure. Once they were back on, I felt somewhat calmer.

My shoes, though! Those didn't go with the dress at all. But as soon as I had the thought, the solution presented itself: a message in tiny letters, written right on the mirror in front of me.

Incurred fines:

-Exiting the dressing room in proper footwear (heels, stilettos) - five spanks from security.

-Exiting the dressing room in improper footwear - ten spanks, and house rules any additional punishment.

-Exiting the dressing room wearing panties - five spanks from security.

-Exiting the dressing room wearing other underwear - present body to security for 5 minutes without restrictions or 5 minutes oral sex.

Swallowing nervously, I shifted my gaze to my own reflection. I looked genuinely terrified. So, that's the worst that could happen--my underwear might cost me a spanking, right at the start, right here, and from one of those hulking brutes waiting outside. Did I really want this kind of entertainment before even getting into the actual club? Was the underwear worth it?

On the other hand, the idea of strutting in half-naked was even less appealing.

I stood paralyzed in front of the mirror, fighting a shamefully fierce urge to run. Was there a window in this dressing room? Because sure, my new friend was attractive and charming, but if there was a way to bolt, I would—

"How long do you plan to make me wait, exactly?"

I jumped. The familiar calm voice jolted me, and I spun around to face Max. It seemed while I was thinking about busting a hole in the wall in hopes of an escape, he had silently slipped into the dressing room and now stood in the doorway, arms crossed, watching. I had no idea how long he'd been there, but long enough for his brow to be furrowed in displeasure. His stern gaze swept over my body before softening, as it met my likely terrified eyes. I even thought I detected a hint of mirth in his tone when he said, "You can leave your underwear on this one time, if you're so shy. Let's go."

"Thank you," I said, quietly, exiting the dressing room barefoot, as per regulations.

It was amazing how glad it made me to keep my underwear on and not get a spanking. Really, people need so little for complete happiness —just let them have their underwear when it counts, and everything else will be okay...

I snapped to attention when Max looked over his shoulder at me as I followed him towards the entrance. Stopping short, I almost rear-ended him this time. I opened my mouth to make that joke, but changed my mind when I saw his serious, appraising look.

"Ready?" he asked.

I forced a smile. "I'm ready. Lead the way."

He smirked, and pushed the doors open.

This was really happening.

Here went nothing.

Chapter Four

The doors opened, and a blast of loud noise, lights, and hot air assaulted my senses. I paused, a bit stunned, but Max pulled my hand, and together, we crossed the threshold.

Inside, the club was warm, bordering on stifling, and fairly busy. As I glanced around, I immediately caught several half-naked men in leather pants unabashedly checking me out. Their stares felt nearly invasive, and I clung to Max for protection, ready to climb him like a tree.

"Easy," he said, taking my hand. "No need to be afraid. You're with me." He patted my hair, and led me through the crowded hall toward the bar.

The crowd wasn't exactly elbow-to-elbow, but people clustered around posts, crosses, and other play furniture. There were about a dozen of these play stations in the expansive hall, and almost all were in use. It felt like watching multiple parallel performances, each with a handful of spectators—semi-nude individuals, adorned and decorated in such sensual garb that my red dress seemed positively prudish. Some women, for example, sported dresses with the neckline cut underneath their breasts to expose them, while others draped sheer shawls over their entirely bare bodies.

"Have a seat," Max whispered, signaling the bartender. "Dima, mix up something light and whiskey-based for my little sub here."

"But I don't really drink!" I blurted, snapping back to reality out of the shock induced by observing the locals. Oddly enough, however, I had begun to calm down, no longer feeling quite so exposed.

Who would have thought that wearing nothing more than underwear and a handkerchief dress while surrounded by a crowd of naked people could strangely evoke a sense of armored confidence?

"Tonight you do," Max insisted, locking eyes with me. "You'll need it. Trust me."

My cheeks flushed, and I lowered my gaze.

It took some time for my ears to get used to the cacophony of sounds in the space—the indelible mix of loud trance music, the swish of whips, slaps of leather against skin, and loud moans. The stuffy atmosphere of the room and my own embarrassment made me blush, and I didn't know what to do with my body or where to look.

"Master and Sir are the same thing?" I asked, trying to mask my shyness with a little light—as it seemed to me then—conversation.

"No, *malysh*," Max replied, condescendingly. He sat on the neighboring barstool, much closer than I'd consider within the limits of propriety, although he wasn't touching me yet. "Sir is any Dom who wants to be called that. But to be master at this club, you have to pass an exam."

"Are there master-submissives?"

"Yes. We call them sweet darlings. Or just sweetlings, for short."

"Is that who you usually play with?"

"For the most part, yeah."

A cheerful, light-haired bartender with an athlete's body placed a glass in front of me, leaning slightly over the bar.

"Hey there, little one. What's your name?"

"Liza," I whispered, embarrassed by the way he was looking directly at my breasts, barely covered by my hanker-dress.

"Her breasts are so nice. Can I get a feel, Max?"

Max must have seen the look of abject horror on my face. "She's a newbie, quit trying to scare her," he snapped, and put his arm around my shoulders. "Don't panic, subby. You're with me. Breathe."

"Max, you brought a newbie?" the bartender smirked, deftly wielding a cocktail shaker. "Did hell freeze over?"

"Stranger things have happened," my companion replied vaguely and shrugged. His warm fingers suddenly touched my chin. "Ready to play a little?"

"Yes," I answered, sounding so terrified I didn't believe my own words. Now that I was here, in this crowded space, being watched by dozens of people, I wasn't at all sure I could get any enjoyment out of a sexual game.

"We'll start slow," Max suggested, unable to hold back a sardonic smile. "We won't move from these seats. I command, you obey."

"Yes, Sir."

"Good girl. Take that glass and start drinking. Then, look around the club and tell me the first thing that comes to mind. Sip, look, speak, sip, speak... you're not allowed to be silent unless you're drinking. Got it?"

"Yes, Sir," I said, reaching for my drink.

Then the meaning of this game hit me—he wanted me to discuss what was going on at the club so he knew what to do with me, obviously. Oh, my god. Oh, no. I couldn't barely bring myself to look at anyone, let alone speak of it. It honestly would have been much easier for me to get on my knees and just... service him.

I sipped slowly and didn't lower my glass until it was almost half-empty.

There was so much going on. Right next to us was a man chained to a post. His partner—a Domme—was whipping him, rather mercilessly, by the looks of it. The poor guy was trembling and whimpering, his body covered with a sheen of sweat. However, the region of his genitals, encased in soft trousers, displayed very obvious evidence of arousal.

"I find that extremely hard to watch," I admitted and looked away.

The next scene, on the other hand, made me swallow and squirm in my seat. A very pretty young woman, her hands bound, knelt before a burly guy, sucking his cock, while another man stood behind her and periodically urged her on by smacking her ass and back with a riding crop.

Gripping my glass, I rushed to bring it to my lips and drink, deliberately trying to avoid looking at the girl. But Max, who'd been observing my face the entire time, had no intention of letting me conceal my reaction.

"How do you like that second scene?" he asked, diligently studying my traitorous, hardened nipples.

"It's... arousing," I admitted, flushing furiously.

"Good. I think so, too." His voice was barely audible. "Next."

Next was even worse. A woman lay on a gynecological chair, her legs spread wide and feet strapped to the stirrups, and a man in a medical mask was giving her an internal "exam."

"Not for me," I said, convinced it was the truth, but Max shook his head, refusing to accept my answer.

"Look again."

Furrowing my brow, I looked at the couple once more. The way she was positioned made a thrill rise up inside me, and one glance at her face was enough to see that she was in the throes of ecstasy. Her enjoyment was something I almost envied. What scared me, though, was how he had his entire hand inside her; it was almost nauseating.

"Maybe, if he was doing something else..."

"Like what?"

"I–I don't know."

"Liar. You can't lie to your Dom. Try again."

"I can't," I said in a pleading voice, and my eyes welled with tears. I wanted to comply, I really did, but simply didn't have the words. Or maybe the courage.

A faint smile touched Max's lips. "All right. You don't have to."

Before I could sigh with relief, though, he added, "But then, you have a choice. You can either give it some thought and share what this scene made you think of, or you can take a punishment."

"What kind of punishment?"

He grinned. "I guess you'll have to find out."

I closed my eyes. This wasn't a choice. This was a trick. Coherent thoughts about fantasies I didn't know I had wouldn't form, yet a punishment sounded terrifying. At the same time, there was no denying the heat he transmitted through his fingers as his hand gently stroked my shoulder, nor the barely containable tremors of excitement. The light touch wasn't enough; the temptation was becoming unbearable.

"Okay, punish me."

"Punish me, *Sir*. This is your absolute last warning."

"Yes, Sir."

"Good girl. Now, stand up and bend over."

My jaw dropped. "What, right here?"

"Yes, darling, right here."

"You wanna spank me?"

My entire body stiffened. I always imagined I would enjoy spanking—in theory. In practice, I never supposed it would happen in a public place, and worse, right by the crowded bar.

"Maybe you'd like to rephrase your question, sub?"

"Yes! I would. Umm... You would like to spank me... Sir?"

"Just a little, just to remind you to be more agreeable next time. Bend over, sweetheart. If you stall any longer, five will have to become seven."

Gritting my teeth, I turned to the bar and froze in confusion, not grasping exactly what position he wanted me in, but Max was already on his feet behind me, pressing down on my shoulders and turning me toward my barstool.

"Like this, angel, belly right on the chair," he instructed casually, as if he were posing me for a photo or explaining an exercise at the gym. "You can hold on here and here, and it's better if you widen your stance a bit, like this." The toe of his boot carefully nudged my bare foot. "See that? You did it. It's really not that complicated. Good job."

The front of my dress had slipped all the way down to my waist, and the back rode all the way up. My only saving grace was the underwear I put on at the last second.

For a moment, I was overcome by the strongest sense of

what I could only describe as un-reality; like I was existing in a dream. But then, Max's palm collided with my buttock in a resounding slap, and I cried out, tightening every muscle in my body, shrinking into myself.

That had been much harder than what I'd expected—and it shocked me.

And I had four more?

There was no way I could have actually heard the sound of the spanks over the din of voices and music in the club, but it felt like I did. The strikes were so painful they made my ears ring. On the third one, tears sprang from my eyes.

I screamed louder when we got to spank number five, but Max was already helping me up gently, enclosing me in his arms as he fixed the hem of my dress.

"Okay, okay," he crooned. "You're done, you did it. It wasn't that bad, was it? It's over. Shhh."

The short punishment instantaneously turned me into a child. I let out a loud sob, wiping my nose on his T-shirt, allowing him to pat my hair and console me.

And that was when a very clear thought flashed in my mind: there was something very wrong with all of this. There was something very wrong with me.

Because the thing was, I wanted him.

I was standing here, embracing the man who just hurt and humiliated me and made me bawl, and I fucking wanted him, desired him so much that it hurt me physically, more than the punishment itself.

Was this something I could tell him? What would he think of me?

Answering my thoughts yet again, Max slid his palm down my stomach to lift up the hem of my dress. "You wet?"

29

His tone was at once conspiratorial and comforting, his low, husky voice betraying his own arousal.

I felt relieved.

Yes, I was excited, but so was he. Therefore, this was normal. It was allowed. And anyway, nothing was up to me, was it? All I had to do was let him take the reins and enjoy myself. Wasn't that why I came here?

My breathing became uneven when Max peered into my eyes, slipping his hand between my thighs. His face was unreadable, but I heard his sharp intake of breath when he found me drenched, just as he predicted. He liked this. His stoic expression of delight heightened mine, like a reward. My surroundings became hazy. I felt weak. All I could do, as he slowly inserted two fingers deep into me, was stare back and hope that was okay.

"I want to take you upstairs. Right now," Max murmured. "Think you're ready?"

The intense pressure of his fingers on the already sensitized bundle of nerves inside drove me to rise up on my tiptoes, off balance. With a jagged sigh, I dug my nails into his muscled shoulders, unsure whether I was trying to draw him closer or push him away.

What could I possibly say? My thoughts were a complete jumble, and my mind wasn't at all sure I was ready for "upstairs." But my body was very clear on what it wanted, and escalating the game down here, with people watching, seemed even less attractive.

I replied, "Yes, Sir."

Chapter Five

He withdrew his hand from between my legs, draped his arm around my shoulders, and led me deeper into the club. My bare feet padded against warm tiles, then sank into the soft texture of a rug as we entered a more private area. The lighting here was dimmer, the scenes more intense, yet somehow quieter.

I turned away quickly from a couple silently playing with fire, grateful Max hadn't demanded I watch or comment this time.

We didn't stop until we reached a set of stairs, where riveting scene froze me in place. A small, slim submissive was strapped face-down, spread-eagle on a spanking bench, while a large man thrust into her from behind—somewhere I wasn't accustomed to thinking of as an entrance. My eyes darted to her face. Tears streamed down her cheeks, a gag muffling her sounds.

My insides turned to ice. I looked up at Max in a panic, momentarily forgetting all the rules. "Max... I don't think she likes that."

"She does," he replied calmly, running his hand through my hair. "You're the one who doesn't like it."

"She's gagged," I protested. "She can't say anything. She can't say her safe word! That gag—"

"She also has a bell in her hand. If she wants to make him stop, she can."

"A... a bell?"

"Turn around—no sudden moves—and look at her right hand. It's free and she can drop that bell at any moment. It serves as a stop-signal."

Breathing hard, I turned back. Sure enough, the girl clutched a small metallic bell in her fist.

"What if he doesn't hear it?" I asked, my voice still hoarse.

"He'll hear it. They're husband and wife, sweetheart. I've known this couple for three years. Rita loves anal. Please, try to relax."

His gentle voice finally reached me, and I took a shaky breath. "Sorry, I just—"

"I get it. You seem to have a thing about gags. We can talk all about it later. But now," he reminded me in a low rumble, "I want to go upstairs." He squeezed my ass.

"Hey! That hurt!"

"Onward, malysh!" he urged impatiently. "Don't make me wait."

"Yes, Sir..." I mumbled, smirking to myself. I was desperately wet for him, and the fact that he was impatient made it even sweeter—he wanted me just as badly.

———

Upstairs, the atmosphere was calmer, with fewer people milling around a semi-dark corridor lined with doors. Max pulled a key from his pocket and led me to the last door. He opened it, and I stepped inside.

"Oh, my," I whispered, when my eyes adjusted to the dim light. The decor was certainly intimidating—chains hung from the ceiling and along the walls. On the other side of the room—paddles, whips, belts, floggers, crops, straps, terrifying-looking bats, handcuffs, clips, clamps, and a whole host of other implements I had never seen before in my life.

Max's hand slipped from my shoulder onto the back of my neck and pressed down gently. "On your knees, sub," he ordered softly, in a voice almost devoid of expression, then closed and locked the door behind us.

Goosebumps prickled my skin as I silently sank to my knees. Could have been from the cool air but, more likely, it was the quiet authority in his voice that left no room for disobedience.

He kicked off his shoes and, without looking at me, crossed to the wall of toys. From the corner of my eye, I saw him pick up a crop before returning to stand before me.

He spoke with the same expressionless tone. "Close your eyes and sit still. I'm going to ask you some questions. If you answer honestly, you won't get a single strike. But if you lie, you'll end up on that bench, and the spanking downstairs will seem like a gentle massage in comparison."

"Yes, Sir."

Why did this excite me? Was it the threat, or was part of me curious to know what it would feel like when things got rough? My thoughts ran wild, almost drowning out his questions, but thankfully, I woke up at the last moment to hear them.

"How do you feel about oral sex?"

"I feel fine about it. To give, not to receive," I answered quickly, without thinking.

Max smirked. "Looks like someone had a bad experience."

"Yes, Sir."

"Want another spanking later?"

"Yes."

"Do you like being on your knees?"

I glanced up, curious. Now, as he looked at me from above, a subtle change seemed to have occurred. The look in his eyes was even more imperious, yet now, it was laced with a newfound tranquility and a touch of tenderness.

For a fleeting moment, I wondered what made his eyes so captivating. Maybe it was the unusual hue of chocolate brown, or his long eyelashes that created this special effect? Either way, I liked how he watched me, patiently awaiting my response, without rushing me and unruffled by the sudden pause.

"Yes."

"Deepthroat?"

"Oh, God, no!" I blurted, terrified.

He smirked again. "Okay."

Using the riding crop, he gently brushed a strand of hair away from my blushing face. The absurd dress had slipped down once more, and there I knelt before him, my nipples unabashedly erect, my face as red as a tomato.

"Anal penetration?"

"No!" I squeezed my eyes shut, my voice almost a plea. His laugh echoed in response.

"Not at all? Not even with fingers or plugs?"

"Oh, umm, maybe. You could try that..."

In the next moment, there was a swish through the air, and his crop struck me sharply across the back.

"Ow!" I cried, opening my eyes wide. "What was that for?"

"I said no lying. I don't need you to agree to things you don't actually want. I don't need your subly favors, I need your orgasms."

"Subly favors?" I couldn't help but laugh at the amusing expression, but the humor faded when I saw the stern expression on his face—then, a little lower, the impressive bulge straining behind the thin black fabric of his pants.

"Try that last one more time," he said, his gaze piercing. "Fingers? Plugs?"

My cheeks flared with heat. The thought of subjecting my virgin ass to any kind of alien invasion unnerved me, but my body's feverish response told a different story.

"I think would like to try it," I said with effort, lowering my eyes. "Eventually. Carefully."

Max set the crop aside and rose. He took a condom out of his pocket and lowered his fly, revealing that he'd worn no underwear. My lips parted on their own when his sizable cock presented itself.

"Oh, wow," I whispered.

Smirking smugly, he rolled a condom down his length.

"Get to it, sub," he murmured almost inaudibly, signaling with his eyes exactly where I should be getting to.

A surge of desire and excitement blossomed in my belly as I playfully crawled on all fours, closing the distance between us.

When I circled the head of his cock with my tongue, I burst out in a short laugh. "Strawberry flavored condom?"

"I thought you might like it," he smiled, running his fingers through my hair.

"I appreciate that," I murmured.

I let myself have free rein, alternating between gentle

suction and playful caresses with my tongue and lips, some-times taking him deep, as deep as I could, other times, merely teasing him. His kept his hand on the back of my head, which unnerved me at first, but it seemed he had no plans to make any forceful movements. He simply stood still before me, rapt with pleasure, eyes closed and breaths ragged.

Eventually, with a deep sigh, he wound my hair around his fist and pulled me to my feet, his eyes raking over me. He said, "Take your clothes off."

I should have known exactly what he'd been about to say, but for some reason, when I heard the words, something tripped over itself in my chest anyway, and a blast of adren-aline hit the back of my brain, leaving behind a pulsing white light.

With difficulty, I focused on doing as he said, disrobing slowly, trying not to feel awkward that I was about to be naked and he was still almost entirely dressed, aside, of course, from his partially unzipped pants.

"Over there," he ordered, pointing to the wall with the chains.

Beneath the chains lay a cushioned mat. Gingerly step-ping on it, I turned to face the wall, lifting my arms obedi-ently to be restrained. With each passing minute, my heartbeat raced faster, especially as Max tightened and secured the wrist cuffs.

My mind raced, too. Terrified thoughts, one after another, like an internal Morse code. *My god, what am I doing? I don't even know him. What if he hurts me? What if he—*

"No thinking," Max barked, and a broad, heavy slap on an already sore spot made me howl and recoil. After a pause, another slap landed on the other side, pitching me forward. I might have fallen if not for my tethers, and straining against the chains that held me fast in my discomfort, all at once, I felt the full extent of my vulnerability. I would have wept if he'd hit me again, not so much from pain, but from this overwhelming sense of helplessness.

But he didn't hit me again. Instead, his hands roamed over my hips and thighs, then higher, teasing my breasts. I'd never heard myself make the sounds I made when Max touched me, a tiny, desperate moan, a plaintive cry, a wordless plea. He stepped closer, as though I'd issued a call he was meant to answer, stopping just behind me, almost flush against me, his breaths feathering my hair. I laid my head back onto his broad chest.

His fingers found my nipples and twisted them sharply, the sensation just shy of painful, before easing off and switching to gentle caresses. As soon as I relaxed, however, once more, the harsh twist. And then again.

He kept going like this, alternating pain and pleasure, pushing me to the edge again and again, testing my limits.

I finally couldn't stand it and cried out.

"Shh. Close your eyes," he murmured. Ceaselessly tormenting my nipple with one hand, he found my clitoris with the fingertips of the other and began to circle gently. If it wasn't for the intense pain in my breast distracting me, I would have orgasmed right then and there—his fingers were astonishingly skilled.

I whimpered and pressed closer against him, and he finally left my breast alone, but then, to my dismay, the maddening simmer of pleasure between my legs ended too. My whimpers got louder, this time in protest and disappointment.

"Step back and bend at the waist," he whispered, pulling my hips back to where he wanted them, then nudging my ankles with his foot, prompting me to spread my legs.

When I felt him starting to push into me, I grabbed on to the chains and let them support my weight. With three harsh thrusts, he was in to the hilt, gripping my hips firmly so my ass was pressed against his body. I couldn't hold back a shudder and a loud, urgent cry.

"Yeah, just like that," Max said. "Scream for me. Scream louder."

Then, he began to fuck me.

He fucked me with such force and abandon that I wondered whether this was another punishment.

But it couldn't be. It felt too damn good.

His warm hands kneaded my breasts, and he gradually sped up his rhythm until it became hard for me to get a full breath in. He didn't have to order me to scream for him—I couldn't have held in my screams even if I tried. At the end, right before the explosive climax, I wasn't even moaning; I was crying, whimpering, like a puppy, feeling myself coming completely apart, turning into molten heat in Max's hands, letting him move me the way he wanted, do with me whatever he wanted. The gasping shock of the orgasm detonated something in my head, blanched my consciousness, and I lost my grasp on reality even when he released me from my binds, scooping me up into his arms to wrap me in a warm blanket.

————

An eternity seemed to pass before the world began flickering back into focus, like an old lightbulb struggling to illuminate the strange room. First, I noticed the contours of the unfamiliar space, then the sensation of being wrapped in something warm, and finally, the presence of another body beside me.

I stirred, and the firm embrace that enclosed me tightened.

"Oh, my god. What is wrong with me?" I slurred when I could finally speak again.

"Subspace, malysh," Max murmured softly, as though afraid to disturb the fragile state between waking and dreaming. "Your eyes look absolutely crazed."

"I've never been fucked like that before."

"I figured. Otherwise, you wouldn't have flown away so easily," he replied just as softly, and smiled at me with endless tenderness, tucking a strand of hair behind my ear and rocking me gently in his lap. "Your sweet little pussy is so tight, and so damn hot..."

"And your strawberry cock is so big and so damn hard."

He chuckled. "Trying to flatter your Dom, little sub?"

"Is that not allowed?"

"Oh, it's definitely allowed," he whispered, brushing his lips over mine.

He skimmed my lower lip with his, softly and slowly working my mouth open, then, slipped his tongue inside to twist with mine for a moment, before backing off, teasing, then going back in. Christ. The kiss was a mini-orgasm in and of itself. How was it possible for one person to be so sexually gifted?

I wound my arms around his neck, kissing him back, and buried my face in the crook of his neck with a deep, satisfied sigh, inhaling that spicy scent, stronger now, after his exertion.

"I don't think I'm done with you yet," he said, cocking his head to the side. "Think you can handle more?"

My heart flipped, and grinning ear to ear, I said, "Yes!"

Only seconds later did I realize it might not have been the wisest idea to let my eagerness show quite so blatantly...

Chapter Six

As I dressed, Max glanced at his phone, suddenly in a rush. "We gotta hurry up and get downstairs. The auction is about to start."

"Auction?"

"Yes, you'll see. Chop-chop, come on." He zipped up his pants and pulled a fresh T-shirt over his head.

Locking the door behind us, we practically sprinted down the hallway toward the club. But when we reached the stairs, our progress halted abruptly. A whole crowd had gathered, spilling over onto the steps, their excited murmurs filling the air. The cellar had been transformed—benches were moved to make room for a small stage, where a busty young woman stood wearing nothing but a tiny loincloth.

"Spanking, oral sex—either kind—wax play! Two thousand, going twice!" shouted a jovial, red-haired fellow in a Club Subspace staff uniform.

The girl on stage posed seductively, her smiles as smooth as her curves, while men exchanged glances and raised their hands to up the bids. In mere moments, she was auctioned off for ten thousand.

"What fresh hell is this, sir?" I asked quietly.

"This is entertainment," Max murmured behind me, his breath tickling my hair. "The money will go toward the buyer's and the girl's membership fees. Thirty percent to the club. Whoever sells for the highest amount gets an annual membership. Same for the biggest spender."

"Do you want to bid on someone?" I asked, noticing a strange smile on Max's face.

"I'm not sure, malysh. For now, I just want to observe," he replied after a slight pause.

Another girl stepped onto the platform, and the process began again. I watched the semi-naked women, trying to imagine standing in their place. The thought of being up there, under those lights, with all eyes on me... I couldn't fathom it. The stage fright alone would be lethal.

"How do you feel about buying someone?" Max asked softly, wrapping his arms around my waist and letting his fingers trace the curve of my belly.

I shook my head, embarrassed, unsure of what to say.

"Have you ever fucked a girl?"

Another shake. But even dazed as I was, I realized the question wasn't random—the current lot was a submissive open to playing with women only.

"Ladies, a rare lot," shouted the auctioneer. "A half hour of whatever you please, including cunnilingus! Ladies, treat yourselves! Gentlemen, treat your ladies! A thousand— going once!"

Max's hands crept up my stomach, grazing my chest until his thumbs brushed my nipples through the thin fabric of my dress. He bent to whisper in my ear, "Do you ever think about it?"

"Yes..." I exhaled, leaning back against him, my legs were going wobbly.

"You want to get your pussy eaten by a girl?" he whispered, dusting his fingertips down my ribs. "I bet she'd know how to lick it so good for you."

"Mmm, yes, master," I murmured, completely submerged in the sensation of his touch and the spice of this new hypothetical question and answer game.

And then, out of nowhere, Max raised his hand.

"Seven thousand!" he shouted, and the auctioneer nodded.

"Seven—going once!"

"What the hell are you doing?" I hissed, pulling on his arm, overwhelmed by embarrassment. A sharp, icy glance from him told me I'd made a mistake. "I'm... sorry," I tried, my voice shrinking.

But Max shook his head. "I'll deal with you later."

"Seven thousand—going twice!" the red-haired guy on the stage yelled.

"Ten thousand!" sounded a raspy female voice from the other side of the room.

"Damn you," Max cursed with a playful smile and raised his hand again, "Fifteen!"

"Twenty," came the same voice, with a cheeky tone, and many in the crowd chuckled, glancing at Max.

"I'll spank you when I see you, Marina," he shouted good-naturedly in her direction, "Twenty-one!"

Whether his jest played a role or the woman opted to withdraw from the bidding voluntarily, I didn't know, but neither she nor anyone else contested the lot.

"Twenty-one thousand, going once, twice!" the lively auctioneer exclaimed, almost bouncing in place, "And the lot goes to his majesty, our magnificent, incomparable, splendid master Max!"

Applause erupted around us, but as the attention

swiveled toward Max, I couldn't shake the unease creeping up my spine. Why did everyone seem to know Max and, judging by their expressions, adore him? But I couldn't muster up the courage to ask him directly what was going on, especially since as soon as the auction ended, he proceeded to glare at me with such burning intensity that I felt compelled to lower my gaze and whisper, "Please forgive me, master. I just got flustered and..."

"Let's go, sub," he replied coldly, gripping the back of my neck like he'd done in the room. Earlier, in the privacy of the room, that control had been arousing. Here, in front of all these eyes, it felt humiliating. He led me through the hall like a captive, the crowd smirking and whispering, anticipating the punishment I was sure they assumed would follow. A few, sensing something exciting was about to happen, even stopped what they were doing and trailed behind us, and as a result, we approached the bar accompanied by a small, merry entourage.

One girl, whom I instantly recognized as the purchased "lot," approached and knelt gracefully before Max.

"Master, I'm at your sub's service," she said in a soft, melodic voice, resting her manicured hands meekly on her lap.

I cast a glance over her. She was slender, with a short haircut that framed her long, elegant neck, giving her an air of fragility. Her bare breasts were small but perfectly shaped. She was beautiful—not that I desired her. I couldn't imagine being satisfied without a flesh-and-blood cock. But I sure didn't mind admiring her.

"Thank you, Lori. Please wait a moment. My sub needs to receive her punishment for her rude behavior first."

"Yes, sir," she replied, her long, mascara-laden lashes

still lowered. But I caught a curious sideways glance in my direction.

A sinking feeling formed in the pit of my stomach. He was going to punish me *here*? At the bar? In front of everyone? I'd said I didn't want public play... or had I said I didn't know? Either way, he was going ahead with it.

No, please, no...

"Dim," Max called to the bartender as we reached the bar. "Come over here."

The bartender emerged, and Max still held me by the back of my neck, which seemed to paralyze me. I didn't dare protest, even as dread tightened around me. If I was being punished for arguing with him earlier, what would happen if I argued harder now?

All those safeguards—safe words, consent—they felt so easy to grasp in theory. But here? How could I dare utter a word when Max was this stern, this displeased?

My master led us to a more secluded corner of the club's lounge and pressed down on my shoulders until I was on my knees in front of a large sofa. Max took a seat opposite me. He had armed himself with a bucket of ice. I exhaled. This didn't seem so bad.

"Dima, would you kindly hold her arms?" Max asked the bartender. My gaze locked on the hollow at the base of Max's neck as I felt Dima crouch behind me. Almost immediately, warm hands gripped my forearms, pulling them gently back.

"And what's in it for me?" came Dima's cheerful, velvety voice from behind.

"I recall you wanting to touch her breasts?"

Heat flooded my face. He couldn't be serious. He *promised*. My eyes stung with the threat of tears.

"Sounds good," Dima said, his tone smug.

45

"Spread your legs wider, Liza," Max ordered, and I obeyed, parting my knees. The word "yellow" hovered on the tip of my tongue, but my cowardice held it back.

Max leaned forward and touched the top of my breast with an ice cube.

I yelped, jerking involuntarily, but Dima's grip on my arms kept me still. The ice cube slid down my chest, agonizingly slow, before Max dropped it down my cleavage.

I gasped as it hit my stomach, sliding lower and leaving a wet, cold trail. Max picked up another cube.

"Please, don't..."

"Oh, come on," he teased. "Be a good girl. It's just ice."

He was right. It wasn't the ice that bothered me—it was Dima's hands. The punishment, the game between Max and me, felt intimate. Dima's presence was an intrusion.

And not just Dima's.

From the corner of my eye, I saw the crowd growing, people watching from a respectful distance but clearly intrigued. One girl in a bright dress craned her neck to get a better view. A Dom holding a flogger smirked, eyeing me hungrily. Even a couple next to us stopped their own scene to watch.

Max, either unaware or uncaring, continued. Another ice cube trailed across my other breast, before dropping it down my dress again. I shuddered as it slid against my nipples, now visible through the soaked fabric.

Suddenly, the dress slipped off my chest altogether, leaving me exposed, my breasts on full display for everyone —Dima, Max, the audience.

But the worst part? My body's apparent shameful betrayal. I was being punished, publicly humiliated, but I was turned on. Insanely turned on. What torture would

Max come up with next if he realized how much I was enjoying this?

I was on the verge of panic just thinking about it, when he leaned toward me and caught a nipple between his lips, warming it.

I would have preferred it if I'd suppressed my cry of pleasure, but alas, it didn't happen. I cried out desperately. Now, the extent of my arousal really was obvious.

My world was suddenly ablaze. Blood roared in my ears, and the room spun — the alcohol I'd drunk, maybe?

His lips switched to the other nipple.

I closed my eyes, trying to forget everything else, just survive the punishment, and when the ice cube returned to my breast, I realized I *wanted* the burn. I wanted more.

And just as soon as I allowed another moan, Max's hand snuck under my dress and up my thigh.

He still held the ice.

My eyes snapped open as I shrieked—the jagged shard was inside the crotch of my panties. My whole body jerked and I cried out in despair as Max firmly held one of my thighs and mercilessly pushed the ice right into my hot, slippery, spastic vagina.

I jerked again, and Dima responded by tightening his grip on me, wrapping an arm around my ribcage to keep me still. I'd almost forgotten about him, and now his grip rudely brought his presence back to my attention. With my movements now completely restricted, my attempts to struggle became even more futile.

"Stop that," Max demanded in a rather severe voice, looking me in the eye. "Sub. Stop this all this ridiculous thrashing immediately."

"I can't... Please..."

"Do I need to tie you up? Bind your hands and feet?

Because I will," Max offered coldly, and I clamped my mouth shut, terrified, shaking my head, feeling my eyes turn into saucers.

Anything but that. Utter helplessness, no way to defend myself—I couldn't imagine anything more terrible.

All of a sudden, breathing became difficult, my surroundings blurred, and my vision swam. In an instant, everything vanished: my arousal, my curiosity, any remaining sense of safety. Only panic remained.

"Liza?" Max sounded different, but I was in no place to figure out why.

"Don't. Don't tie me up, please." I managed to force out. "Yellow..."

"Okay. Okay. Breathe. I won't tie you up, malysh, calm down. Seems like we've found another hard limit, right?"

"Hard... hard limit?"

"Something you absolutely won't do," Max explained gently, signaling to Dima to let go of me. He adjusted my dress and tried to pull me into an embrace, but now free, I shoved him away.

"No! Don't touch me!"

"Why? What's wrong?"

"Nothing," I muttered angrily, rising from my knees.

"I asked you a question, Liza." Max repeated slowly, rising as well, only to pierce me with a harsh, stern gaze. But I wasn't having it. It didn't work this time. This time, I met his glare head-on with an equally grim look.

"How could you do that?" I whispered, unable to speak louder, my throat tightening with tears.

"Do what, exactly?"

"Let him touch me!" I spat out what should have been obvious.

Max blinked, confused. "What is the issue? I didn't see him hurt you."

"That's not the point."

"Then, what is?"

His tone grew colder by the second, and I shook my head. Tears started to flow uncontrollably, because suddenly, I realized it was no use. He was obviously the kind of person who was always right, and I wouldn't be able explain or make him see my point of view.

But I tried anyway.

I said, "The point is... You hurt me."

"Because I punished you?" he clarified, still not getting it.

"Because it wasn't just *you* punishing me. You made another man hold me down. While all those people watched."

Max frowned. "Liza, you're in a BDSM club. People come here to play in public, swap partners, and participate in each other's games. What exactly were you expecting?"

"I don't know what to tell you. I didn't enjoy this."

"It was punishment. You're not supposed to enjoy it, that's the whole idea."

Was he growing angry? I cast my eyes down in misery. It was like we were speaking different languages. Worse still, I couldn't even fully understand my own feelings. Of course, I failed to explain them. Max, strictly speaking, hadn't done anything terrible to me — on the contrary, he succumbed to my nagging, led a fantastic session and gave me a mind-blowing orgasm, and then, shelled out a decent bunch of money for a woman who, as far as I understood, was there solely for my pleasure.

So why did this seemingly insignificant episode upset me so much?

"I just wasn't ready to play with other men. Sorry if that disappoints you," I explained quietly. "I liked being with you, just the two of us, and you—"

Warm hands rested on my shoulders interrupting me mid-sentence. I'd lost hope and didn't expect Max to understand, but when he spoke his voice was suddenly different.

"I understand," he said. "Shit. I get it. Sometimes Doms make mistakes too, and this time, I did. I'm just not used to someone with zero experience. So... yes, I made a mistake. I should have explained the club rules better, and clarified your limits. I should have shown you more patience. I am truly sorry. "

Hearing his apology was as surprising as it was comforting. Glancing up, I was almost expecting to find he was mocking me, but I only saw sincerity and calm sort of confidence in his eyes. I didn't want to be mad at Max, didn't want to believe he would do something malicious or uncaring, and didn't like feeling like we weren't understanding each other. His gentle look soothed my hurt, and I smiled at him through my tears.

"I accept your apology," I said.

"Good." Max smiled back, tousled my hair and took my hand. "Ready to get back in the game?"

I smiled wider. "Yes."

Chapter Seven

Back at the bar, Max's purchase was casually chatting with Dima, sipping on a piña colada. I lingered a few steps behind, doing my best to avoid eye contact with Dima, timidly taking refuge behind Max.

"Lori," Max called out softly. "This is Liza. Liza, meet Lori. She's yours for the next half hour."

Before Lori could even rise from her barstool, I blurted out, "I want a private room!"

Max's smile was easy. "Wouldn't have it any other way."

Lori studied me with frank curiosity, and something unexpected stirred inside me—something I'd only felt when looking at an attractive man before.

The moment Max shut the doors to the familiar bedroom, Lori gracefully sank to her knees by my feet and looked at me with such a delightful, unabashedly affectionate expression that I found myself unable to resist reaching out to stroke her hair. Just a heartbeat ago, the notion of doing such a thing to a grown woman would have been utterly unimaginable.

"Go ahead, sweetling, make my baby feel good," Max said gently, patting Lori's shoulder before moving to the far corner of the room, where he settled into an armchair, evidently preparing to watch.

Although the phrase *my baby* made my heart flip and melt treacherously within my chest—I knew it probably meant nothing—the idea of engaging in intimate activities with another woman, particularly while Max watched, sparked a nervous flutter. What if I... couldn't follow through?

Rising gracefully from the rug, Lori towered over me. She stood very close, too close for comfort, but her gaze radiated warmth and such eagerness to serve that my anxiety began to ease. We studied each other in a moment of silence, my eyes sweeping over her perfectly made-up face, the chic cut of her blonde hair, the oversized ornate earrings, and the plush curve of her lips.

Taking another step forward, she leaned in, offering her lips but leaving the final choice to me, pausing just a breath away.

Exploring my own emotions, I tentatively touched her parted mouth, ready to retreat at any moment, but the girl was a wonderful kisser and handled me with the utmost delicacy, only reciprocating what I gave without any attempt to lead. It was as if we were getting acquainted. Gradually, I eased into the moment and ran my hands over her body, experiencing an oddly captivating sensation, especially when her bare breasts ended up under my palms.

It wasn't strange, I realized. It was... pleasant.

Lori wore little more than a semi-transparent skirt, her

body gleaming with fragrant oil, and intricate gold-painted shapes adorned her shoulders, throat, and thighs. Her skin felt soft and delicate, like butter under my fingers.

"Lie down on the bed," she whispered into my ear, responding to my caress by grazing my breasts with her fingertips.

Feeling clumsy, I climbed onto the bed, and Lori slipped in beside me. She helped to ease off my dress and her lips began exploring my skin, sending waves of goose-bumps with every soft kiss. The warmth of her tongue over my nipples, stomach, and inner elbows was electrifying.

Filled to the brim with warmth and pleasure, I started to float away, finally surrendering to the moment, eyelids fluttering shut.

But they snapped back open in alarm when Lori peeled off my panties, dragging them down my hips, bent my legs at the knees and spread them apart. Then, she paused, as if contemplating the view that had opened in front of her.

Having someone examine me was bad enough, but my face really went up in flames when Lori turned her head, and quietly asked Max, "Master, may I shave her?"

Oh, my God.

I'd already realized—almost as soon as I entered the club—that I was probably the only woman in the whole place with any growth below the lash line. There wasn't much, but compared to everyone else, I felt like a cave-woman. Lori's frank question knocked the wind out of me, stealing my ability to take a breath for a few seconds.

Meanwhile, receiving a regal nod from Max, Lori quickly sprung into action, retrieving a towel, razor, and basin of water from a bathroom I hadn't noticed.

"Please relax," she said softly, smiling as she delicately

began to wield the razor before I ever got the chance to object.

I stayed frozen in mortified surprise as she worked, but the gentle touch to my intimate area, the jangle of her earrings, and her soft jasmine fragrance slowly coaxed me into relaxation and filled me with a delightful anticipation. Embarrassment aside, the process was unexpectedly sensual.

As Lori gently dried every crease with a fluffy, slightly damp towel and began applying some sort of oil from a small tube, the anticipation turned to desire, and I started to moan softly, arching into her touch. To feel the caress of her lips and tongue between my legs... The intense longing nearly consumed me, erasing any initial shyness until it became a distant memory.

And soon, I felt them.

Lori began with a few gentle kisses on my inner thighs, close to where they met my buttocks, moving up slowly toward the apex, until finally, she touched her tongue to my swollen clit.

I jerked with an agonizing moan, and her tongue responded with more pressure. I was lost in the way she caressed me, moving in widening circles and back and forth, around and over, each round sending waves of pleasure through me, almost shameful in its intensity, and escalating by the second. I bit the back of my hand to stifle any sounds, and my eyes involuntarily squeezed shut. A warm touch on my wrist made them open again to see Max standing over me.

Gently but firmly, he moved my hand away from my face and pinned it above my head, then did the same on the other side, exposing my flushed face, as though he wanted to clear his view for observation. After a second, I felt something encircle my wrists, followed by the unmistakable metallic clang of chains. I was now helpless, tethered to the wall.

Max returned to his watch post, and Lori, after a brief pause, smiled softly before continuing her attentions to my clit. Pleasure washed over me in waves, leaving me feeling as though I were floating, swinging high above the ground.

Eventually, I couldn't hold back any longer. My hips rocked in a shockingly obscene way, and I whimpered as Lori added fingers—two or three, I was far too gone to be able to tell.

I could feel the climax approaching, swelling inside me, taking over everything. I arched my body, digging my heels into the mattress, strained through the last few moments, and when I came, the orgasm hit with such intensity, it felt like my ears popped. Lori slowed down, riding out every shudder with me, before lifting her head.

"Thank you, sweetling," Max quietly told her, coming closer and peering tenderly into my eyes. "And how are you, love?"

"I'm super," I smiled blissfully.

But the longer I looked into his eyes, becoming aware of the demons dancing in their depths, the faster my calm gave way to alarm. Naked and defenseless, I felt vulnerable under his implacable stare as he stood over me fully dressed, and clearly aroused.

"Would you be so kind as to free my hands, master?" I asked, seized by a fit of mild panic.

"Nope." His smile turned playful, but there was an unmistakable glint of mischief. And then, as if he was really seeking an opinion, he asked Lori, "Sweetling, should we add a little spice?"

Of course, he didn't need an opinion; his mind was already long made up.

My heart raced faster as I watched him unwind a chain attached to the ceiling. "Wait, what spice?"

"Give me your foot, sub," Max commanded, extending his hand.

"My foot?"

Instead of obeying, I instinctively squeezed my legs together.

"Sub," Max's voice dropped to a warning tone.

"I just wanted to know what you—"

"Lori, crop."

Obediently, like the perfect submissive, Lori nodded and fetched a riding crop, kneeling to offer it up with both hands.

"Your foot, sub," Max repeated, this time accompanying his order with a sharp strike of the crop.

Giving him an indignant look, I stretched my leg, silently expressing exactly what I thought of his threats. Max clipped a leather cuff around my ankle, fastened it to a chain, and pulled—raising my leg straight up at a ninety-degree angle. Twirling the riding crop in his hand, he circled the bed leisurely, his intense gaze never leaving me.

"Other foot," he said a little softer, holding out his hand again.

Flaring my nostrils, I lifted my foot, barely resisting the overwhelming urge to give him a good kick him. Once both ankles were secured, Max inspected his handiwork, pulling the chains tighter until my legs were stretched just shy of discomfort.

"So, what were you saying about anal penetration?" His voice was casual, as though we were resuming a normal conversation.

"Ohh, no," I exhaled, eyes widening.

"No? I remember otherwise," Max declared, shaking his head. "I remember 'I think I'd like to try it--'"

"Eventually!"

"—Carefully." He turned to Lori. "Sweetling, what do you think, how many strikes of the crop on her cute little ass has my sub earned for fibbing and refusing to do as asked, when asked?"

"At your discretion, master," replied the girl courteously, still kneeling on the rug by the foot of the bed, where I could barely see her. I did manage to notice, however, that she suppressed a smile.

"We'll start with fifteen," Max nodded, as though Lori had suggested exactly that. "And while we're at it, keep her mouth busy. Liza, I want you to reflect on how to correct your behavior during this punishment."

Lori said, "Yes, master."

I, on the other hand, attempted a defiant silence. But the look on Max's face grew frankly menacing, sending a peculiar shift through my body—an intermingling of helplessness and alarm ignited an acute arousal I had never felt before, not even during my wildest, most secret fantasies. My mouth opened, and words spilled out before I could stop them.

"Yes, master."

"Very good," Max approved, a feral smirk playing on his lips.

The first strike stung my left buttock, and my mouth fell open in response. Lori's lips were there to meet mine, in a gentle, sweet, soothing kiss. The next blow came just as her tongue grazed my lower lip, and I whimpered, my body jerking, painfully aware of my helplessness—my legs raised, hands secured above my head, and my bare ass fully exposed for punishment—a profoundly degrading position.

It was unbearable.

By the seventh strike tears of pain and humiliation streamed freely down my face, a welcome relief to the pressure behind my breastbone. I could safe-word—it occurred to me, somewhere far away in the background, but God, it was all so delicious, so intoxicatingly sweet, the pain *and* the humiliation, that the idea faded.

"Do you know what I'm doing right now?" Max's voice cut through the haze of my heightened state and echoing cries.

Barely breathing, overcome with emotion, I fixed him with a surprised stare. I couldn't quite make sense of his words, and found it impossible to predict what he wanted to hear as a response.

It seemed he wasn't waiting for one. He said, "I'm teaching you, because you asked to be taught. Remember that audacious girl who tried to blackmail me in the car three hours ago? She asked for it, all of it. All of *this*. And now she's getting it."

"What—I—"

"I didn't want to do it. I tried to avoid it. But you insisted. You wanted it so badly, you threatened me. Didn't you?"

Was all that really only three hours ago? Seemed like an eternity.

"What do you think of that girl now, Liza?"

"I'm sorry, master," I sobbed, squeezing my eyes shut.

How absurd and naive was I to try to mess with a man like Max? I had no idea how much he could hurt me... and how much I could like it.

"Aww, are you sad because this hurt?" he teased, as if

plucking the thoughts from my mind, and then broke out in merry laughter at the terror etched in my face. "This doesn't hurt! This is just routine discipline for a disobedient newbie. It's for your own good."

"You..."

The intended insult fizzled into nothing as Max swung the crop again, forcing a scream from my throat. Another strike landed right after, extinguishing what remained of my defiance. My buttocks burned and throbbed, and when he gently stroked the sorest spot with his palm, I surrendered and reached out to Lori for solace. I kissed her greedily, as if her lips provided some kind of anesthetic—for my tormented body and bewildered mind.

Not to mention, her kiss was astonishingly arousing. *I could kiss her forever...*

"Lori," Max called, and I let out a groan of protest when she separated from me. Without realizing it, I'd slipped into a strange state of half-sleep. My eyelids weighed heavily, making it a struggle to lift them, even though I was dying to look at Max and Lori, and listen to what they were whispering about.

"Liza?" Max said, coming closer and bending to look at me.

"Yes..." I said at length, opening my eyes with a deep sigh.

"Are you okay?"

"Yes. But I'd love to know what else you thought up."

"Just a couple more things, malysh. Now Lori will show you how to use a butt plug."

"What?"

"Just a little one."

"I—"

Arguing would be pointless, I could see that in his face.

Lori's delicate fingers played with me for the next five minutes. Up and down the clitoris, in and out of the vagina, until they finally slipped down to the back entrance.

A citrus scent reached my nostrils.

"Mandarin oil," Lori said softly.

Something warm trickled between my legs and down between my buttocks, and then, without warning, Lori slipped a finger inside.

My eyes flew open, mouth opening wide, and Max murmured, "You're so fucking sexy when you look at me like that, malysh. That's just a finger. Imagine what you'll do when I finally fuck you there."

I shook my head. "You're way too big. It won't fit."

"Oh, really, is that so?" he smirked.

"Yeah."

He smiled so broadly that I could see dimples appear on his cheeks. "Oh, my lovely girl, you have so many wonderful, fascinating discoveries ahead of you."

Lori pushed in a second finger, thrusting slowly in and out, and I moaned again, and then again.

Max leaned in, whispering with sadistic enjoyment, "Yeah, that's it. There you go. Make some noise for me, sweetheart, that's good."

He covered my mouth with his in a tender kiss, simultaneously caressing my breast with the palm of his hand.

When he freed me, I whimpered, "This kind of hurts."

No one paid me any attention.

A third finger. I began to writhe in an attempt to escape my fate somehow. I didn't think I was ready for something like this.

Lori's fingers slipped out for a moment but quickly came back, and I cried out, mouth open wide again. *God, no.*

Max bent to me. "Liza?" he asked softly.

Our eyes locked for a moment. "I'm scared," I whispered.

Max nodded and straightened. "Lori, why don't you give her a nice, long kiss," he asked, looking her way, and she smiled agreeably.

To my surprise, she didn't stand up and reach for my face, but rather kept finger-fucking my ass and put her mouth on my pussy instead. I cried out, long and loud, when she sucked my clitoris gently between her lips. I was already so sensitive, but she had no mercy for me, teasing me with her tongue again and again, speeding up, revving up her intensity, until I twisted my whole body, shuddering in another shocking, explosive orgasm.

———

When I finally gathered my wits and blinked my eyes open, Lori hummed with approval. Max was still grazing my lips with his, as if he wanted to swallow my breaths. I almost forgot all about my ass, when something cruelly unyielding and jarringly cold pressed against my oiled up little hole.

"Noo!" I cried, twisting away, but it was too late. Lori worked the plug in with a few firm and rather merciless movements, after which she gave my clit one last kiss, this time without any real caresses, as if she was just giving me a goodbye smooch. Then she licked her lips and smiled at me.

But I wasn't in the mood for smiles by then. My sphincter throbbed, the plug causing a very palpable discomfort, and my pride smarted. Breathing hard, I glared at Max, then burst out in a desperate plea: "Master, please. Please, can I take this out?"

"Depends what you'll offer to do in return," he smirked. "We'll discuss that in a second, let me walk Lori out."

"No, now! Please! Take this thing out now!"

"Sub," he laughed. "You're really asking for it again. Don't you ever learn your lesson?"

Overcome by desperation mixed with anger and pain, I bit by tongue as I watched Max tenderly hug Lori, his arm around her shoulders as he walked her to the door. He whispered something in her ear, and she nodded with a serious expression. She joined her palms in front of her chest in a gesture of gratitude and left, shutting the door softly behind her.

"So," Max said loudly, redirecting his attention to me. "What's going on over there? I believe I wasn't quite finished with spanking that beautiful red ass of yours."

"You're not serious."

"Dead serious. I promised you fifteen. How many did you get?"

Our eyes met, mine, filled with trepidation and his with fake clueless innocence. Was the bastard openly fucking with me?

"Nine," I answered honestly, certain of the number because I had diligently counted each strike in my head, eagerly anticipating the punishment's conclusion."But--"

"But what?"

"They were pretty hard."

"I know." Max's eyes gleamed with a sadistic light. "You can ask me to ease up on the last six strikes, if you like. But politely, little sub, otherwise, it might have the opposite effect."

"Uh... Please?"

"Please, what?"

"Please, master?"

"Please, master... what?"

He was definitely fucking with me. What exactly did he want me to say?

"Please, master, ease up on the last six strikes," I said, speaking through gritted teeth, barely containing my righteous rage, voice full of loathing for him and his infuriating smirk.

He seemed to savor my frustration. "Hm. I don't think that was polite at all. I actually don't appreciate your tone and am wondering if I should go harder."

Tears welled in my eyes. My tolerance was almost at its limit.

"Please, master..." I pleaded, feeling my lips start to quiver.

"That's a little better," he replied, softly stepping closer. "By the way, did you notice you started calling me 'master' after we fucked? It hits different, right?"

"Yes?" I answered, confused. "I--"

I met Max's eyes and suddenly understood that he was getting a serious kick out of my suffering, making me beg, changing the subject, underlining his own superiority. A furious flush crept over my cheeks, while a new wave of wicked arousal swept over my body.

He sat down on the bed, and reached between my legs, caressing my pussy lightly with his fingertips. I gasped, and he said, "Good. Again."

I tried not to, just to spite him, but holding in sounds was impossible, and finally, I moaned. Max made a pleased noise and bringing his face closer, kissed my mouth lightly, barely touching my lips with his, as he penetrated me with his fingers.

Oh, God...

Everything felt so transgressive—the plug, Max's

fingers, my feet pointing at the ceiling, even the way he seemed to consume my exhales, feeding off my excitement and embarrassment. With the plug in my ass, everything was tighter and more responsive. The sensations were infinitely more intense. I opened my mouth wide, realizing I was about to come again, just one more second, and—

—and Max stopped.

That underhanded, horrible, impossible top snatched his fingers away at the very last second.

"No! Please, don't stop... Please!"

My eyes flew open, and I began to struggle within my bonds, whimpering and begging. Why had I turned into such a pitiful, sniveling mess? Was it the chains, or was it because I was increasingly giving in to his power over me? I had no idea. At that moment, the only thing that mattered was my throbbing, disappointed flesh and the orgasm I'd been denied. I needed it and was ready to plead, beg, bargain for it... please, please...

Except Max's mischievous face above me made it abundantly clear none of that would have any effect whatsoever.

He gave me a brilliant smile, and got up. I went slack, sniffling, and watched with increasing alarm as he picked another weapon and implement of torture by the wall. He strolled about the room as though he was in no hurry at all. And he wasn't—his arms and legs weren't restrained, and his body wasn't desperate with desire.

Suddenly, I was overcome by fatigue. My feet were starting to go numb, my ass still throbbed, though not as severely as a minute ago, my mind was foggy.

"Can I have some water?" I blurted out, realizing I was parched.

"Of course, sweetheart." Max's voice, unexpectedly tender, surprised me. He returned holding a terrifying round rubber object with a long handle and, completely unperturbed by my look of terror, put a bottle of water to my lips, raising me slightly with an arm around my shoulders.

I took a few sips, and couldn't hold back a moan.

"Whatever's the matter, malysh? You seem frustrated." His eyes were full of mocking over my current pathetic situation.

My throat was tight with tears, and my heart palpitated. The muscles of my vagina were contracting in and up, spasming with the utter lack of satisfaction. I stopped understanding what it was he wanted from me. I looked frustrated? No shit. I lowered my lashes to conceal the exact degree of my frustration, in case it earned me more strikes, and took a few more gulps of water.

"This is a paddle," he informed me, when I lay back on the pillows again. "What do you think it'll feel like with that plug up your pretty ass?"

My face fell when he winked at me. "Max—"

"You're about to find out, sweetheart, and I, personally, cannot wait to see your face. Six strikes."

My whole body tensed with fear. Again, the vague thought of using a safe word flickered in the back of my mind, but the rest of me was unwilling to use one. Now? After all that? No way. I had something to prove here.

"Max. This is a bad idea."

"Seven strikes, sub."

"Master, please, I'm sorry."

"I said seven. You'd better close your mouth. It's doing you no favors, malysh."

"I am so fucking sick of you and all your fucking favors!" I shouted, suddenly losing any self-control I had left.

Max froze, paddle in hand, then turned slowly. "Eight."

He put his words into action immediately, and I began to wail immediately as well. The pain was scalding, and Max wasn't merciful. I screamed without holding back every time he doled out a blow.

"I hate you, I hate you, I hate you!" I hissed right into his face as soon as the punishment ended, losing control of my own rage.

Responding to my anger, Max flared his nostrils, and tossed his weapon to the side. He unchained my feet, unzipped his pants and roughly yanked my thighs apart, holding them down. I fought him like a wild animal, and even tried to bite him when he put his weight on me and snaked his hand between our bodies.

I screamed when I felt him pull out the plug.

Gathering my hair into his fist, just like he did in the car, he bent my head back. "Should I fuck you here?" he asked, the head of his cock pressing against my ass. "Think about how that would feel right now, right in your tiny, tight little—"

"No!"

With a low growl, he drove into me the regular way, all in, all at once, filling me, his hips pinning me to the bed. For a short while, I kept fighting, but my strength was leaving me, and after the fifth or the sixth generous thrust of his hips, I gave up completely. Like the last time he fucked me, my body was starting to shake, and the liquid heat flowing from my brain down my spine and into my belly was impossible to resist. I forgot why I was fighting.

"Max..." I exhaled, pressing my whole body to his. "Yes. Don't stop, please don't stop."

"Stay strong," he whispered, reaching up a hand to free my wrists. "It's about to get bumpy."

It seemed impossible, but he fucked me even harder this time, demanding and accepting nothing but total submission. I screamed until my voice went hoarse, and when the orgasm hit, it felt like losing consciousness. The world went black.

———

When I came to, I'd been freed and covered with a fuzzy blanket. Max lay next to me, and my head rested in the crook of his elbow.

Blinking at the ceiling, I waited for the fog to clear. I wanted to tell him it had been the best sex of my life, but the words wouldn't come out, so instead, I rasped something about being ravenous.

"We'll go down in a moment, grab a snack, malysh," he said. After sex, his voice had also become somewhat raspy, and it made it sound even more velvety, more soothing. "How do you feel?"

"Okay. A little tired."

"A little? I think you've just insulted me."

My eyes snapped open, terror zinging through me, and I even lifted up on my elbow, mouth slightly open, ready to argue, but unable to conjure up any words of defense.

Max laughed. "Nice reflexes! But this time, I was just joking."

I sighed with relief, and fell back on the pillows again, smiling at him. "For real, though, I'm exhausted. You really wore me out."

"Those are good things. Come, let's eat and chat, and then I'll take you home, sound good?"

I said yes, but my heart squeezed with an unexpected

wistful ache. Would that be it, then? And we wouldn't see each other again?

We took turns in the shower, I worked myself back into the impossible non-dress, not the least bit embarrassed anymore about going commando. I felt like if Max ordered me to go downstairs butt naked, I would, and without much difficulty. After this second time, something had exploded in my brain and parts of my mental make-up were swept away with the blast.

Only—was it the last of my inhibitions or what remained of my common sense?

Chapter Eight

By the time we made it downstairs, the playspace had thinned out. Faint moans and cries still echoed from behind the closed doors of the private rooms upstairs, but downstairs, the atmosphere had quieted. A scene played out in a far corner, out of sight, while the music had shifted to something soft and soothing.

We passed by empty benches and abandoned crosses on our way to the bar. Most of the club-goers were still present but had migrated to a different section that had been empty earlier in the night. The space, located behind the bar, was outfitted with low tables, sofas, and armchairs—perfect for unwinding with a drink or snack.

"What time does the club close?" I asked, more out of curiosity than anything else.

"Seven a.m. It's around five now, so some people might still be playing—the endurance champions," Max explained with a grin as we navigated between sofas and tables, exchanging greetings with the Doms and subs relaxing there.

A little farther on, I spotted Lori, kneeling at the feet of an immaculately groomed Domme in a vibrant burgundy dress. However, unlike the outfits worn by the subs, this dress looked perfectly decent and would be suitable for a cocktail party or dancing in any regular club.

"Jealous?" Max teased, leaning close to my ear.

We stopped to watch Lori massage her Mistress's feet as the latter lazily petted her hair, periodically caressing her neck and shoulders.

"A bit," I admitted, my attention fixed on the Domme's fingers.

I was still in a pleasant trance when Max helped me sit down and arranged me on the couch, then walked to the bar to place an order.

A contented smile played on my lips. Focusing my eyes, I turned around and finally made eye contact with the bartender. My head was so empty of thoughts, I couldn't for the life of me remember his name. Then, it floated out of nowhere—Dima. The fear I'd felt around him earlier had melted away, flooded by endorphins. I smiled at him, and he returned the smile knowingly, as if we now shared a secret.

I glanced back toward Lori and her Domme—and my eyes widened. The submissive was now draped across her Mistress's lap, receiving a spanking severe enough that it hurt me just to watch. What could Lori have done to deserve that?

"Malysh?"

I hadn't even realized Max was back until I heard his voice. He smiled as he followed my gaze. "Don't worry about her."

"Why is she being spanked?" I asked, wincing at the impact but unable to tear my eyes away.

"Because she gives a nice foot massage. This is a reward, lovely."

"A reward?"

"Lori is a bottom with masochistic tendencies," he explained, sitting down by my side. "Hey. Look at me."

Reluctantly, I tore my eyes away from the scene and met his gaze. Something about his expression made me uneasy.

"What?"

"You would like to come back to the club, am I understanding correctly?"

"Yes, Master," I replied, suddenly anxious. Was there an issue with returning? Maybe there was a high fee or a limit on admissions? I wasn't a millionaire, but I did okay. On the other hand, I did live in the most expensive city in the country... I didn't know what a membership to a BDSM club cost, but around here, a membership to a good sports club could be considered a frivolous expense.

"We have certain rules and requirements for new members," Max said, confirming my suspicions. "And there is an entrance challenge. The good news is, if you pass it, you get a free trial membership, for three months."

"What's the challenge?" I asked, gripping the edge of the sofa cushion nervously.

"The auction. Today, the submissives were offering specific games, but as a newbie, you'd be presented without any defined conditions. The scene would be whatever the buyer decides, but only masters are allowed to bid."

"What if no one buys me?"

Max smiled. "That won't be an issue, trust me. You're way too beautiful." He tucked a strand of hair behind my ear as I blushed. "But in the case of that fantastical, hypothetical, very unlikely situation, the lot goes to the hands of an available master, and they will scene with you."

"Can't you buy me?" I asked softly.

Max shook his head. "Let me tell you why I won't, malysh. The philosophy of this club is open opportunity: partner swapping, non-monogamy, or at least, public play and kink with others. Members have to know they will always have people to play with here, and if Doms know they won't get a chance to play with you or Lori, or whoever, it takes away half the fun of being here. Same for the submissives. They like the element of surprise."

"But... what if the master decides to do something I can't—"

"All the limits are discussed prior to the scene. But they have to be real limits, sunshine, not something fabricated by your nerves."

The allegation that I would fabricate limits seemed unfair, but as I looked into the emptiness in front of me, imagining myself on stage, available for anyone willing to spend some money to do with as they please, I couldn't form a coherent objection.

"Look at me," Max said, and I looked up. "The auction and the challenge exist because we want certain kinds of individuals to join this club, people whose interests align. The point of the auction isn't to trip you up, or make you fail. It's not even really for us. It's for you. For you to self-assess, and decide whether you even want this kind of adventure. If you find the exercise impossible, then maybe this is not the place for you."

He said it so matter-of-factly, but my stomach clenched. I didn't want to stop coming back here, but a vague sense of manipulation twisted in my gut.

"I bought Lori at the auction. Did I do anything terrible with Lori?"

"No, but--"

"Just answer me, sub. Did you like what we did tonight?"

"Yes."

"Do you or do you not want to come back here?"

"I do, but—"

"So? Don't you trust me?"

"Don't pressure me! Jesus!" I snapped, and in the next instant, heard my own loud gasp and nothing else.

Max was in my face, his hand fisting my hair, pulling painfully on my scalp, bending my head back until my neck strained. My breath got trapped in my chest. All I could do was stare into his ice-cold eyes, my mouth open, frozen.

"Don't you dare talk to your Dom like that," Max said, his voice steely.

"I'm sorry, Master," I mumbled, my mind scrambled. My body tingled and buzzed in response to his touch, despite or even because of the roughness. The sharpness of his control sent shocks through me. Why did I react to him this way? At this rate, I'd be running after him, begging to be hit, like Pavlov's dog.

He let go of my hair and sat up. "On your knees."

Heat shot through my body, lust pooling between my legs, pussy drenched in mere moments, before I even moved. How was this happening? It should have been impossible for me to become aroused again tonight, not after all the madness, not with how tired I was. Yet, by the time I ended up on the floor and knelt on the cool tile for him, my flaming, wicked desire was causing me physical pain.

"You'll be eating right there, kneeling on the floor," he continued, his voice icy. "You will be silent for the duration. If one word comes out of your mouth before I put my fork down, so help me God, I will drag you buck naked through the whole club and fuck you on the bar in front of every-body, is that clear?"

"Yes, master."

Ripple after ripple of shivers coursed through me. As I locked eyes with an evidently infuriated Max, food was the absolute last thing on my mind. His expression was colder, harder than I'd seen all night—maybe except when he ordered me to take off my panties in the car for the second time. By the look on his face, it seemed his patience had genuinely worn thin.

Oddly, at that moment, I wasn't the least bit afraid. It dawned on me that I was becoming attuned to Max's mood. Despite the steely tone and stern expression, a glimmer of mischief flickered in his eyes. I had a hunch that he wasn't planning to make good on his threat to drag me naked to the bar and fuck me there. He was testing me.

A topless waitress in a miniskirt appeared, carrying two plates. "Shrimp Caesar or Asian duck?"

I opened my mouth to answer, but Max slapped a hand on the table right in front of my nose.

"Not a word," he warned, his tone so cold that even the waitress flinched in fear, taking a step back.

Max smiled at her, softer this time. "Not you, sweet-heart. Come here."

Right in front of me, he pulled the girl onto his lap, his lips grazing her neck as his hand stroked her back. "I owe you a scene," he whispered against her lips, and I watched as she flushed with delight.

Meanwhile, my heart fluttered in a painful twinge and my jaw clenched.

"Thank you, master," exhaled the waitress, taking his hand in hers to kiss it. Then, she got up and went back to work as if nothing had happened.

Without saying a word, Max claimed the Asian duck and pushed the shrimp Caesar in my direction. "Eat."

At first, I couldn't. My appetite had vanished, replaced by arousal and a rush of jealousy. It confounded me. I wasn't a jealous person. I could be territorial at times, but not usually with casual partners. But watching Max touch and promise a scene to someone else was unbearable.

The waitress returned with two large glasses of orange juice, this time retreating in silence. Reluctantly, I picked at the salad, working hard to focus on anything but Max. Gradually, as I chewed, my hunger returned, my body remembering tonights rigorous energy expenditure. Before I knew it, I'd finished the plate.

Max was halfway through his own meal when he took a gulp of juice and turned to me. "So. About the auction. Next Saturday, you'll show up wearing something nice. You'll be topless. Stilettos are a must, body art is allowed, the rest is up to you. Hair down. No underwear, unless you go with a see-through thong. Skirt—any length, but if it's long, it has to be sheer. Understand?"

I very nearly answered, but at the last moment caught myself and nodded silently instead.

"You can speak when I ask you a question. I don't think I'll be dragging you all that way just for a 'yes, master,'" he said smugly, his grin making me want to hit him with something hard—then have him fuck me anyway. My pussy had been throbbing the entire time I ate, and now it was sore, my nipples tight and aching.

"Is this getting you hot and bothered?" he asked, his grin widening as his eyes dropped to my chest.

"Yes, master," I muttered, flushed with embarrassment.

At that moment, someone called out Max's name, and another Dom approached. He was taller than me, dressed in

75

dark clothes. He looked young, but his sharp, green eyes suggested he was closer to my age, maybe older, just "well-preserved," like me.

"Max, you're very much needed upstairs. Irina has a... situation," he said vaguely, clearly trying not to let too much slip.

Max stood and looked at me. "I have to step away," he said. "You can sit on the couch while I'm gone. This is Nik. You can trust him. Nik—"

"Got it, no problem," nodded Max's friend, looking at me with encouragement as I got up off my knees, embarrassed.

I gave Max a nod. I didn't want him to leave me, but it was clear there was some sort of emergency.

"Hey," said the stranger, jovially, sinking on the sofa next to me when Max was gone. "I'm Nik. I'm Max's partner."

"Partner?" I blurted. My brain must have truly been jammed and my reasoning in shambles, because I was truly shocked by the idea that Max also had a male partner. So, he swung both ways? How broad were his carnal interests, exactly?

Nik burst into laughter, catching my wide-eyed look. "Not that kind of partner. Business partner. Here, at the club."

"The club?" I stammered, choking on my juice, embarrassed.

"We. Co-own. This. Club." Nik explained this softly, as if talking to a someone with a severely limited under-standing of the world. When he said "this club," he made a sweeping circular movement with his arms, suspecting, I imagined, that I might be confused about the meaning of those words—"this club."

I felt foolish. Of course, Max wasn't just some guest—the evidence was there from the get-go. From the way the staff treated him to his conversation with Dima, to the way the crowd cheered at the auction—it was obvious. Here's what I couldn't decide—was this good news or bad news? Did I like knowing Max wasn't just a casual kinkster but that he was so invested in the lifestyle, he made a business out of it?

"Was tonight your first time here?" Nik asked, his tone softer, almost intimate. His curious gaze made me blush.

"Yes, master," I said automatically, by now accustomed to the club's protocols.

"Nik's fine. I'm not big on protocol," he said, tilting his head to get a better look at my face.

I breathed a little easier. I liked that he wasn't gawking at my body, and that he talked to me like we were equals, without trying to play with me without a negotiation.

"Protocol?" I clarified.

"Yeah. You know, all the formal etiquette between Dom and sub. How you talk, how you kneel, all that shit. Max loves it, but I don't care much for it."

Sighing, I tried to decide what I liked better. Probably Max's way. It gave a certain spice to the entire game.

"Thanks for explaining," I said politely, unsure what else to say to fill the silence.

"You'll be presented at the auction next week?" he asked, slowly, his eyes gliding over me, down to my bare knees.

"Yes," I murmured, my cheeks heating up again.

"I'll be bidding," Nik said casually, standing up as Max returned.

I got up to greet him, and he touched my shoulder. "All

okay over here?" inquired my master when Nik was gone. "What did you think of him?"

"Oh... I don't know," I replied, completely bewildered. At first glance, Nik was perfectly nice, but his promise to bid on me was a bit unnerving. An absolute stranger had plans to buy me and declared so without a trace of shame. It was enough to confound anyone.

"Lori mentioned she liked you very much," Max said, non-chalantly. "Would you like to play with her again next weekend?"

"Really?" I exclaimed.

"Indeed," he replied with a barely noticeable smile.

"Yes, I really want to."

"And with me?" Max tilted his head slightly, looking at me in a way that melted everything inside me—a clear, calm, and penetrating gaze.

"Definitely."

"Good." He paused a moment, then added. "You do understand that next time, I'll demand more?"

"Yes."

A warm wave ran along my spine, and my knees unhinged. He invited me to play with him again. So... I would come here again.

"All right," a slight smirk curved across his lips. "Come on, then, malysh. This has been a long night, and I suppose, it's time to go home."

I nodded and followed him out without even attempting to fully process our "long night."

Chapter Nine

I awoke that evening with the distinct sensation of being in an alternate universe. I was at home, but at the same time, everything seemed new and unfamiliar: my bed, my phone, the wall hangings I made last year, when I was experimenting with oil paints. My whole apartment seemed sort of unusual, and for some time after getting up, I observed my surroundings, searching for what had changed before realizing everything was exactly the same—the change was me. Something had shifted inside me, setting off a chain reaction that left me buzzing with euphoria and an odd sense of clarity. It felt like being on drugs, where even the lines on my hands suddenly seemed fascinating—a trip, but without the substances, just the thrill of a new and changing perspective.

Usually, I'd start my day by making coffee and collapsing onto the sturdy kitchen sofa. Tonight, though, when I tried, I yelped and jumped up, my hand instinctively pressing against my sore ass. Bolting to the mirror, I yanked down my pajama pants, and the sight of my it made goosebumps ripple over my skin. The bruises were much worse than I expected.

Actually, I hadn't expected any bruises at all—the pain from Max's spanking hadn't seemed all that terrible, not enough to leave marks and swelling like this! A shiver raced through me, as I took note of my own arousal by the memory of Max's hot palms, the lingering scent of his cologne, the commanding tone of his voice, the stern look on his face.

"Well, well, doll. Welcome to the thug life," I muttered to my reflection, rubbing soothing cream into the bruises.

As I applied the cream, I caught myself thinking it wouldn't be a bad idea to bring some next time. When did I decide that there was going to be a next time? Maybe there wasn't. My feelings toward Max were all over the place—the warmth and trust I felt from an undeniable otherworldly physical connection clashed with his aloofness and icy demeanor, clearly intended to keep me at arm's length. Plus, that particular deviant had emphasized that partner swapping was the whole idea over at Subspace, and was more than prepared to let any guy in that club have me to do with as they pleased. And truth be told, I'd never had much pull toward swinging, or even exhibitionism.

I sighed, replaying our conversation from the car ride home. Max had taken my number and even offered to pick me up next Saturday. But when I showed any excitement or delight at the consideration, he quickly added, "If you have doubts, it's better if you don't come. You won't disappoint or upset anyone."

I didn't know what to make of that. Was it meant to reassure me that there was no pressure? Because it could also be a rather non-equivocal brush off. Either way...

"Yes, master," I'd answered, automatically.

"You can just call me Max, malysh. We're not playing anymore," he corrected, as he pulled into the lot by my building.

"Max, why didn't you tell me you were the owner?" I blurted, suddenly realizing I'd forgotten to ask.

He seemed surprised by my question. "Does that change anything?"

"I don't know. Just... seems like it would be logical to tell me something like that."

A faint smile touched his lips. "Logical, huh? You spend too much time in your head, malysh. Tonight probably did you some good."

"I had fun," I nodded, looking him in the eye, ignoring the patronizing tone that didn't bother me as much anymore.

"I did too," he said, pulling the car to a stop. "I'll text you Friday."

There was a silence. Then, Max's eyebrows went up in an expression of mild dismay. "Everything okay?"

Shit. Obviously, informed by regular, normal-people dating, I had expected some sort of good bye, a kiss or a hug, and it didn't hit me right away that Max had no plans to give me either.

"Yes. All good. I'm going."

I hopped out of the car before my face could turn red again, and he drove off almost immediately.

Watching the tail lights recede was the moment I decided I didn't want to ever see him again.

At least, I thought so.

But by the next day, that decisiveness was gone.

As I stared out the dark window, sitting on my sore ass, my mind wrestled with my emotions. Processing what happened wasn't going too well. In my head, chaos reigned, but my body was still blissed out from last night. Whatever my brain thought, clearly, my body was convinced it was great.

I felt good, so good, that I was still on cloud nine, and even the sore bruises on my ass didn't scare me away—the opposite; they summoned a dreamy smile, called up memories.

And Max, damn him, had been so fucking impressive, even though he didn't exactly provide me with a gentle or even smooth first experience.

I remembered the anal plug suddenly and squeezed my knees together. One of the sharpest and most frightening sensations of the entire night—but hell if I didn't love it. In fact, most likely, I would have been disappointed without something like it. And despite hitting our few snags, despite feeling enraged sometimes and wanting to strangle him, I hadn't felt in danger once the entire night.

Max inspired confidence and trust in me at first glance, for some reason, as though I were meeting a friend from a past life or a parallel universe... a kindred spirit.

For a long time, I'd been curious about BDSM, but I'd never acted on it. The idea required careful thought, and I'd always hesitated. I'd even joined a BDSM site a year ago but backed out of every date. Most men either repulsed me with their crude demands or bombarded me with endless questions, asking me to plan out every detail of a scene. Back then, I didn't understand why it irritated me so much, but now it made sense. I didn't want to dictate the experience—I wanted to trust someone to take control.

And... what could an experienced dom do with me? A wave of shivers cascade through my body as I considered the question. Locking eyes with my reflection in the sleek black glass, I asked that enigmatic woman: what else could you be capable of? With every passing second, I realized that I didn't actually have an answer, but really wanted to find out. Expanding curiosity pulled me in like a vortex.

———

The feeling that everything had changed, that I'd been reborn, lingered well into the next morning. I felt like a hot spring of energy and vitality, laughing with my coworkers, chatting up the barista at the corner coffee shop, even flirting with a stranger in the elevator. He seemed so taken by me, in fact, I was sure he would've asked for my number if we hadn't arrived at my floor.

Not that I would've been interested—my mind was elsewhere by then. A text from an unfamiliar number popped up while I was eating lunch: *Would you like to grab a cup of coffee? I want to get to know you outside the club. Lori.*

Grinning from ear to ear, I quickly replied, *I'd love to. When and where?*

Within a couple of minutes, we managed to connect on WhatsApp, coordinate the meeting time, but it didn't stop there. I thought we had it settled, but the phone buzzed again.

> Lori: I'm happy we're meeting up. I've been thinking about you.

> Me: all good things, I hope...

> Lori: great things. Your face when you come, for example.

I nearly dropped the phone, at a loss, and when I didn't answer, another text came through:

Lori: I'd like to see it again. Maybe even tonight.

Me: haha... tonight? at the coffee place?

Lori: why not? they've got great bathrooms.

Me: ? What do you mean?

Lori: I mean, their bathrooms are great if a friend wants to eat another friend's pussy, is that more clear?...

I couldn't respond. My hands were shaking too hard to type, and I was way too flustered to think of anything witty.

Oh, the feel of Lori's warm, teasing tongue on me... my panties were soaked at the mere thought as I made my way back to work, and my nipples were hard behind my thankfully sturdy bra. Amazing how swiftly I reacted to Lori's sexy suggestion, and how strongly.

Still bewildered and abuzz from my maiden voyage into the uncharted waters of BDSM, I hadn't even had the chance to wrap my mind around my first experience in bed with a woman.

I. Had sex. With a woman. Holy shit—who wouldn't be shaken by that? I mean—I realize, many wouldn't, but up until Saturday, I believed I was planted firmly in the hetero camp. Although, truth be told, I hadn't lied to Max when I let it slip that I'd thought about it, but any thoughts I might have had about women were always nebulously non-specific, hypothetical, without any plans to make them reality or, indeed, any belief that such a reality was possible.

Now, here I was. Deflowered, if you will, again, this time, by a woman.

And what a defloration it had been! Sweet, electrifying,

tender and uncomplicated in a way that was simply not possible when dealing with a man. In short, more than I could have hoped for. Of course, I wanted more now! I was itching to find out where this would lead me, what else we could do.

As these thoughts swarmed in my head, any drive to be productive at work went out the window, and I had to force myself to get anything done at all.

I couldn't wait until tonight!

Chapter Ten

By evening, the rain was pouring down, and my shoes and socks were soaked before I even got into the car. Normally, this kind of weather would keep me curled up at home, wrapped in a blanket with no desire to go anywhere. But tonight was different. I was still buzzing with energy, and wet feet weren't going to slow me down—even if I did manage to splash my pants with mud while dodging puddles on my way to Chaykhana.

I'd always liked this place. It wasn't fancy or expensive, but it had a warm, welcoming vibe with great food and good service. The spacious tables and cushioned booths were cozy, and they had these oversized, almost human-sized teddy bears you could cuddle up to if you wanted a little extra company.

Lori had picked the perfect spot. It was ideal for getting to know each other better, sharing an intimate conversation, and maybe... flirting a little?

Or... exploring the bathrooms?

Did I want to flirt a little bit with Lori?

By all indications—my drenched panties, for example—I

did. But how would that work? And how attractive could I be to another woman, especially one so bold and experienced?

I tried not to think about the other thing. The thing she'd said about seeing my face when I came. I didn't dare let myself daydream about that. I wasn't sure I'd stay conscious if I did.

———

Lori was waiting for me at a table by the window, looking impeccable despite the rain. She wore a mini-skirt with red stockings and patent leather shoes, her white blouse barely containing her ample chest, held up by a complex push-up bra. The whole outfit screamed "stylish metropolitan woman," like she'd stepped straight out of a fashion magazine. Even though her raincoat and umbrella on the windowsill told a different story, it was hard not to think she had magically materialized here, wearing this pristine outfit, looking like perfection.

"Hey, sunshine," she greeted me with a smile, her eyes openly traveling up and down my body, making me flush with embarrassment. She was everything I wasn't at that moment: polished, sexy, confident—not to mention dry and clean. I, on the other hand, looked like I'd barely survived the weather.

Who's supposed to go down on whom in light of this?

"Hey," I replied, feeling awkward as I ducked into the seat, trying to hide my wet boots and pants. Lori didn't seem to mind; she smiled, her gaze lingering briefly on my chest before she tossed me a flirty glance.

"How are you feeling after... everything?"

"Good," I smiled, unable to stop myself from checking her out, too. "I enjoyed it."

"Max is good, huh?"

"Yeah, not bad," I replied noncommittally, then, studying her face added, "Did you... have a thing with him?"

Contrary to my expectations, Lori's smile dimmed. "No, sunshine. I only play with girls. It's just, everyone always says Max is an excellent play partner. And he did help me, but not in that way."

"Helped you?"

"Well, yes, he's a psychologist and sex therapist, you knew that, right?"

"Uh... no," I said, surprised but at the same time not. "But that explains a lot." Max's ability to read me so well, to push my boundaries without scaring me, for example. It all made sense now.

"So, you don't really know each other at all?" Lori asked, raising a perfectly sculpted eyebrow. "Like, at all?"

"We just met on Saturday." I confessed with a sheepish smile.

Lori listened to the rundown of events leading to my night at the club, shaking her head and eyeing me with renewed interest. "Wow. He must have seriously liked you if he picked you up and took you in so fast."

"Maybe he just wasn't excited about waiting for the cops," I suggested, signaling to the waitress.

"I don't think that's it."

The significant, expressive look Lori threw my way said, *you're missing something, kiddo*, but I didn't know what to with that, so instead, I asked, "Have you been a member long?"

"About a year."

The waitress arrived, and we ordered coffee and dessert. Then Lori looked up playfully and bit her lip. "Want to have a little fun?"

I was lost and taken aback.

"What do you—"

"Come on!" she whispered.

Her charm was impossible to resist—that much became clear at the club. Everything is very easy when I'm with people like Lori: they suggest things and I agree, even if deep down, an incredulous little voice is screaming "Is this really happening?"

Before I knew it, I was following her to the bathroom like a conspirator in some thrilling heist. We slipped into a spacious corner stall with a window and a sturdy wooden sill. Clean, discreet, and oddly cozy—it was perfect.

"See? I told you—the bathrooms here are very convenient for this sort of thing." She winked at me. "Why don't you get those pants off? And don't get nervous—the doors are locked, total privacy, just the way you like."

I stifled a nervous laugh and stared at Lori, disbelieving. What did she say? Did I hear her correctly?

"Take them off," Lori commanded then, and the subtle change in her voice reminded me of Max. It was the same tone he had used—authoritative yet somehow comforting. Without thinking, I obeyed, my rational thoughts falling away as my fingers hurried to comply.

Lori gestured toward the windowsill, settling beside me. Our lips met in a fervent, hungry kiss, laced with the taste of coffee and a hint of mint. If I'd been nervous about keeping up, I found I knew what I was doing quite well. Dizzied by her ardor, wanting to return the sentiment, I wrapped my arms around her waist, sneaking my hand under her silky blouse and trailed my fingers along the warm, soft skin of her lower back.

Blood roared in my ears, and the scent of her jasmine perfume intensified around me as her hand slipped between my thighs. She found me already wet with excitement, and teased me with weightless caresses of her delicate fingers, until I arched into her hand impatiently, a soft, plaintive moan escaping my chest. Only then, did she gracefully lower herself to her knees in front of me, and spread my knees open with the same irresistible gentle confidence as Saturday night.

When I felt her lips on me, I gasped and immediately swallowed the sound, conscious of where we were, but Lori didn't seem bothered. For the first few minutes, I jumped at every noise and clang coming from beyond the doors, tensing when I heard footsteps outside. Unlike the club, this was not a place meant for such games, locked doors or no. How was Lori so relaxed? How was I supposed to let go and really enjoy myself?

But Lori's warm, slightly rough tongue patiently continued its steady, increasingly insistent caresses, and soon, any of my misgivings lost importance. The sounds of dishes and silverware clinking and the din of conversation outside faded into the background, while the soft music coming from the speakers in the ceiling seemed to get louder, filling my slowly relaxing consciousness. A thick, honeyed, slow-building ecstasy took over the rest of my senses.

Soft sounds of pleasure echoed against the tile walls, and I wondered why Lori was moaning. Then, it hit me—the moans were mine.

When Lori suddenly switched from licking to a gentle sucking, my breath caught, and the orgasm covered me instantly. I had no control over what my body was doing by that point, and had the wherewithal only to cover my own mouth with the back of my hand, and dig the fingers of the other hand into Lori's hair, to keep her where she was until I was done. That wasn't necessary, however, as Lori had excellent instincts and skills, and didn't go anywhere until my breathing began to even out.

When she rose, we kissed again for a long time. Seized by a wave of tenderness and gratitude, I peered into her large, perfectly lined eyes. "What can I do for you?"

"You don't have to do anything for me. I like eating girls out, malysh."

"Don't you like it when they return the favor?"

"That's nice too. But I'm good for now. Let's go have some coffee?"

"Sure," I agreed, pulling my pants up. "Would you teach me how to do it? I'd like to try it with you."

"Of course. We can do it at the club. You'll be there Saturday, right?"

"I think so. Though, I'm really freaked out by the whole auction thing."

"Oh, don't be. It'll probably be Nik, he loves newbies. Always gets into a bidding war over them."

"What does he do to them?" I asked, my voice suddenly hoarse, various frightening versions of future events playing out in my head, sending an unpleasant chill down my spine.

"Nothing special, don't worry," Lori laughed, opening the door for me.

———

Outside, we bumped right into a young guy, who looked at us, coming out of the same bathroom stall, with surprise. I felt my cheeks grow hot when he smirked suggestively.

My thoughts scattered as we made our way back to the table, but as soon as I took my first sip of coffee, I focused back on the crux of my issue. "Lori, please, tell me what they do to newbies. I'm terrified—to the point where I'm actually not sure if I want to go next weekend or not..."

I was mumbling, throwing short embarrassed glances her way, but she merely laughed again, tossing her head back, which made her oversized earrings clink like wind chimes.

"That's the whole point," she said. "Max has it structured so that any submissive or bottom who comes into the club does so voluntarily and consciously. Sometimes, people have no idea what they really want. I want or maybe I don't want, or maybe I want but not like that, or want but can't... That ruins the fun for everyone."

"I get that, but I still don't understand why the auction," I objected. "I would think it would be easier to go slow, get used to things. This feels like he's throwing me right in the deep end."

She laughed again, gulping down her cooling coffee. "Wherever he might have thrown you, this is actually quite far from the deep-deep end, trust me."

Watching her lips move and her throat bob, I squeezed my legs together involuntarily.

God, you're beautiful...

The thought flitted by, but I wasn't liberated enough to say it out loud yet.

"Okay, I understand this is just the tip of the iceberg, but a public scene... that's a serious challenge for me."

"For a lot of people." Lori nodded. "After I went through the auction, I couldn't show my face at the club for three months. I also thought I'd never take part in an auction again, only that one time, to get the membership. Gradually, though, I came around to the idea. It's actually kind of a buzz, when you're the center of attention, and everyone is impressed."

"When they're impressed, sure," I sighed, trailing my eyes over her pretty face and chest.

"Relax," she replied. "You're beautiful *and* impressive. And anyway, if you came with Max, all exams are as good as aced."

I sighed again, nodding as I brought my demitasse to my lips. "Thanks."

"Also, you have a great ass."

"Thanks..." I repeated, lowering my gaze, but unable to suppress a smile. "You're very beautiful, too, Lori."

"There, see? Now we understand each other." She reached across the table, grazing my forearm with her fingertips. "Would you like to come over my house and play? Let's say, tomorrow, or even today."

"Yes!" I answered quickly, without giving it a second thought. "Except... my great ass is covered in bruises. It's sort of embarrassing."

"My ass is too," Lori shrugged. "Does that bother you in any way?"

"No."

"Me either." She was so matter-of-fact, that we both burst out laughing, looking each other in the eye.

Chapter Eleven

By the time we left the cafe, it had ceased raining, and the floodwaters had receded, allowing me to walk down the street without making an absolute mess of myself. When we got to my car, Lori made a circle around it, examined the bumper and remarked, "Hm. What a surprise. Max hit it hard and from behind. So predictable."

We broke into giggles and kept laughing as we got into the car.

"Where to?" I asked, turning on the ignition.

"That building over there, see? Cross the intersection, go right, and into the courtyard."

It took no time at all before I was staring at a gate, confused, but Lori already had her remote at the ready, and the gates slid open. Once inside, I understood I was in some sort of elite community.

There was a security guard, a well-organized parking lot, a playground, manicured flower beds and even a fountain right in the middle. The only things missing from this paradise on earth were a few angels with harps, and maybe some cabana boys to feed the residents grapes while fanning them off with feathered fans.

I parked between a Mercedes SUV and a sports car that looked like a spaceship. Next to these gleaming vehicles, my little Ford felt like a rusty Wall-E among brand-new Eves. If I remembered correctly, Wall-E was identified as a contaminant and chased across the spaceship by a horde of horrible maintenance bots.

Without Lori, I'd probably face a similar fate here. Even with her, I kept expecting someone to declare my car—and me—too awkward for this place and bodily eject us both from the complex. "Us both"—me and my poor little Ford, not me and Lori.

My discomfort didn't ease once we were inside. Even the door-woman behind the glass by the elevators looked better dressed than I was. Her eyes seemed to say the same thing as she watched us cross the lobby. But once the elevator doors slid shut, Lori flashed one of her brilliant smiles, and I couldn't help but smile back, the anxiety fading.

Lori's apartment looked like a five-star hotel suite. I'd stayed in a place like this once—on a business trip. Not because my company had booked me a suite, but because the hotel had overbooked, and it was all they had left.

My astonished gaze glided across the warm pink tiled floor with radiant heat in the mudroom, then transitioned to the polished parquet in the living room, taking in the bamboo, shiny mirrors, plush poufs, tapestries, and uniquely shaped lamps, accompanied by sturdy brand new-looking furniture.

The bathroom was even more impressive, with natural stone, bamboo accents, and smooth river rock underfoot in the shower. It was an Asian-inspired spa haven, and I felt myself relax as soon as I stepped inside.

"Will you bottom for me tonight?" Lori asked softly, unbuttoning her blouse in front of the mirror.

"I—" curiosity surged upward through me, like champagne bubbles. So, Lori could bottom and top? "Yes. I will."

"I'm only starting to experiment with topping, so if something is bothering you, speak up," she said. "The safe words are the same."

"Okay."

Lori continued undressing, shedding her skirt and stockings, unfastening her bra. I stood behind her, watching. When I saw the blue and purple marks on her toned ass, my eyes widened, and I swallowed. They looked much more intense than mine.

Our eyes met in the mirror, and she said, "Take your clothes off."

"Completely?"

"Yes, completely. And hurry up."

A subtle change in her voice sent a steamy rush over my skin. This was the second time I heard those commanding notes from her, and I wasn't sure whether I liked this Lori—top Lori. My body, however, had no objections. Almost automatically, my clothes were off and neatly folded on a footstool in the corner.

Lori reached to an overhead cabinet, extracting a large tube of arnica cream. "Take care of those bruises for me, love. But be careful. I'm not in the mood for pain right now."

"Yes, mistress," I replied without thinking, unscrewing the tube, and when I realized what I'd said, froze.

Lori met my eyes in the mirror again, giving me a

knowing look. "Max really did a job on you Saturday, didn't he?"

"I guess so, yeah," I forced myself to say, as my cheeks turned pink.

I squeezed a good amount of cream onto my fingers, and bent at the waist to get started on Lori's bruises, but she looked over her shoulder, eyes flashing. "On your knees."

"Yes, ma'am."

Surprisingly, I found myself comfortable in this position, as if it felt natural for me to be there, on my knees, tending to Lori's battered buttocks.

I nearly stuck my tongue out in concentration. Part of me was simply striving to do the best job I could, but another, bigger, part of me was reveling in touching her skin, being close to her, feeling her relax under my fingers. I wanted to go further, wanted... more. What "more" was, exactly, still eluded me, but I held onto the hope that Lori knew better than I did.

She said, "Good girl. Let's get in the shower."

The shower was a secluded nook, separated by a small glass wall. Lori stepped onto the smooth stones lining the floor and fiddled with the handles until a gentle rain shower descended on us. We stood beneath the warm cascade, enjoying the soothing sensation.

Turning towards a wall adorned with jars and bottles of all shapes and colors, Lori singled out a few. "This is what I want to use for now. You have foot and body scrub, face wash. Shower gel, shampoo, hair mask. Go for it."

After a moment of contemplation, I grabbed the shampoo and began lathering her hair, trying to be as gentle as possible. I couldn't remember the last time I'd done something like this for anyone—if I ever had. Yet, I found I enjoyed it. There was something satisfying about focusing on someone else, taking care of them, making them feel good.

When I rinsed off the shampoo and began to apply the hair mask, Lori turned the shower off.

"Hey, don't leave yourself out of the pampering party," she said with a playful tone, her fingertips gently tracing the contours of my cheek in encouragement.

Giving a sheepish grin—it was true, I might have forgotten—I lathered up my own hair. Rinsing off the shampoo, I grabbed the conditioner. Then, I snagged the face scrub, getting back to taking care of Lori, mimicking what I could remember from my last facial.

With body scrub smeared across my palms, I grew bolder, rubbing her shoulders, arms, and breasts. Tentatively, I traced my fingers over her nipples, slightly hardened from my movements across her chest—and locked eyes with her. Lori smiled faintly and leaned in, brushing my lips with a soft kiss.

"Don't be shy," she whispered.

No longer holding back my curiosity and exploratory spirit, I resumed caressing her breasts, then tracked my thumbs down her stomach, to the area around the navel, and a bit lower—where everything was smoothly shaved and incredibly soft. Her quiet moan told me it was okay to go further, but I hesitated, timidly running my fingertips along her intimate area.

My heart raced at double speed, and my cheeks flushed.

Then, Lori parted her thighs slightly, letting out a breathy sigh. "Wash me everywhere. Come on."

Urged by her stern voice, I snapped out of my trance, I rinsed off the scrub, and began to soap her up with gel. However, when I reached the lower abdomen, I hesitated once more.

"What's going on? Do we need a little incentive?"

There was a threat in her voice, and she didn't need to clarify that incentive would be a punishment.

"No, thank you."

Overcoming my shyness, I trailed my fingers along her soft skin between her legs. So unlike a man—of course—but the realization still hit me like a pleasant surprise. Bolder, I repeated the process, noticing the slight tremor of Lori's thighs, how wet she was becoming, clearly aroused. Seeing the effect I had on her steadied me. Maybe I could do this without humiliating myself...

"Good job. Now, I want a foot scrub," Lori declared, her voice noticeably huskier than before.

I grabbed the jar eagerly and crouched down to give her a foot massage. This part came naturally. I'd taken a massage course years ago and was confident in my skills. My efforts were rewarded with a soft moan.

"You're so good at that," Lori said, smiling. "I want more of the same with massage oil when we get into bed."

"Yes, mistress," I replied, smiling back.

"Get up. Turn around, hands on the wall."

There was that shift in her voice again, and as she hung up the shower, I could barely breathe with anticipation. Lori's soft, soapy palms glided over my entire body—then began caressing my back, shoulders... breasts... down to my stomach... lower...

When her hands reached my pussy, I moaned softly, closing my eyes, waiting—but she didn't touch me. Instead, she grabbed the shower head, turning it to an intense massage mode.

"Woah, there," I said, half-joking. The other half was legitimately nervous when I realized what she had in mind.

"Face me and spread your legs."

"Umm...Lori..."

"Now."

I obeyed the order and watched, my fear turning to curiosity and then to excitement, as she first directed the stream to the tender skin on my inner thighs, left, right... and then... there, right there, between my legs.

The intense pressure sent an abrupt jolt through my whole body, and I jerked, letting out a loud gasp. That was way too strong; I wouldn't have called it pleasurable. Lori smiled, adjusting the stream to reduce the pressure. "Better?"

"Y-yes," I gasped. It was better—much better.

I played in the shower by myself, too, and normally, my escapades didn't take much time. With someone else there, I wasn't so sure. Lori, however, clearly knew what she was doing. All she did was run the stream of water up and down my clit a few times, unhurriedly, almost leisurely, and I exploded in a sudden orgasm, gasping for air, helplessly scratching the stone wall behind me with my nails.

"I love the way you come. Let's go again," she said, grabbing the shower again, barely waiting for my spasms to subside.

"What? Wait..."

I involuntarily straightened up, shaking my head. But Lori surprised me, putting her hand around my throat—not hard, not to affect my breathing. Only enough to pin me back against the wall and immobilize me. Her right foot stepped on mine, helping keep me in place.

"I said, one more," she whispered gruffly, locking eyes with me, and repeating her previous maneuver with the shower head.

I froze under her stare, letting the water pulse against my sensitive clit. She was pleasuring me, yes, but her hand

101

around my throat, her foot pinning me in place, made it feel like more than that. She wasn't just holding me—she was controlling me, trapping me. This wasn't the same Lori I'd known: not the docile submissive from the club, not even the playful girl from earlier. Something different had taken over, something more intense, and as the arousal surged through me, so did a mix of emotions—excitement, confusion, a flicker of discomfort. But the pleasure overwhelmed everything else, building relentlessly until I was helpless under her gaze, her eyes locked on mine as she pushed me toward the second orgasm, unrelenting, merciless, and in complete control.

Right as I came for the second time, I was overcome by the fierce urge to burst out crying, and I heard an uncontrollable jagged half-sigh half-groan escape my chest.

"Very nice," Lori smiled, placing a soft kiss on my lips again, and only then releasing her grip on my neck.

I was in a slight trance as I dried off, my mind preoccupied, trying to figure it out: what was that just now? Who was that stranger in the shower? My body liked her, my will responded to her, but at the same time, I recognized that uncomfortable emotion the change had evoked—it was fear. I feared her—possibly even more than I feared Max armed with a riding crop.

Was it strange to want to be afraid this way, get aroused by it?

"Are you okay?" Lori asked softly, touching my shoulder.

"Yes, mistress," I replied, shivering.

"Then let's go to bed. Grab the massage oil—that pink bottle over there."

Chapter Twelve

I n the bedroom, the sense of being with a stranger only intensified. This new place, with its dim lighting and unfamiliar surroundings, felt almost ominous. The quiet was strange, the scent of massage oil sharp in the air, the sheets foreign beneath me. Everything was different—except for Lori's body. Her slender, nubile form was the one constant, grounding me in the midst of all the uncertainty. I smiled to myself, realizing this was my first true opportunity to explore her fully. She was giving herself to me, trusting me with her body.

My hands on Lori's beautiful body. I was quite literally all aflutter.

As I soothed both of us with the massage, I entered into an almost meditative state.

It was so strange. A week ago, the possibility of sex with a woman hadn't even crossed my mind, and now, here I was, almost pouncing on her body, eagerly touching her all over, overtaken by a powerful yearning, as if this, *this* was what I'd been missing my entire life: this velvety skin under my hands, these smooth and silky curves, these subtle and exquisite tactile nuances that only a woman's body could provide.

Carefully avoiding the bruises on her buttocks, I noticed older marks—healed over welts that looked like they came from a bullwhip. Like the one I'd seen in Max's car. They also looked like something that would result from skin splitting, from deep wounds. My breath caught, and I had to make an effort to exhale. Fresh, purple bruises—hers and mine—turned me on and excited me with memories of a good time, but this? This was horrible. I felt nothing but rage and rebellion, from the bottom of my very rapidly beating heart. Who could have hurt Lori in such a cruel way? How could she have allowed something like this? Or did they do it without her consent? Was she assaulted and beaten? The thought was too horrible to consider, and I pushed it down, as far away from my consciousness as possible.

I spent some time massaging the backs of her thighs and her calves, trying to calm myself before asking my mistress to turn over, but she knew as soon as she saw my face that something had changed.

She frowned. "Are you uncomfortable?"

"No, mistress," I replied, continuing to massage her. "I was just... a little upset by your scars."

She sighed softly. "That's in past. I don't play like that any more. Don't think about them. Relax."

With this, she reached for her phone, and after scrolling around for a bit, turned on quiet background music, something a fancy spa would play: soothing trills of the flute, a babbling brook, birdsong, interspersed with occasional notes of the piano.

As my fingers drifted higher on her body, Lori began to moan softly, and I let the massage evolve into something more intimate—starting with her small breasts and taut, dark brown nipples, then her flat, toned stomach, her muscles tensing with each light touch.

And then her velvety, wet pussy.

As I started to stroke the silky tissues with the tips of my fingers, Lori spread her legs wider, bending them at the knees, and arched her back slightly.

"Yes," she whispered, the sound barely audible, but the desperate plea fueled an irresistible urge to kiss, taste, caress; to give back for all the pleasure she had so generously bestowed on me Saturday at the club, and earlier today.

Shifting to lie next to her, carefully, I put my mouth around her nipple, sucking gently, as my fingers continued caressing her pussy. I was careful not to be too intense; I only wanted to tease. I was curious to see if I could drive Lori to that state, the state where she would lose control?

Of course, I might be the one to lose control first—I was flooded with lust.

Nevertheless, I spent some more time licking her areola, warming her nipple with my breath, and even nibbling a little, all while I gradually sped up my fingers on her clitoris.

"Sub..." she whispered, finally, but it was a whisper that had the effect of the crack of a whip.

I startled, and without any other commands, slipped downward, positioning myself between her legs. I took a breath, hesitating for a moment in a rush of uncertainty, but the sight and sensation of the supple beauty before me urged nothing but the desire to please. The newfound intimacy overpowered any apprehension.

With caution, I tentatively brushed against her with my tongue for the first time, and Lori jerked her entire body.

Looking up, I realized she was restraining herself, breathing heavily.

Lost in thought, I pondered the astonishing effect of my gentle touches on her, and a faint smile graced my lips as I pressed against the tiny hardened peak with a soft moan, teasing it with the tip of my tongue.

Almost right away, Lori arched her back, raising her hips, gripping the sheets tightly in her fists. A hoarse moan escaped her chest. She was coming, I realized with surprise and almost dismay. Her thighs clenched, trapping me between them for a moment, before she relaxed fully, going limp on the bed.

Wow...

I thought I would have to work a lot harder to achieve this. In fact, I doubted that my limited skills as a novice bottom could elicit such ecstasy in someone as experienced and passionate as Lori. In fact, most likely, it wasn't any bodily sensation that led to this at all. By all indications, something special and unknowable was at play in her mind, beyond mere physical sensations.

I knelt back on my heels by her side with a blissful smile, enjoying the sight of a relaxed, satisfied Lori as she caught her breath with her eyes closed.

Finally, she opened them slowly, and looked at me. "Come here. Kiss me."

Her eyes shone from within, and I suddenly noticed their unusual color: grey and green at the same time, and the hue seemed to change depending on her mood.

Keeping my eyes locked on hers, I crawled up the bed until I reached her and covered her mouth with mine. Her kiss was as I remembered—soft, delicate, cool. Then, Lori put a hand on the back of my head to hold me steady, and abruptly flipped me over, ending up on top.

Her kiss suddenly changed, too—became greedy, demanding, like she was aiming to own my mouth, invading me with her tongue, asserting her dominance. She pushed a thigh between my legs, and pressed it rhythmically against my pussy, pinning me to the mattress with each movement.

With a rush of adrenaline, that feeling came back—the fear, the discomfort, the understanding that I had no control of the situation. But I tampered down the urge to resist and fight, willing myself to relax, and once I did, pleasure began to spread through me, heat filling my veins and arteries, infiltrating my skin.

Gradually, that was all I could feel, and what Lori was giving me wasn't enough. I threw my arms around her, pulled her tighter to me, responding to her plundering mouth with the same ardor. We rolled around on the bed, kissing hungrily, thighs intertwined and pressed against each other, both of us wanting to get closer, harder, higher.

We came almost simultaneously this time, and stayed wrapped around each other, freezing that moment in time, the two of us alone in the world, with our labored breathing and our quivering, exhausted bodies.

Chapter Thirteen

Usually, I wake up with my alarm, sometimes because I had a bad dream, more rarely because I'm thirsty. Never had I woken up like I did the morning after my impromptu playdate with Lori—because I had an important thought. A bright red, neon sign flashed before my mind's eye in my sleep: *A woman is the answer!*

It hadn't occurred to me on Sunday morning, when Max explained the requirements, but now, after yesterday's experience, it was so obvious.

I had a decent time with Lori, didn't I? Oh, yes, more than decent, although there was something about her dominant side that unsettled me—a strange inconsistency, or maybe a hidden motive. It felt like a wild beast was simmering just beneath her surface, ready to devour me whole. Then again, maybe she was just struggling to fully realize her dominant persona, overcompensating for the submissive lurking underneath.

In the shower, and again over my coffee, I couldn't help but smile imagining Max's face as I strode onto the stage, with the auctioneer announcing that I was reserved exclusively for women. A small thrill coursed through me—he'd probably want to punish me later. Which would be... well, I wouldn't mind.

And if Lori ended up winning me, I'd be more than okay with that. Honestly, I'd be fine with any woman. The thought of being spanked by the Domme who'd spanked Lori didn't cause any panic. I could handle the pain, make it through the scene, and be done with it.

But the moment I replaced that image with a man, my whole body tensed. The idea of Nik, Dima, or—God forbid —one of those brutish, brooding security types in Lori's place made my jaw clench. I couldn't bear the thought of going through a public scene with just any man. Not every man was worthy of my trust.

On the way to work, I sent Lori a text.

> Me: If I do the auction, will you bid on me?

> Lori: Of course, I will!

My mood soared, and by suppertime, I was ready to think about what I couldn't even fathom the day before: what I would wear when I walked across the stage on Saturday.

I messaged Lori again, and she immediately offered to take me shopping on Friday. That settled my nerves. I knew she'd help me find the perfect outfit, and limiting the bidders to women felt like the perfect solution to all my anxieties.

The next day, I got an unexpected call from Max. My reaction his call was so immediate that it astounded me. One glance at his name on the screen, and I broke out in red splotches across my chest and neck, while my pussy clenched involuntarily. I answered the phone in a voice so soft I barely recognized it.

"Hello, malysh," he said, his tone calm. "I wanted to check in about Saturday. Have you decided?"

"Um. Yes. I'll be there."

"You sure?" His voice dropped an octave.

I nodded, as if he could see me. "Yes, definitely. I'm sure."

"Good. The reason I'm calling—our clinic is open tomorrow. All applicants need to get an STI test and a doctor's clearance. Does that work for you?"

"Oh. Yes, of course. I understand. The only thing—I work during the day."

"Right. The doc will be there through the evening. I'll text you the address, and you text me the exact time so I can let her know."

"Thank you. That's fine."

So, condoms weren't the only method of protection over at Club Subspace. Smart, considering their policy for swapping partners.

After hanging up, I sat still, staring at my computer screen. It was really happening. The upcoming medical exam made everything feel official—more real, grounding the entire situation in my mind. Oddly, I found that reassuring.

———

However, by Wednesday evening, I was languishing in anticipation and regretting putting off my shopping plans with Lori until Friday. The looming inevitability of the auction still frightened me, but not nearly as much as before. Most of all, I was looking forward to playing with Max again, and couldn't wait to start getting ready. Unfortunately, there was nothing to be done at the moment—hair salon, manicure, bikini wax were not until Saturday, the shopping trip scheduled for Friday.

Gritting my teeth, I decided to kill time by going to the movies with two colleagues. Then, on Thursday, I arrived at the club so eagerly that anyone would think I was there to play again—not just for a medical exam.

Since Max hadn't specified whether he would be at the club, I took extra care to apply makeup and wore a flirtatious skirt with a fitted blazer and high heels, just in case.

At the entrance, one of the guards I recognized from Saturday greeted me. He asked my name and who I was there to see without batting an eyelash or showing any sign of recognition.

"Liza... I'm here to see the... doctor," I finished lamely, realizing how absurd that statement sounded in the lobby of a nightclub.

But the burly man nodded and gestured toward the entrance. "They're waiting for you at the bar."

Taking a deep breath, I stepped inside, half-expecting the same chaotic scene from last time: hordes of doms and their submissives, the rhythm of slaps and moans, trance music pulsing, and muffled conversations. Instead, I found complete silence. The space seemed to have quadrupled in size, with all the equipment moved to the far corner, leaving an open area up to the bar, now closer to the opposite wall.

Soft, relaxing piano music drifted from the speakers. Drawing closer, I heard voices behind the bar counter, so I circled around it and immediately spotted Max in the company of a man and a woman, whom I recognized with a slight delay as Nik and the same Domme I had seen with Lori.

The delay in recognition made sense—their attire and overall manner was far more casual today. They were lounging lazily in armchairs, their conversation slow and relaxed. Max smiled as soon as he saw me, and I couldn't help but beam back at him.

His eyes quickly scanned me head to toe, and I did the same to him. Dressed in jeans, a plain T-shirt, and sneakers, his hair tousled, he looked worlds away from the stern Dom I'd met on Saturday. He seemed like he was just a young guy, hanging out with friends.

Nik was dressed similarly but appeared a little worn out, while Irina, in a simple maxi dress and messy bun, looked all business. As soon as she saw me, she straightened and stood. Max followed suit.

"Irina, this is Liza. Liza—Irina. She's the doctor."

"Nice to meet you," I said automatically, suppressing the urge to take a step back. I didn't like this woman, hadn't liked her since I saw her spank Lori. Even knowing it was something Lori wanted didn't help my antipathy.

"Is everything alright?" Max asked, narrowing his eyes slightly.

I forced myself to relax my shoulders and smiled at him —that part was easy. "Yes, of course."

Irina's attentive gaze lingered on me for a few more seconds before she nodded. "In that case, follow me, Liza."

Without another word, she led me to the staircase I remembered, but instead of going up, she opened a door behind it, leading us into a utility corridor.

"The clinic is on the other side of the building, but we can go through here," Irina explained, glancing sideways at me.

"Got it," I replied, trying to sound as soft and sweet as possible, to try to conceal my unease with all my might.

After passing through another door, we entered what looked like a typical doctor's office: narrow halls with doors on either side, staff in green and white coats moving about, and a few patients in disposable shoe covers waiting their turn.

I didn't have to wait—Irina opened the nearest door with her own key, invited me inside, and locked it behind us.

Despite my initial dislike, I had to admit—she was a professional. I'd never had my blood drawn so quickly or painlessly. In just minutes, she examined me thoroughly, diagnosing everything from mild photodermatitis to occasional knee pain and insomnia.

"And how did you figure that out?" I marveled, momentarily forgetting my reservations. She merely smiled.

"Now a quick internal exam, and we're all set," she said instead, pointing to the curtain opposite the desk.

I trusted her enough to undress and get on the table without hesitation, though I couldn't resist asking, "Are you a gynecologist?"

"I trained as one, yes," Irina replied, pulling on her gloves.

"And in this clinic?" I persisted.

"In this clinic, I'm the chief. Relax, Liza."

I still blushed when she began her examination. It turned out that it wasn't quite the same when you knew your doctor was into women. Same as the few times I'd been examined by a male gynecologist, I couldn't help but wonder what they thought of me... and my nether regions. It was dumb. But there it was.

"Liza, please relax," Irina repeated, her tone soft.

I took a noisy, deep breath and closed my eyes, though I

still couldn't fully let go of my tension. Fortunately, the exam was quick, and I reached for my clothes with relief.

"And it had been a while since you had sex before last Saturday?" Irina asked as I emerged from behind the curtain. She quickly filled out an empty form. "A year? Two?"

"A year," I whispered, confessing almost as if it were a crime.

"Things get intense around here, Liza, you can tire yourself out if you go too hard right away. Some new submissive get frenzy."

"Frenzy?"

"Yes. It's a known phenomenon: when new subs discover subbing, they want to try everything and all at once, and up doing unsafe things. I'll remind Max to be mindful of that, and if you play with anyone else this week-end, remind them too. Other than that, you're fine. Drink plenty of water, pee after sex to avoid a bladder infection, use some lube to avoid soreness... and have a great time!"

"Yes," I replied, inadvertently straightening up and nodding as if I were a soldier in front of a commander.

"May I ask a question?" I ventured when Irina glanced back at the form and began writing again.

"Yes, of course."

I hesitated a bit longer, allowing her to finish writing out her sentence, involuntarily studying her fluffy lashes and eyes moving across the lines.

"Are you... a sadist?" I finally blurted out, not taking my eyes off her.

Her hand paused mid-sentence, and she raised her eyes to fix me with a penetrating gaze eerily similar to Max's.

"Is that an interest of yours?" she asked, arching an eyebrow. "You don't seem like a masochist."

"No. No, I'm not interested. I just... I saw you with Lori on Saturday. I mean, on Sunday, in the morning—there, on the couches," I awkwardly explained, stumbling over my words and making nervous abstract gestures.

Surprise on Irina's face was replaced by cheerful understanding. Following the ironic look at the figures drawn by my hands in the air, she smiled broadly.

Her surprise faded into amusement. She smiled broadly. "No, sweetheart. I'm not a sadist. But in the club, compromises are part of the game. Finding someone with perfectly aligned interests is rare."

"I understand. I'm sorry."

"Don't apologize. You're a newbie; asking questions is normal. Do you like playing with women?"

Irina's face now reflected genuine curiosity, which unnerved me greatly.

"Well... I've only tried it with Lori," I muttered, lowering my gaze.

"Did you like it?"

"Yes."

"Great," Irina beamed and flipped over the cover of the form. "Do you have a primary care doctor? We'd be happy to have you as a patient here."

"Sure, why not. Can I see you personally?"

"You're already seeing me. I work with the club under contract, it's included in the cost of your membership. If you're a patient of the clinic, that takes care of tests, and being seen by other specialists, if needed, and so on."

"Got it." I smiled at her. And Irina responded with such a sweet smile that I couldn't help but change my mind about her once and for all.

Chapter Fourteen

When Irina and I came back into the club, we found Nik and Max hadn't moved since we left them.

"Need a ride?" Nik offered Irina, and she nodded.

Max stood, stepping toward me. "Ready to go? I can drop you off at home." He glanced at Irina and back at me. "All good?"

She gave him a thumbs up, and I smiled. Signed, sealed, delivered. Healthy. I didn't think anyone suspected me of having any sexually transmitted illnesses to begin with.

"How are you feeling?" Max inquired casually, as we settled into his car.

"What?" His question caught me off guard until I remembered the lingering bruises on my ass and flashed him a bashful grin. "I'm fine."

"Are you? Come here, let me look at you." Max's hand trailed gently along my hair and cheek, turning me to face him. My lips parted, suddenly dry, and a bolt of liquid lightning shot straight from his hand to the pulse between my legs.

"You been thinking about me?"

His voice was velvety and soft; mine was just an exhale. "Yeah."

"Do you want to do more?"

Holding his intense gaze was unnerving. I found myself averting my eyes, feeling as though he was trying to read my mind—maybe because he didn't trust my answers or didn't believe what I said, which made me doubt my own judgment.

But then again—More? More of what? How was I supposed to answer his question if I wasn't quite sure what he was asking?

"Yes," I said anyway, even though that hadn't been part of my plan.

Max fisted my hair and pulled me close, leaning in. His whisper scorched my ear. "You're scared. But you're submitting. My favorite combination."

Warmth spread somewhere behind my breast bone—he was pleased, and that was worth taking risks.

His lips hovered just over mine for what felt like an eternity. Whether he realized it or not, Max had drawn me closer and tilted his head; we were poised for a kiss.

Then he abruptly pulled away.

"Has Lori called you?" he asked.

"What?" I didn't register why he was asking at first, then realized that he must have been the one to give her my number. "Oh. Yes, she called me."

"Did you have a nice chat?" He'd been about to buckle his seatbelt when he glanced at my face and stopped, turning. "Did you meet up?"

"Well... um... yes?" I hesitated, startled by his question, uncomfortable, unsure how he'd feel about the news that I'd met with another person.

"Look at me." Lifting my chin with his fingers, he urged me to meet his gaze.

Despite my discomfort, his pull was irresistible. His eyes held me captive, and suddenly, I struggled to hold onto a single thought, my body turning soft and boneless. I had no recourse against him.

Neutrally, he asked, "Did you fuck her? Did you like it?"

"Uh... Yes. And yes."

"Tell me."

"Well... we just met for coffee, and she just... invited me over," I said.

Forced look him directly in the eye, I took the opportunity to study his face. Getting the words out made me feel calmer and his reaction no longer scared me. In fact, I wanted to tell him all about it--brag about it, maybe. I almost wanted to provoke him, poke the bear. If offering that waitress to scene right in front of me was a-okay kind of behavior, surely, me meeting up with a lover he introduced me to wasn't a big deal. Wasn't the point, like he said, to change partners, play with others? Let's see how he liked that I did.

Judging by how he gripped my hair, he wasn't a fan.

"She invited you over to her house?" he asked, lowering his voice.

"Yes," I grinned defiantly right into his face.

"And what did you do at her house? Did you have yourself some nice, sweet girl on girl time?"

"Not exactly."

"You topped?" He seemed genuinely surprised.

"No! Lori did."

"Lori dommed you?" An astonished look spread across his face, his eyebrows rising. Then, a thought I didn't fully understand flashed in his eyes, and he turned serious. "So, that's why you're so zen all of a sudden. You got topped by a girl, liked it, and now you're thinking of having a woman bid on you at the auction. Right?"

"Basically." I shrugged.

"But that's gaming the system, malysh. The auction isn't for testing your creative thinking."

He continued to scrutinize my face, so I deliberately turned and looked out the window. "It's not against the rules, is it?"

"No, it's not—if you plan to play exclusively with women. But you obviously prefer men. So I can't allow it."

"That's unfair, Max," I said hotly, flashing him a discontented look and crossing my arms tightly in front of my chest. "You said I could choose the gender of the partner."

"Yes, in accordance with your actual preferences, not to avoid confronting your fears."

"And what if I just... what if I just don't want to get up on that fucking stage? What if I..."

Choking on emotion, I was unable to say more. A lump rolled up to the back of my throat, and my nose filled. How did Max manage to do this to me? Why was it that in his presence I invariably turned into a helpless crybaby?

"Shh..." His face and voice softened, and he put a soothing hand on my cheek, feathering my hair away from my face. "Shh... it's okay. Breathe. Deeper. Like that. Want some water?"

"Yes."

He reached for a bottle in the cup holder, untwisted the top and held it to my lips, tipping it so I could take a few gulps.

"Good. Now, let's talk. What is it that you're so afraid of? Is it the stage or playing with a strange man?"

"Both!" I shot back.

"Sweetheart, I'm sorry but you're lying," he accused mildly.

I gave up, leaning back in my seat. "Fine. A strange partner."

"That's what I thought... And you figured, if you knew Lori was your buyer, you'd feel better?"

"Yes."

"But you realize another woman could buy you, right? A hard domme or a sadist?"

His attentive gaze remained fixed on my face. I made a valiant effort to meet it but failed, and once again, found myself staring into my lap.

"Liza?" Max prompted.

"Yes, a domme or sadist could buy me, but I'm not afraid of them," I replied with a sigh, feeling bright red heat disseminate from my cheeks to my ears and down my neck. "Not like a strange man..."

"Sunshine, but you played with me on Saturday, and I was a completely strange man, too. How is this different?"

"It is different. I won't have a choice."

"Of course, you'll have a choice. You can always, always use a safe word."

"No... I can't. I won't be able to," I whispered, tears suddenly spilling from my eyes and down my cheeks. I realized suddenly that Max's line of questioning had helped me identify something of importance, though I wasn't yet fully aware of what it was.

"Liza. Hey. Malysh?"

I covered my face with my hands, unable to respond to either his words or his concerned touch, until the car door opened suddenly, and I realized that Max had gotten out and was offering me his hand so I could do the same.

"I'm sorry, I'm sorry. Give me a moment, I'll be okay. I'm okay," I said, between sobs.

"Come on, you," he said tenderly, wrapping his arm around me and guiding me back into the club. We crossed the expansive first floor, ascended the stairs, and soon I found myself at the entrance to the private room where we had played on Saturday.

Regaining my composure, I hesitated in the doorway. "You... want to... now?"

"No, love, it's just a quiet place to talk. Nobody will bother us here."

"Fine." I agreed, shoulders sagging, allowing him to nudge me inside.

"Sit," he offered, pointing at the armchair.

Feeling increasingly awkward, I sank into the buttery leather seat. Now that I was a little calmer, I regretted my inexplicable and embarrassing outburst.

Max dragged another armchair over, and sat diagonally across from me, leaning forward slightly.

"If I understand correctly, the problem is you're afraid you won't be able to use your safe word when needed, right?" he asked. "Specifically, when playing with a man you don't know?"

His tone was steady—unnervingly steady. I glanced up to see if his expression matched his voice. It didn't, though; behind the stoic, expressionless facade, I could sense an entire storm of suppressed emotions. Compassion, maybe, or empathy. Anger, too. He wasn't numb to my distress— alive after all. He was experiencing it second-hand while trying to stay calm and strong for me. This eased my discomfort—not completely, just a bit, enough to make speaking possible.

"You understand correctly," I whispered, averting my gaze.

Nodding, he said, "In that case, that is not a good situation, and you have every reason to feel uncomfortable with an unknown partner."

I sighed in agreement.

He shifted in his seat. "Liza, tell me, did you at any point experience a similar feeling on Saturday? With me?" he asked carefully. "That you want to use a safe word but can't?"

"N-no... I don't think so," I replied. "Maybe... a little, when... the thing with Dima. You seemed so cold, I didn't know how you'd react. But then I said it after all."

"Right, you did. That's good. And we dealt with it. So, why are you so convinced you wouldn't be able to do that again?"

"Because... cause..."

My mind went blank in an instant, my ability to articulate coherent thoughts disappearing into thin air. I glanced at Max, feeling utterly helpless, silently begging him to grasp the nature of my issue without the need for words, knowing it was futile, drowning in a sense of despair... And then, he nodded, as if he understood me perfectly.

He said, "Malysh, will you allow me to venture a guess?"

I nodded back at him, silent still. The desire to tell him everything, talk it all out, free myself of the burden, was rapidly becoming overwhelming, yet talking remained an impossibility. The effect was torment worthy of a nightmare —when you're trying to run, but your legs won't obey.

"Liza... Were you ever sexually molested as a child?"

My lips parted, and my breathing quickened. My vision went black for a moment. Unbelievable—I'd worked with a psychologist before, and she only got an inkling of such a history in my past after several weeks of intensive therapy, and even then, she asked about a history of rape, and it's not like I was raped, not really. Anyway, I never did gather enough courage to tell her what really happened. And here was Max, "venturing a guess," and hitting the bullseye with impressive precision. How did he manage to piece it all together so quickly?

"Come here," Max demanded suddenly, reaching for me, pulling me from the chair and into his strong arms. His embrace was as I remembered, warm and calming, and I let out a broken sigh of relief—at not having to talk, not having to look at him, not having to keep a straight face.

I waited for more questions or suppositions, but Max remained silent, rocking me in his lap, holding me tight and secure.

"I've never told anyone," I finally whispered, realizing it was a struggle to breathe. "It's so hard to explain. If you hear the story, it sounds like I wanted it, but I didn't. I didn't."

"I know, malysh. How old were you?"

"Eleven. He didn't really force me into anything, he just sort of... talked me into it. He told me I was a big girl and this was what... big girls do."

"Breathe, love. It's okay. It's not your fault."

"He wanted me to... " I whispered, living that day over again in my mind. Unable to say the words, I gestured vaguely, then gave up. It didn't really matter, anyway. "And for some reason, I felt like I had to. But in the end, I couldn't —it was too repulsive."

Max smoothed my hair and touched his warm lips to my forehead. "It's not your fault."

"But it's not like I resisted or anything..."

"It's not your fault," he repeated firmly, which gave me a

painful twinge of irritation. Why did he keep repeating the same fucking thing? Especially when it wasn't true!

I felt it then—the fierce accusation, rising up like lava from deep within: your fault. Your fault. Your fault.

"I—"

He turned me so he could look directly into my eyes, and with a solemn look, repeated the same phrase for the fourth time. "It's not your fault."

And that was when I lost it. Furious tears choked me even as I struggled to hold them back, but my efforts were in vain, the momentum was too great. I broke out in miserable sobs.

"It's okay to cry," Max said softly. "Sometimes, it's what you need."

He held me while I bawled my heart out, soaking the front of his shirt completely. Once I calmed down, he allowed me to rest my head on his chest. For a time, we sat together in silence, as our breaths synchronized.

Finally, he said, thoughtfully, "You're right, Liza, it's not a good idea for you to do the auction."

"Really?" I exclaimed, sitting up to search his face. "And you'll still give me a membership?"

"Yes, sweetheart. But there still has to be a public scene."

"Wait..."

"But I'll do it myself."

"Thank you!"

I exhaled with relief, but Max shook his head.

"With another master. I'll pick someone. And no objections."

"Two at the same time?"

"Yes, malysh."

I was still stunned by his suggestion-no-objections, dizzy from the proverbial emotional roller coaster, but then Max's hand suddenly moved from where it lay on my waist, sliding under my jacket to trace a heated path up my ribcage, and all coherent thoughts evaporated.

Pulling back, I locked eyes with Max, mine still teary, wide open with surprise, and his guarded and intense. A heady sensation took over, as if all the adrenaline of the previous hour transformed into a deep carnal yearning.

The buttons on my jacket popped open easily. Underneath, I wore only a revealing silky top. Max squeezed my nipple with his fingers, his gaze locked on mine, twisting it until my mouth opened in a quiet gasp of delicious pain. He leaned forward, resting his forehead on mine.

"You know what I'm wondering?" he whispered against my lips. "I'm wondering, should I go ahead and fuck that pretty pussy of yours right now?" his face took on a vaguely hungry expression, and he nodded, as though answering his own question. "I don't really see why not."

Chapter Fifteen

I probably looked like shit. How could Max want to fuck me, when my make-up was smeared all over my splotchy cheeks, my eyes were puffy and red, and—oh shit! I remembered my lack of grooming down below with horror. Widening my eyes at him, I vigorously shook my head. "No, I'm not ready."

"Don't you worry. We'll get you ready."

He reached for me, but I slipped away.

"No, that's not what I—I didn't shave," I admitted, bursting into flames, and sliding off his lap.

I searched his face for signs of disgust, but he only directed his eyes toward the ceiling, and signaled toward the bathroom door. "There are razors in there. You have exactly fifteen minutes. If you make me wait, I will make you regret it."

"Yes, master," I said, grinning ear to ear, and bolted for the bathroom.

I found everything I needed—it was impressively stocked. Choosing a brand new razor and some gel, I hummed as I took care of business as quickly as I could. My nerves got the better of me, and I nicked myself a few times. After a good warm rinse, I emerged, wrapped only in a towel.

He was still in the same chair, scrolling through his phone, but his posture had changed almost imperceptibly. Now, he was clearly in his Dominant role. A mere scorching glance in my direction made me feel it.

"Fourteen minutes, twenty seconds," he smirked, glancing at his phone. "Not bad. On your knees."

He rose from the chair at the same time as I sank to the floor sitting back on my heels.

"Eyes," he reminded me, coldly, as soon as I made the mistake of glancing up at him, and I immediately directed my gaze at the floor.

Max kicked his shoes off and crossed the room toward the implement wall. This time, I made sure not to follow him with my eyes or turn my head, sitting meekly in my spot. I was suddenly curious how it would feel to be completely obedient, to do exactly as he said.

Something clanged right by my ear, and I startled, though I was able to keep my eyes on the floor.

"Good girl," Max murmured, and something tough touched my neck. "Relax. This is a leather collar. Is that all right?"

"Yes, master."

He buckled it at the nape.

That was it—that was all Max did, put on the collar and buckle it, but it was enough for a heavy wave of heat to roll from my racing heart straight to the pulsing core between my legs. My skin peppered with goosebumps, and my nipples stood at attention.

"You're going to be my good little puppy today," Max declared, scratching the back of my head under my hair. "Puppies, as you know, can't speak—except to say their safe word—and must walk on all fours. A puppy can, however, whimper, nod, sit by its master's leg, rest its head on his master's leg, and so on. Is that clear?"

"Yes—oh."

"Bad puppy," Max said with a mischievous grin. He extended his hand and beckoned me up with a playful gesture, "Up."

I almost hopped to standing, but at the last moment, realized what he wanted and got up on all fours instead. Hot color slowly rose to my cheeks—this game was humiliating! But the most horrible thing was that my entire being responded to the humiliation with an almost painful influx of lust. God damn you, Max, how could you possibly have known this about me?

Suddenly, one of Max's heavy smacks landed on my ass and made me jump with my whole body. I would have screamed if not for the towel softening the impact.

"Bad puppies get punished," Max explained, as if I didn't get it, and there was an audible smile in his voice. "It's time for puppy training. Puppy, heel!"

He walked toward the opposite wall. His cheerful tone brought on unpleasant and defiant thoughts, but a few vivid flashbacks to Saturday night reminded me that it was better to do as he said. So the "puppy" in me immediately began to wander around the room by Max's heel. To be extra playful, I even raised my paw by the bed, succumbing to the mood.

"No!" Max commanded with a laugh. "Puppy, run!"

What? How was I supposed to run on all fours? He was being ridiculous... but I wasn't eager for another consequence, and so I tried. However, speeding up even a little hurt my kneecaps, and the towel I'd wrapped around my body began to slip. I grabbed with my hand and earned an immediate consequence—Max strode toward me, rearing his arm back, and smacked me like before, except on naked skin this time.

He yanked the towel all the way off. "Bad puppy! Puppies can't hold anything with their paws, and they certainly don't have a need for a towel," he said, doling out a second smack.

I huddled involuntarily in response, pressing my elbows and forehead against the floor—just as dogs do, incidentally —and Max softened slightly.

"Puppy, speak."

Oh god. "Awooo," I attempted quietly, but Max shook his head.

"Speak," he repeated, his tone firm.

He wanted me to bark. In my shock and embarrassment. I wasn't sure my vocal cords would work, and even to me, my attempt at barking was terrible.

Max nodded with a resigned sigh. "Sit."

Returning to my original position, I froze, watching out of the corner of my eye as Max rummaged through one of the drawers. In my line of sight, one by one, Max tossed several objects onto the bed that instilled immediate fear in me: a dog's tail with a clip and a metallic butt plug.

Whimpering pitifully, I threw him a pleading look, but all that got me was a condescending smile. "You're a good little puppy. You deserve a pretty tail."

He ruffled my hair and scratched behind my ear.

I whimpered again, hoping to soften him somehow, stay my fate, but it seemed that even my best behavior and most pathetic begging couldn't sway his intentions.

"Puppy, up!"

Panting with agitation, I got up on all fours, trembling. There was no denying my response to this degradation: I could tell how slippery I'd gotten, could feel the throb of shameless desire. There was no hiding it either, of course—Max could see everything, from my tight nipples, to the surge of goosebumps on my skin, to the quivering, wet mess my cunt had become.

The conflicting feelings overwhelmed me to the point that for a moment, I wanted to scream in frustrated confusion. On one hand, my entire body trilled with anticipation; on the other, shame and resulting rage adrenalized my blood. I was a puppy? Clearly, yes, since I wanted to maul Max and even my teeth itched to sink into his hand.

How could he treat me like this? Debase me utterly, turn me into an animal, reduce me to a sniveling mess, but in a way that removed me from any of my real world emotion or bad memories, and at the same time, stirred up the most intense, lustful longing? The most horrifying part of this whole thing was how well he seemed to grasp my needs, needs even I didn't know I had.

It only made me want to sink my teeth into him even more fiercely.

He twisted the cap off a bottle of lube and squeezed a generous amount onto his fingers, stepping behind me. His warm hand on my buttock made me shrink and tense, but he patted me lightly. "Easy, puppy. Up."

Suddenly, he grabbed the leather collar and pulled me down, forcing me to arch my back, then knocked my knees apart with his foot. Before I got a chance to get scared, I felt something warm and slick slide between my asscheeks—his lubed up fingers.

My entire body jerked, attempting to wriggle away from the from the merciless, slippery intrusion, but Max held me firmly in place, bracketing my hips with his legs to restrict my movements even more.

"Quiet. Stand, puppy," he ordered brusquely, moving his fingers in and out, deeper into me with each thrust.

Involuntarily, I started moaning, tensing a little less with each movement of Max's hand, feeling everything—discomfort, mild pain, fear... Fortunately, the pain faded rather than intensified.

"Good puppy. Stand," he repeated, taking his hands off me.

He took a step to the side to reach for the plug, but it was enough of a lapse in his physical control of me that I straightened up and sat back on my heels, shaking my head desperately. The prospect of getting plugged wasn't any less terrifying the second time around. I remembered perfectly well how unpleasant and painful it was to have that thing in me, at least for the first few moments.

"Bad puppy," Max said, lowering his voice, and grabbed the collar.

My only recourse was some sad whimpering. Max smirked, lifting me up on all fours again, forcing my back into a deep arch rather unceremoniously, and without further ado, inserted the plug.

A loud wail of protest escaped, but instead of consoling me, Max laughed to himself as he attached the tail—and only when he was done with that did he let go of the collar. "Walk," he ordered evenly.

I was rendered petrified by the magnitude of my humiliation and couldn't move. Never in my life had I felt this way, including the fateful moment when Max rubbed ice over my erect nipples for everyone to see. I didn't think I could get any more humiliated than that. However, it seemed that turning into an animal took me to a whole other dimension of shame I never knew existed. And the tail, which, soon as I moved, started to sway and graze my inner thighs and buttocks, made it almost unbearable.

Circling around the bed, laying my hands and knees on the floor slowly and carefully, as if I were crawling over broken glass, I shot Max an incinerating glance over my shoulder.

"Eyes!" Max snapped, and I flinched and looked away.

With a sense of resignation, I realized that simply looking away wasn't enough of a show of obedience, as he beckoned me over.

"Puppy, come," he commanded, and patted his thigh. That denigrating sound instantaneously took me to the brink of madness. I craved being near him, but at the same time, the urge to sink my teeth into some meaty part of his body became even more overwhelming. Fortunately, common sense hadn't yet abandoned me completely, and I approached him and sat back on my heels by his chair.

"Breathe a little," he said a little softer, reaching to scratch behind my ear and to run his fingers through my hair. "You're doing great."

His unexpected tenderness caught me off guard. For a while, I sat in silence, letting Max's gentle strokes calm me. My mind went blank, and I drifted into a strange, vague sense of joy. Then, a growing, all-encompassing, and insane urge flooded over me: I longed to kiss Max's hand.

But I couldn't. I couldn't allow myself to stoop so low, even within the confines of our game. I'd been humiliated enough today. I willed myself to stay still.

"What's that face?" Max asked softly. "What's troubling you?"

When I lifted my gaze, it must have looked unhinged,

because Max's eyes narrowed with concern as he immediately crouched down beside me.

"Liza? You may talk. Answer me. Are you okay? What's the matter?"

"I'm fine," I replied quietly, meeting his intense but unusually kind eyes. "I'm just entertaining the notion that I might be losing my entire damn mind."

"Ah, I see," he said, and the corners of his mouth lifted in a gentle smile. "And what happened to make you entertain such a notion?"

"I can't tell you." My voice dropped to a whisper, and my face flushed.

"But you have to. That's part of the game—the sub doesn't lie to her Dom and doesn't conceal her thoughts."

"Please, don't make me," I whispered, but Max's face turned stony.

"Do you want to get spanked again?"

"No, please, Max—"

"Please, master," he gritted out, and my whole body tingled as I counted how many times I'd said the wrong thing or called him the wrong name, and how many strikes of his crop that earned me.

"Please, master!"

"Sub, this is your last chance. If you don't comply, I'll use the cane, and you'll have to show your glowing red ass to the entire club on Saturday. Do you want that?"

"I wanted to kiss your hand," I blurted out, tears welling up from the frustration of confessing such a shameful, ridiculous desire. Couldn't Max see that he was pushing me too hard?

His face remained even. "Okay. So, what's the problem?"

I said nothing, diligently studying the blank wall, but seeing nothing from behind a blurry curtain of tears.

"Sub?"

"I thought, no one in their right mind—"

"Because it came from *your* mind?"

"Yes."

"But you wanted it?"

"Yes."

"Kiss my hand."

"Please, sir, don't—"

"This is an order. Now, Liza."

Max didn't move, forcing me come to him. I sighed deeply, inching forward, and took his hand in both of mine, turned in palm up and pressed my lips to it. The intention was to touch it symbolically and then let go, showing my disdain for the entire process, but I found I couldn't do that. In fact, having his hand near my face was such a relief, I kissed it again. And then, pressed my cheek into it, sighing with delight.

Max had done it again. He'd known exactly what I needed.

"There's a good puppy," he said quietly after a while, caressing my cheek with his thumb before extricating his hand. Gently, he grasped the collar at the back of my neck. "Heel, puppy."

We circled the bed, and Max indicated that he would like to see me on it. I climbed up and sat in the middle, looking down, but watching from beneath my lashes as he extracted a condom from his pocket, then took off his clothes.

As I looked on, my mouth dried up immediately, and an electric surge radiated from somewhere around my solar plexus out to the rest of my body—my elbows, my hands, the tips of my fingers, my chest and nipples, down to my belly and between my legs. Between my nerves and all the excitement of the night, I hadn't gotten a good look at him on Saturday, but now, I had the chance to really study him.

He looked solid, though not overly muscular—clearly, a man who worked with his brain rather than his body, although he was fit. Even if he had visible flaws, it wouldn't have mattered. He possessed two things I valued more than a sculpted physique: a brilliant, adaptable mind and a nice, big dick. This combination made him irresistible.

The mattress shifted as he got on the bed. I gasped and tensed when Max grabbed the collar and forced me onto all fours with my back in a deep arch. Then, he gently spread my knees wider, and moved the tail out of the way, draping it over my back. I felt the thick press of his cock against my thigh.

Sweet lord. He was about to fuck me with that plug and tail still in my ass. He had no plans to remove them.

I suddenly found I couldn't exhale.

"What are you thinking about, malysh?" Max whispered, leaning down to me. "Don't you want to get fucked? You're wet like you do."

His hard, hot flesh pulsed against my cunt, but he wasn't quite trying to penetrate me yet. His right hand squeezed the back of my neck when I tried to lurch to the side, and I felt a piercing helplessness, especially when I realized my inner thighs were slick with my own arousal, despite everything.

"Please, sir, I'd like to remove the plug," I muttered, realizing that unless I said it, it would stay in.

"Oh, would you, really?"

"Yes. I'm afraid it'll hurt if it stays in."

"It might. But what if it would please me to cause you pain, sub?"

Goosebumps ran down my spine, not the kind you get when you're excited, but the kind that form when you're terrified. My fingers tightened reflexively, clawing at the sheets. I jerked once more, but Max kept his grip tight, unaware or ignoring of my struggle.

"Please, sir, I really don't want this."

"Sub. I've had enough of your whining."

Max shifted slightly, to my horror, I felt the tip of his dick against the entrance to my vagina. The pressure bordered on pain, threatening to become more intense by the second, and I clawed at the sheet again, panting like a dog. My vision blurred and darkened, and I heard my own desperate cry: "Max, no! Yellow!"

"Hmm," he responded from behind me, and the sadistic undertone in his voice made my hair stand on end.

He still had me by the back of the neck, and without much delay, I felt another attempt at penetration.

Oh, god. What the hell was happening? I couldn't believe this. Max? The owner of this damn club? Had he lost the plot? Had he gone completely mad? Why was he not reacting to a safe-word?

"Max, I said, yellow!" I cried out, in an aggressive, belligerent shriek, which was somehow simultaneously full of the trembling rasp of fear. Anyone would understand I was no longer playing.

"I heard you," Max replied, pressing me into the bed even harder. "Yellow..."

...and I finally got it.

"Red!" I shouted before he could cause me any more pain. "Red, red!"

"About fucking time!" he exhaled with obvious relief, instantly setting me free.

What?

Leaping from the bed, I stared at him, wide-eyed, my breaths coming in heavy, ragged gasps, my hair a disheveled mess. I felt like a startled cat facing off against a towering dog.

"You... You...."

"Calm down, Liza," Max raised his hands palms out, to indicate he was harmless and unarmed.

"Calm down?" I rasped. "Calm *down?*"

"I'm sorry. I know that was scary. But I had to test you. Now I know you can do it, and you know it, too. Although, you should have said red as soon as I didn't respond to your initial verbal request. Ignoring repeated requests like that, especially when the submissive is tense and terrified is unacceptable. That's an immediate red. I would want to know about it if a member here committed such an offense."

My mouth fell open involuntarily. Did he not realize how he sounded? "You're saying this was my fault somehow? After you just sat there and repeated fifteen times that *it's not your fault?* You're choosing this moment to stand there with that grave look on your face and read me a fucking lecture?"

Max shook his head, not understanding. "Not how I meant it at all."

"I don't care how you meant it!"

"I meant any dominant worth his salt should have stopped and—"

"I trusted you," I whispered, too consumed by anger and rabid helplessness to listen. "I trusted you, bastard!"

"Liza," he said placatingly, almost apologetically—

almost but not quite enough. He reached out to touch me—a big mistake—and I pounced, turning into a creature, reacting to his approach as though it was a clear and present danger, swatting at him, hitting, and scratching.

"Liza, Liza... Knock it off! Stop it right now!" he bellowed, shielding his face with his arms but not before I got him with a few stinging slaps and numerous scratches. Dodging and seizing one of my hands, Max swiftly flipped me face down onto the bed, pressing me into it with his weight. Pinning my hands, he murmured into my ear, almost tenderly, like he was trying to placate a child having a tantrum.

"That's enough. It's over now. Shh. Come on, sweetheart, enough. It's just a little flooding therapy. Face your fears. I know it was a mean trick, but you did so well. You used all the safe words. A little late, yes, but that's only because deep down you knew I wouldn't have—and you were right. I would have called it if you hadn't. You're right —you trusted me. You still do."

"I don't trust you anymore," I hissed, "because you're a traitor!"

I twisted, working with all my might to throw him off me, escape to freedom, and then punch him in the face. Best if I hit the nose or the eye. But I was pretty well pinned down, and soon, lost my momentum.

"Of course, you trust me," Max said evenly, as if we were just having a conversation, and not wrestling to the death. "And now, you will allow me to remove that plug, after which, you will beg me to fuck you."

"What? Absolutely not."

"We shall see," he whispered tenderly, and pulled at the plug.

Chapter Sixteen

His whisper in my ear enveloped me in a strange, dream-like haze, the air thick as molasses. The desire to give myself over was overwhelming, and I knew if I did, I would be in ecstasy for every millisecond of the ten minutes he promised me. But remnants of my wrath gave me the will to shake off the hypnotizing effect of his voice, and I hissed at him, "You have the worst delusions of grandeur I've ever seen in my life. The size of your—"

His fingers came to life, gently gliding up and down my clitoris, then all the way to the tip of the cleft and all the way down past the vagina, my flesh slick, quivering, shamelessly open for him. My breath hitched and my mouth fell open. I completely forgot what wise-ass thing I'd been about to say.

"The size of my what, exactly, darling?" Max inquired, with an infuriating faux courtesy, speeding up his caress.

I tried to lurch away from him, gain some control back, hold on to my righteous rage, but he had me in an iron grip

—one hand pinning my wrists, his knees on the backs of my thighs keeping my legs spread wide.

His free hand reached my clit again, grazing it, but departed as soon as it arrived, leaving me gulping for air.

"Max..." I exhaled, but it made no difference; I didn't even think he heard me. His hand played everywhere but where I needed him most, moving faster and faster, but keeping the sharp sensation I craved just beyond reach. I could feel my brain shutting off, my body giving up; I'd forgotten—why was I resisting? Why would I ever want to fight this?

"Max!" I exclaimed, impudently arching back into his hand, and in response, he flipped me over in one unexpected, rough move.

"Shut your mouth, hands behind your head and don't move, or else I stop," he said on a single breath, shifting down, impatiently spreading my thighs with his hands.

By then, I could no longer think straight. All I could focus on was trying to keep my hands where he said, shut my mouth as he ordered, and enjoy.

Although, shutting my mouth was a big ask. Max must have known it would be impossible—as soon as his tongue grazed the tip of my nipple, I began moaning, and by the time he finally touched my clitoris with it, my moans had turned into desperate cries.

I'd never heard such shocking noises come out of anyone, and certainly didn't think I was capable of producing them myself, but what Max was doing to me defied comprehension. I didn't know a human tongue was capable of such machinations. He alternated between firm pressure and barely-there flutters so fast, they felt like the wings of a god damned hummingbird. At times, he would press his tongue against me, seemingly motionless, yet eliciting electric vibrations that surged from the point of contact up my spine, culminating in a detonation within my brain.

One moment, every fiber of my being—the arch of my back, the undulation of my hips, my erratic breathing—screamed how much I wanted and needed him. The next, I was writhing on the bed, trying to escape the too-intense sensation, ecstasy bordering on agony.

Attempts at escape were futile, however. Within the first minute, he propelled me into a staggering, panting orgasm, and to my horror, persisted, prolonging my time atop that euphoric peak into an excruciating eternity until I could barely stand it. And even then, the ruthless bastard was nowhere near finished. After a mere second's respite, he pursed his lips around my already sensitive clitoris and gently sucked on the tip. The acute sensation made me twitch all over, and I let out an anguished cry, not sure if he wanted me to beg him to stop or keep going, or if he was just trying to sentence me to death by unbearable pleasure.

The state I was in, I wouldn't have been able to say my name if asked. It was sheer madness, a relentless cascade of sensations, an endless orgasm followed by a string of non-stop explosions, each wave crashing into the next in an unbroken chain. Or perhaps, the first orgasm simply never stopped, propelling me through a ceaseless cycle of ecstasy. I wept, and even my neck ended up wet from the tears streaming down my face, or maybe, from the sweat of exertion. Between my legs, a torrent of heat surged, leaving me feeling hollow, famished, and utterly desperate.

I clawed at him, not in resistance but in a desperate plea for mercy. No longer a sentient being, I was a clump of nerves and need, begging Max to stop the torture and fuck me—just as he'd predicted.

"Please, please..." I whispered over and over, burying

my tear-streaked face into his chest as he rose up, digging my nails into his arms, his back.

Only when he heard my desperate pleas did he bend my legs up and possess me, keeping his eyes open and locked on mine, burning right through any remaining defenses. I felt him inside me, hard and aggressive, the owner of his domain. Still not quite done with the previous orgasm, I convulsed around him, gripping him as if trying to hold him captive.

After that, every thrust felt like another explosion, all my nerve endings firing at once. He was in so deep, it jostled and hurt sometimes, somewhere deep in my core, but I liked it, and didn't want him to stop even for a second, ready to hold him inside me until the next morning, the next week, the next... forever.

Pressed to the bed as he fucked me, immersed in the moment, drowning in sensation, I could hear and feel everything all at once—his racing heartbeat, his damp skin, his hot, heavy breathing in my ear and against my neck—right up until, with a wild and desperate grunt, he succumbed to his own shudder of an orgasm.

———

An eternity later, I gradually regained awareness of my body: first the softness of the pillow against the back of my head, then the sensation of the sheets against my clammy skin, followed by the chill in my toes and fingertips, until finally, I felt myself as a whole, flattened and sprawled on the bed.

"Maa—" I moaned, my attempt to utter his name foiled by lips and tongue that refused to cooperate.

Max, lying beside me, equally breathless, reached out

and placed his weighty, warm hand clumsily on my belly in a gesture of comfort. Neither of us spoke, and I surrendered to the urge to close my eyes, drifting into a dark, semiconscious slumber.

Through the haze, I felt Max rise from the bed, heard the door to the bathroom creak open and shut. For a long while, the only sound was the steady flow of running water, until the bathroom door opened once more. Despite my reluctance to wake or move, a gentle pat on my shoulder eventually drew me back.

"Liza?"

"Hmm?"

Struggling to crack my eyes open, I shot him an unhappy glance, letting him know waking me up was completely unnecessary.

"You should get in the shower, malysh. Time to get up."

"Mmm... ten more minutes..."

"Liza," he chuckled, sitting down on the bed next to me, and shaking my shoulder a little more vigorously. "Get up."

"Can't."

"Sure you can. Rise and shine, subby. It's late, I'll drive you home."

Lifting my heavy eyelids to look at him again, I finally acknowledged that I would, indeed, need to get up, and with some effort, sat up. "What time is it?"

"Ten."

"Oh," I said, and trudged to the shower.

The hot water snapped me out of my woozy state, and by the time I emerged, I felt relatively fresh, though a little embarrassed that Max had to see me without any makeup.

But he only smiled, scanning me from head to toe. "You look so young like this."

"Do I?"

"Uh-huh. Like a schoolgirl. A very naughty schoolgirl."

"I might be," I smiled back, channeling all my strength into the effort not to gaze at him like the proverbial enamored schoolgirl. Saturday had felt like the pinnacle of my sexual experience, but tonight had taken me to a whole new dimension, and now I was intrigued by how far this man could take me.

"A very naughty schoolgirl who forgot to wear panties under her very short skirt..." Max murmured as I finished getting dressed. "What do you think about that for Saturday, sunshine?"

"Um... this Saturday?" My head snapped up as I grasped the full meaning of Max's quiet words. "You mean..."

"Our upcoming public scene, yes."

Standing still in the middle of the room, he watched me, unblinking. He was the embodiment of casual power—the regal turn of his head, the relaxed slant of his shoulders, his hands buried in his pockets...and I would have sworn I could make out the outline of his straining erection. Jesus, where did he get this much stamina?

Unlike Max, I was the epitome of tension. Furthermore, since he'd sprung his brilliant idea on me just as I was hunched over attempting to slip my foot into a shoe, I was now stuck in the awkward hunched position, holding my shoe in my hand.

"Yeah, you'd be so good as a schoolgirl," he said, as though speaking to himself—just as he had an hour ago, trying to decide whether to fuck me or not.

Chapter Seventeen

That night, I had a strange dream. I was on my way to school, yet at the same time, somehow aware I was actually headed to play at the club. In the hallway near the classroom, I spotted Max and Lori. He looked like he was giving her a stern talking-to, while she knelt before him, begging for forgiveness. Then, he brandished a yardstick, poised to beat her with it, except in an instant, it was me in her place, shielding my face with my hands, frozen in terror and unable to move my lips in order to scream out my safe word.

I awoke before dawn, drenched in cold sweat, unable to shake off the residue of terror. Despite my best efforts, sleep eluded me, and eventually, fed up, I abandoned the venture, crawled out of bed, and made my way into the kitchen. Even a massive mug of freshly brewed coffee failed to breathe life back into me, and for the first time in years, I decided to call in sick. I sent a text to my boss, citing a sudden respiratory illness, and returned to bed, feeling extremely relieved. To my surprise, I fell back into slumber relatively quickly, especially considering the dose of caffeine I'd just self-administered.

By midday, I woke up again, this time feeling fully rested. I spent tome time lounging in bed before taking a long soothing shower and had myself an extended lunch. When I was almost done savoring my food, a random momentary flashback of my dream hit me out of nowhere, dampening my newfound joy.

Maybe I shouldn't have told Max about Lori and me. The night before, as I retired to bed, a pang of doubt about confiding in Max had crept in—and probably provoked that awful nightmare. It felt like I'd betrayed Lori in some way, like maybe what we'd done at her house was against the rules. Otherwise, why would Max react with such disapproval?

Initially, I entertained the notion of jealousy, but quickly dismissed it as improbable. If he was capable of being jealous, why would he share me with another Dom in the entrance exam scene? No... this was something else.

I toyed with the idea of reaching out to Lori, especially since we had plans to go shopping that day. However, I hesitated, opting to wait for her call instead.

While I waited, I decided to treat myself to a mani-pedi, since my day had freed up anyway. I'd canceled my wax after shaving for Max yesterday and thought I'd spend Saturday relaxing with a TV marathon and a nap to prepare for a long night at the club.

Relaxing wasn't happening.

Despite trying to convince myself I should be relieved that the public auction no longer loomed over me, I couldn't shake off the anxiety about the prospect of a public scene with two Doms, and with each passing minute, Lori's conspicuous silence worried me more and more.

At six o'clock, just as I was finishing up drying my nails, I couldn't take it anymore and called Lori myself, but she didn't pick up. Fearing the worst and at a complete loss I left the salon, I walked into the nearest coffee shop and spent the next hour watching my screen, waiting for it to light up with a call or a message. When seven o'clock arrived and there was still no response, I decided to call Max.

"Yes, malysh." He answered right away sounding out of breath, as if he were out and about. Suddenly, I lost my nerve.

"Hi... Um, Max, I'm calling to talk about yesterday."

"Let's talk about yesterday."

"I mean, I want to say the things I said about Lori... about me and Lori... I mean—"

I hadn't felt this tongue-tied since seventh grade, when I forgot about an oral report in history class, and the mean teacher made me stand in front of everyone and improvise from memory. Fortunately, unlike that witch from my past, Max didn't plan on using my discomfort against me.

"I understand what you mean, Liza," he interrupted in a calming tone. "What was it you wanted to discuss?"

"Lori. She's not answering my calls. Is this because— Did you say anything to her?"

"I spoke to her earlier today," he confirmed, his voice still soothing, but this time, it made my stomach knot with dread. My premonition had been right. I'd gotten Lori in trouble.

"You didn't do anything wrong," Max added quickly, as if reading my mind. "Lori knew what she was doing when she violated certain agreements, and she will have to face the consequences. And she's not answering your calls because I forbade her to."

A muddy, unsettling feeling settled in my chest and

stomach. Shit. Why didn't Lori warn me that I couldn't talk to Max about what happened between us? And how could he *forbid* her anything outside the game? She wasn't even his sub, not to mention, she never played with men at all.

"But... you were the one who gave her my number in the first place?"

"I did, yes. I thought it would ease your nerves about the auction if you could speak to an experienced person you already knew, but instead..."

"So you *forbade* her to talk to me."

"Yes."

"I... I thought rules applied only while playing at... the club," I mumbled into the phone, paralyzed by confusion, hurt feelings, and a continued sense of dread, as if I'd stepped on a mine.

"This isn't play, malysh," Max sighed. "It's a bit more serious. Look, Lori will be able to speak to you again, eventually, maybe Sunday. And then, it'll really be up to her if she wants to tell you the whole story. I'm sorry, but I can't share any more than that. It's not my place."

"But it was your place to make me feel like shit by *forbidding* her from calling me?" I snapped, suddenly angry. All these secrets smacked of adolescent games of power, despite Max's assurances that it was not about play.

"Hurting your feelings wasn't my intention, Liza."

"Yeah, well..."

A silence stretched between us, until Max finally prompted, "Well?"

He was clearly ready to end this conversation.

"What about that second Dom?" I blurted before I could bite my tongue.

Shit.

"What about him?" Max asked when I said no more. He

didn't sound annoyed or like he was trying to intimidate me, so I took a chance.

"Am I at least allowed to know who it is?"

"I'm still thinking," Max replied in the same soft voice, but the effect was no longer calming. "You're just going to have to wait and trust me."

"Trust you?" I snapped shrilly, desperate, hoping against all odds to break his composure. "Do you even understand how much I'm freaking out?"

"But why?"

He sounded so genuinely surprised by my confession, that I felt I'd said the stupidest thing in the world. I breathed into the phone without answering. What could I say in response to that? *Why?* Was there any woman, any *person*, in the whole entire world who *wouldn't* be nervous stepping out onto a stage, half-naked, to perform an intimate act, with two guys, in front of a bunch of people she didn't know, for the first time in her life?

Finally, Max must have realized I simply couldn't bring myself to speak and said, "Listen, malysh. I'm going to tell you something, and I want you to really grasp its importance. Your ability to understand it correctly will actually determine whether or not you should get involved in BDSM at all."

I nodded, forgetting that he couldn't see me, and when I remembered, added, "Yes, master."

"Good girl," he said, and I heard the smile in his voice. "So, here is the thing. You're new to this, but you're the one who asked for it. I'm willing to guide you through the basics, and while I expect some anxiety, if it's at the point where you don't think you can bring yourself to trust me, then maybe, there is no point in us playing together after all."

I clutched the phone in my hand, utterly stunned and

breathless, feeling as if I'd just gotten slapped across the face. *Willing to take me through the basics... maybe there is no point in us playing together...* I swallowed hard, and parted my lips, drawing a painful inhale. I whispered, "I'm sorry—"

"Nothing to be sorry for," Max interjected, sounding impatient. "That is not why I said that, nothing to do with what I'm trying to convey."

What was he trying to convey? Whatever it was—I didn't get it.

And then, like a dam breaking, the question that had been simmering at the edge of my awareness probably since last weekend finally erupted before I could hold back. "Max, do *you* want me there? Do you even *want* to play with me on Saturday?"

The pause that followed felt interminable. It probably wasn't, but it was long enough for me to curse myself fifteen times for showing him my hand, letting him see my insecure side. Now he'd get irritated, snap at me, hang up. Or worse —tell me not to come.

"Yes, malysh," he finally answered. "I do want you there. I do want to play with you."

His voice was even and smooth, and perhaps even a measure more firm than usual, which made it somehow more reassuring, and heat flooded my neck and chest at the affirmation. My face broke into an involuntary grin, though I still couldn't speak.

So, that was what had really been bothering me, what I'd really wanted to know— I wasn't actually particularly worried about who the second Dom would be. I worried about whether Max wanted me there for himself—and now that I knew he did, I finally felt some of that relief I'd been chasing all day. I tried to sigh, but my heart was racing too fast and my ribcage refused to expand.

Meanwhile, Max was back to business. "Please don't forget what we discussed yesterday. Skirt. White top. Stockings. High heels."

"Yes, master," I said, and then, suddenly remembering the rules as they were written out above the mirror, asked, "Will security let me in wearing heels?"

I was still smiling, and when Max said, "They'll make an exception for you, malysh. For you, they will," I could tell that he was smiling too.

Chapter Eighteen

On my way to the club on Saturday, doubts and anxiety seized me once again. I envisioned myself sitting on the bar, wearing that dumb catholic schoolgirl uniform, with the entire club staring at me in dismay, wondering why a grown-ass woman would put on such a ridiculous get-up. I imagined looking to Max for reassurance and finding he wasn't there—replaced by some faceless stranger.

The mere thought of it caused my brain and body to revolt so fiercely that I had to pull over to the side of the road to catch my breath.

I shouldn't go.

Should I?

No.

Yes.

Glancing at the clock, I realized I needed to decide quickly. There wasn't much room to indulge in endless doubts and deliberations. Not wishing to arrive early and end up feeling awkward, I'd given myself just enough time to arrive by ten on the dot, like Max had ordered.

Placing my palm over my solar plexus, I closed my eyes, urging myself to relax at least a little, attempting to feel my body as a whole and calm the epicenter of my fear. Opening my eyes, I looked thoughtfully at the package in the passenger seat. Inside were brand new suede stilettos, a provocative schoolgirl costume, fishnet stockings, and a garter belt.

All as ordered.

Slowly flipping the visor down, I peered into the mirror to examine my face again. I almost didn't recognize myself, with my unusually bright makeup and frivolous pigtails, fastened with colorful ribbons, a hairstyle I deemed appropriate for my overall image.

With a sigh, I released the visor, and it snapped back in place with a thud. How ridiculous did I look, exactly, on a scale of one to ten: twenty? A hundred? One thousand?

Just as I was about to get seriously upset by my own doubts and thoughts, a loud ringtone made me jump and snapped me back to the real world.

Startled, I grabbed for my purse and pulled out my phone, answering the call almost faster than I could read "Max" on the display.

"Hi, Liza. Are you here?" he asked in such a demanding tone that I involuntarily swallowed.

"Um... almost."

"Get here, malysh. I want you kneeling before me in ten minutes."

His voice sounded a bit impatient but also, supremely confident. He allowed no room for doubt that I would come, and I felt embarrassed that I ever considered standing him up. I would go. If not for myself, then for him. It was almost calming—the idea that I *had* to go, for him, for Max, like it took the difficult decision away from me—a relief.

"Yes, master," I replied quickly. "On my way."

"Good girl. Get a move on," he said and hung up.

Tossing the phone into my purse, I zipped it shut, flung it aside, and then peeled off onto the road so quickly that I didn't even realize how I fast I was going until, within a couple of minutes, I was turning into the courtyard by the club. I pulled over near the entrance, and throwing the car into park, hopped out, bag with costume clutched to my chest. I followed some unfamiliar man— a regular, by the looks of it—through the unmarked dark door... and froze, my hand clamped to my open mouth, as soon as I stepped inside.

————

The lobby looked same as always, except now, bouncers were occupied with mercilessly spanking some unfortunate half-naked girl, right there by the entrance. My cheeks instantly burned crimson from the shock, and my whole body stiffened in sympathy, my fingers tightly clenched around my bag. The girl looked tiny and utterly defenseless in the hands of the two brutes, and with each resounding slap they doled out, she let out a shrill, pitiful scream that squeezed something inside me—every time.

They had her bent over one of the elegant reception chairs, her short skirt hiked up to her waist and her whispy panties pulled down to her knees. If my assessment was correct, they were the reason for her current predicament, along with the bright red high-heeled shoes she wore. They made her already slender legs look positively scrawny.

One of the hulks had briefly diverted his attention to open the door, but his right hand still held the unfortunate girl down by the neck as his eyes glided over me and the man who had entered before me. Then, he calmly returned to his task - namely, manually restraining the poor girl, as she struggled and his partner continued to spank her tiny, naked ass.

It took a good several seconds and the loud slam of the door for me to snap out of my shock. The man who entered the club with me had already moved inside, while I still stood there, gawking, my mouth hanging open. Realizing that the guards were about to finish with the girl and then, they would all catch me staring, I sidled over to the entrance of the dressing room and, sharply turning, fell through the door.

Once inside, I stood on the threshold for a couple more seconds, hand on chest, breathing heavily and trying to regain my composure. And only once I was able to hear myself think through the incessant banging of my heart, did I realize I wasn't there alone.

"Hi."

Startled, I looked up. A red-haired girl about my height and build, in a stunning knee-length black lace dress was fixing her hair by another locker. "They still haven't finished with Marishka?"

"What?" I asked.

She sharply nodded towards the foyer, then waved her hand dismissively. "Never mind. You must be new."

I nodded, choosing a locker as far away from her as possible and deliberately taking my time - for some reason, I didn't want to take my clothes off in her presence.

"I'm Anastasia, Nik's sub," she introduced herself, her voice full of pride, almost boastful. "He's the owner of the club, so if you have any questions, just ask."

"Thanks," I muttered barely audibly, opening my locker.

"When did you do your auction?" she asked, coming closer.

"Um... I didn't." I replied absently, pulling my clothes out of the bag.

The redhead threw such a pointed glance at my costume that my cheeks instantly flushed. Was it not adequate? I wasn't exactly well-versed in erotic dress and bought the cheapest set from the first online store I found. I didn't even know if I would need it more than once.

But at that moment, under the derisive stare of this snobby redhead, I wished I could go back in time and purchase something... better. Fancier. More expensive. My pitiful little outfit contrasted way too starkly with the other girl's gorgeous, sophisticated dress.

"A schoolgirl costume?" she sneered. "Honey, you're unlikely to impress any decent Dom with that trashy piece."

I froze with the skirt in my hands. Something inside me clicked, shifting from feeling upset with myself to feeling aggressive toward an external enemy. Why in the world was it so difficult for people to mind their own damn business?

"You know something, if I'm ever need of a second opinion, you'll be the first to know," I gritted through my clenched teeth.

Anastasia's eyes narrowed, but an instant later, her face spread into a deliberate saccharine grin. "Don't get all worked up now, little girl, or I might have to ask my master to buy you and give you a nice little treatment with his whip. Your auction is tonight, right?"

"Wrong," I barked in her face. "And you can keep your nasty to yourself, *little girl*, or else *I* might have to ask *my* master to give you a nice treatment with *his* whip. He just got a really pretty new one, too. Nice and stiff."

Anastasia stood, legs akimbo, hands on hip, smirking.

"Well, aren't we mouthy. You won't do well here like that, darling, so don't get too comfortable after your auction—I'd say you'll be out on your ass as fast as you arrived."

"You know what, you can fuck right off, you—" I growled, completely losing my temper, but then my phone vibrated in my purse again, and all words instantly evaporated, my heart stopping.

Max. The time. Damn!

"Aww, what's wrong?" she said with another sneer. "Is your mommy looking for her lost little girl?"

Her laugh sounded downright sinister right before she slammed my locker door shut with a bang inches away from my face, and, still chuckling to herself, sauntered off toward the exit.

My body was trembling with rage and frustration. Who would have known that my schoolgirl role would include getting bullied before I ever got changed or started the scene? But soon, as I rummaged in the depths of my purse trying to get at my vibrating phone, I didn't give a shit about her anymore.

"Sub," Max's sharp voice rang in my ear. "It's been ten minutes. Did I not make it clear where you should be right now?"

"M... Max, I'm in the dressing room. I just need sixty more seconds," I pleaded, feeling frightened in spite of myself.

"Hurry up, Liza. I'm at the bar," he ordered abruptly, and my adrenaline instantly shot off the chart.

I changed as fast as I could, thinking only of one thing: not getting punished before ever getting to the stage, especially not in plain view of that bitch, Anastasia.

Rushing, I pinched my finger in the locker door, groaned, cursed, slammed the locker shut, only to realize I'd left my purse out. Cursing again, I unlocked it once more, tossed the bag inside, spilling its contents, shut the locker, worked in the padlock, put in the combination, made sure it had snapped in...

and then, pressed my hot forehead against the cold metal.

This was madness. I needed at least ten seconds to calm my breathing. Nine... eight... seven...

———

Six seconds later, I stepped out of the dressing room with a face and posture as if I had not a care in the world and my mind was clear and free of everything—except, perhaps, the simple wish to enjoy a tasty cocktail in pleasant company.

"Good evening," I said to the two guards, who now looked bored, as if they hadn't been executing that poor girl here just five minutes ago.

"Good evening, sub. Have a pleasant night," one of them responded in a practiced voice and opened the door for me.

Well, Max hadn't lied — they really did let me in with my shoes on and... damn... my panties on, too. I stumbled at the threshold, remembering that I hadn't been supposed to wear them. It was too late now. Or was it?

Yes, it was, I realized as I met eyes with Max across the room, as he stood up from the bar stool to meet me. In his hand was a paddle, and in his eyes a delicious hint of threat.

He made a beckoning gesture, then widened his stance and waited, shaking his head in mild reproach. Blushing, I walked towards him through the entire room, feeling dozens of eyes on me. Just as I approached the bar, I noticed Nik in the company of the obnoxious redhead — she sat next to her master, massaging his shoulders, her cold gaze fixed on me.

161

With tremendous satisfaction, I noticed the dismay on her face as she realized who I was meeting, then forgot all about her when I locked eyes with my Dom.

"On your knees," he ordered quietly when I stopped within arm's reach of him.

Kneeling before him, which was not very comfortable in my stiletto shoes, I carefully sat back on my heels, looking down at the checkered hem of my tiny red-and-white skirt, barely covering the apex of my thighs. The top of the costume was a short white crop top, more a bra than a shirt in concept.

"You're late, sub."

"Forgive me, master," I mumbled.

"Can't hear you."

"Forgive me, master," I repeated, lifting my face.

Max snapped his fingers loudly, and I flinched, involuntarily looking at him. Fortunately, he didn't notice it, as his gaze was directed somewhere into the distance.

"Get up, little one," he softened, lightly tapping me on the shoulder with the paddle. Jumping to my feet, I stood humbly beside him, lowering my eyelashes.

"Look at me," Max ordered quietly.

Our eyes met, and my breath hitched at the back of my throat again. His gaze burned as if he were ready to fuck me right at that moment, without further preamble. Pressing me closer, he wrapped one arm around my waist and ran the other over my chest, squeezing my nipple painfully — I gasped — and then brought it even lower, lifting the hem of my skirt to reveal the thin white panties underneath.

"Panties?" he tsk'd. "Bad girl."

He held me tighter, not allowing me to move, and worked his hand under the thin layer of cotton, sliding over the slippery skin and roughly penetrating me with one finger. "What do you think, what sort of punishment do you deserve?"

"Please, master, I'm sorry." I pleaded, thinking only of the repulsive redhead behind me, and the unbearable prospect of withstanding a punishment within her fiend of vision.

Max's eyebrows rose slightly. "And what will you do to make amends?" he asked with a slight smile, pressing against a sensitive spot inside me.

"Anything you want," I whispered, instinctively closing my eyes.

"Anything I want? That's interesting. But you're making a mistake, my beauty," Max chuckled, pressing me even closer, but withdrawing his hand. "My imagination is far broader than your boundaries."

"So, does that mean you will forgive me, master?" I whispered, raising my eyelashes and smiling at him.

His gaze softened, and as further evidence of his leniency, I received a tender stroke on the cheek with the tips of his fingers.

"You've become very clever in just two days," he said, studying my face and lowering his voice to a whisper. "Are you ready for our scene?"

"Honestly, not really," I whispered, back, closing my eyes again. The realization that the infamous scene was upon me made my stomach clench tightly.

"Don't be afraid. Let's go," he said and, taking my hand firmly, led me through the room.

Chapter Nineteen

We strolled past several play stations, where people watched scenes unfold, just like last week. Ahead was an open space, free of equipment and clutter, except for a large desk, upon which sat Nik, absent-mindedly playing with a flogger. This is where we stopped.

I instantly broke out in a sweat. Nik? I couldn't believe my eyes—wasn't he just at the bar?

Shit. Shit. I'd really hoped it would be Dima, or someone else. Anyone else! That red-haired sub of Nik's was still in my peripheral vision, lurking somewhere among the spectators, boring a hole through me, her eyes full of bitter loathing. If what had happened between me and that woman in the changing room could be considered a chance encounter, judging by the feral look on her face, she'd just declared war. To the death.

Definitely—at this point, I would have preferred a complete stranger.

Shifting my gaze to Nik, I had to wonder if he understood the degree of this woman's jealousy, and if he did, why he was doing this to her.

In the next instance, however, I stopped thinking about anything or anyone but myself, because Nik spotted me, rising from his seat, and Max nudged me forward, until I stood in the middle of the empty space, facing the spectators. I now had an audience of about forty people and counting. Or, to be more precise, Nik and Max, the two best-regarded masters at the club, now had an audience of forty people and counting.

With Nik no longer seated on the desk, I noticed, with horror, the objects displayed on it. The purpose of each of them was to administer some sort of corporal punishment: a long ruler, a cane, a belt, several—oh, God!—canes and switches. Cold sweats returned, and my knees threatened to buckle. I was not prepared to endure the use of all these items.

"Liza?" Max whispered into my ear, "Breathe. And hop up on that desk."

Shaking myself out of my trance, I cautiously climbed onto the desk, stealing a glance over my shoulder to see Nik holding the flogger.

Maybe it would help me to get into my role a little. Experimentally, I swung my legs back and forth a few times.

There was gum in my pocket!

I took it out and shoved three pieces into my mouth at once, blowing a massive bubble, as I stared right at the backs of my two executioners, who stood facing the audience, awaiting their attention. Once silence settled over the crowd, I burst the bubble with a deafening pop, causing both men to startle and turn around, while some of the spectators chuckled.

Back to my senses, I was feeling much better. I flashed Max a dazzling smile and shook my head side to side, letting my ridiculous pigtails bounce. My Dom didn't react, his facial expression growing inscrutable, as he faced the public.

A few moments later, when the space was deathly quiet again, in a quiet voice he announced, "We request complete silence. A math examination is underway. Any disruption will result in removal from the premises. Both proctors are present, and the student has just arrived. We will commence in two minutes."

He repeated, "Complete silence," and both Doms turned around slowly, approaching me and closing the distance between us.

I glanced at Max with apprehension, edging away, but he gently shook his head, stroking my hair. "Liza, it's just a game," he soothed, his whisper barely audible. "We'll ask questions, you'll give answers. If you're wrong, you get a smack with a paddle or a strike of the flogger. Have you used a flogger before?"

"No."

Max turned to Nik, who lightly slapped the falls of the instrument across my bare lap. I tentatively touched the strands of suede with the tips of my fingers, and took a relieved breath.

"It's a soft toy, malysh. There won't be too much pain, I promise," whispered Nik, catching my eye, and I nodded, immediately looking away.

"Okay. And then?"

"Then... we'll do some other things," said Max evasively, glancing towards the implements laid out on the desk. "Don't worry about getting the answers right. The whole point is to fail the exam."

"And then what?"

I looked at him, terrified, but he only smiled.

"Depends on your behavior."

"Max. Please. Tell me what you're going to do?"

"Sub, don't make me mad, it's not in your best interest. And spit that gum out, right now."

He really did sound just like a teacher...

Stuffing the gum, wrapped in a scrap of paper, into my pocket, I lowered my eyes, and for a while, my senses were overwhelmed by the pounding of my own heart and the roar of blood in my ears. There was nothing else.

————

And then, Max took several steps back and in a loud, frighteningly stern voice asked, "What is your name, Miss? And why are you tardy to the examination?"

"I... um..."

"Ium? That's certainly an original name. Never heard that before. Young people these days, don't you agree, Professor?" he addressed Nik, who nodded, studying me as if he were seeing me for the first time.

Color rising up my neck, I mumbled, "Liza. My name is Liza."

"So she has an actual name. Look at that," Nik said, in a deliberately obnoxious nasal voice. "Well, Liza, why, pray tell, are you tardy? Do you think it's appropriate to make two professors wait?"

"I didn't mean to be late, Professor... There was a detour and I had to take the back way—"

I licked my dry lips, thinking I did well coming up with that excuse on the spot, but several people burst into laughter, and even Max raised his eyebrows.

"Oh, she took the back way—this sounds promising," he remarked. "Ladies and gentlemen, it looks like this student might be more advanced than we thought."

The audience laughed again, and I felt myself turning crimson to the tips of my ears. Meanwhile, Nik made a circle around the table, and touched my shoulder with the handle of his flogger, as though caressing me. "Here's your first question, then, Liza. What is three times seven?"

"Twenty one."

"Good. You studied?"

"Yes, Professor." I smiled.

"And why are you grinning?" Max's voice turned icy all of a sudden. "Professor, don't you feel like this student isn't taking her academic standing seriously?"

"Perhaps," Nik replied almost lazily from somewhere behind me, and then, his flogger whacked against the table so suddenly and so loudly, that I gasped and actually jumped.

In the audience, someone snorted in laughter.

Max came closer, looming over me, and asked, "Quick, seven times eight."

"Forty eight!" I burst out, startled, only to be met with more laughter from the audience, which told me my answer had been incorrect even before the belated it's fifty six, idiot, could float up from the depths of my consciousness.

"Tsk, and she's trying to tell us she studied," Nik reproachfully chimed in, his voice condescendingly sing-songy. "How embarrassing for you, Miss. Now, how about we raise eight to the third power?"

Max gently spread my knees apart and moved in close, standing between them. His expression was unreadable, but his gaze locked onto mine was absolutely hypnotizing. With each passing second, the audience, the room, the lights faded away. All that remained was his scent, his gaze, and the warm touch of his hand.

To the third power... to the third power—Christ, right now, this sounded completely nonsensical in my brain. Eight times eight is eight squared, which is the same as the second power, so the third power is...

"I don't know..." I whispered in despair, feeling utterly tormented at my inability to come up with an answer.

"That's no good," Nik said, stretching out the vowels. He was somewhere very close to me. "Wrong answers incur punishments, if you recall. I suppose we could try something a little simpler. Subtract ninety-seven from one hundred and eight, my dear, and that'll be the number of strikes with the flogger you will receive. But if you can't manage the subtraction, then, hmm... then we'll have no choice but to use multiplication—multiply the numbers of strikes by two."

Max eased me down onto my back, his grin devilish as he loomed over me, his hand slipping under my shirt and sneaking upward until it covered my breast, caressing it gently, and squeezing the nipple.

"Oh..." I arched when it passed the point of pain, and gazed at him asking for mercy.

"I'm still waiting for your answer, Liza," Nik said in a smarmy tone, trailing the flogger down my arm.

"Professor, please could you repeat the question?" I pleaded.

"Certainly. One hundred and eight minus ninety seven," repeated Nik, patting my arm with his palm, while Max pitilessly continued caressing my breast.

"Eleven!" I burst forth, catching an elusive moment of mental clarity.

"Excellent. Now we have two right answers, and two wrong ones. What shall we do, Professor?" asked Nik.

"This is a great question, Professor. What do you think, Liza?"

"Me?"

Max's lips curved into a smile in response to my surprise. "You, of course. Perhaps you'd like to suggest something to us instead of punishment? Or maybe you'd prefer eleven lashes with the flogger?"

"I... I don't..."

"It's possible we might enjoy it if you unbuttoned your fancy little blouse. Professor, how would you feel about playing with her charming breasts and lovely nipples?"

Nik didn't say anything, but I almost felt him shrugging, as though it didn't matter to him.

Carefully, Max pulled me up to sit, helping me lower my feet again, and suddenly, there they all were, the entire club, and I was facing them head on. My cheeks and ears flamed with heat.

"Well, Liza? The professor is waiting for your decision. Flogger or blouse?"

"Flogger," I forced out, without having to think about it much. A lashing sounded infinitely better than a striptease.

"You disappoint me, my dear," Nik sighed. "Well, what can you do? I suppose you'd better get up."

Max stepped aside, shaking his head. My heart sank for a moment, thinking he was genuinely displeased with my choice, before I remembered this was the idea behind the whole game. As I hopped off the table, I found myself face to face with Nik.

"Turn around and bend over the desk, Liza," he commanded impassively, toying with the flogger.

I slowly turned and took a deep breath. The good news was, now the audience was behind me, out of sight. The bad news... I still couldn't bring myself to bend over. The mere thought of everyone watching made something twist inside me. Yet, there was no denying that my body was in flames, my nipples swollen from Max's ministrations, a heaviness settling between my legs.

"Quit stalling. Bend over," Max commanded in a stage whisper from across the table.

Meeting eyes made it easier to obey the order—as if his words and voice somehow managed to provide moral support.

"Hands," he whispered again, in that private tone clearly not meant for Nik or the public at large, and held his own hands out in an impatient gesture. I let him cuff my wrists and only once I was restrained, did Nik hike up my skirt and... he lowered my panties to my knees. Oh, my god...this was the real bad news—I didn't have to see the audience, but now they could all see my bare ass! My whole body lurched when Nik's hand caressed my skin there, prepping it.

"Shh, it's okay, just relax," Max murmured, grabbing my wrists with one hand, and pressing on the back of my neck with the other.

The first few strikes of the flogger were softer than I'd expected—soft, careful slaps of the suede falls. They became stronger gradually, and the last two brought real pain; nothing too severe, but definitely palpable.

The worst part came after: the realization that Max had no intention of letting me go, and Nik's plans included the continuation of my "exam" in this exact position, ass up, panties down.

Petting warm skin with his palm, Nik, began again. "So then. Shall we go on? Liza, would you be so kind as to remind me what the square root of four is?"

"Two!"

"Hm. She sounds awfully excited by square roots. What if we checked how much?" With a deft movement, he used the toe of his shoe to slide my right foot gently to the side, parting my legs as far as my panties, now slipping down to my ankles, would allow.

My body tensed. Max had used this exact move to spread my legs during our first encounter, just before he went on to fuck me like I'd never been fucked before. It was incredibly arousing, yes, but I didn't want Nik to actually touch me. Or... Did I?

Nik's skilled fingers didn't wait for me to decide, slipping between my buttocks and down past the vagina toward the swollen nub of my clitoris. I let out a soft moan when he found the epicenter of my excitement, and pressed on it gently a few times with an implacable fingertip.

"Huh. Looks like she rather enjoys those square roots. I have to wonder about exponents. And integrals."

Once again, merry laughter came from the audience, but my heart raced and my ears rang, blocking out all noise other than the sound of my own labored breathing. When two fingers smoothly found their way inside me, I melted in pleasure and dissociated completely.

But this wasn't good. This was terrible.

My body was betraying me.

And not just me—it was betraying Max, with another man, right in front of him and a whole bunch of strangers.

The next two questions never reached my consciousness.

Trapped in Max's grasp, I might have tried to get away, and he held me down more and more firmly, until I felt a serious pressure on my neck. Meanwhile, Nik's fingers were everywhere at the same time: inside, outside, on the clit, in the pussy. The two Doms exchanged jokes and remarks, entertaining the audience. Then, the fingers disappeared, and I realized that someone was picking up the yardstick, which had been patiently waiting by my head.

"Ah!"

I snapped back to reality. I arched my back with the mild pain of the impact. I was being spanked again—by Max this time.

Max?

It was only then that I realized the two men had switched roles. Max had released me, and now Nik was the one who held my hands, while Max administered the punishment. I sighed and closed my eyes. This was much better. It hurt, but let it hurt. Max's punishment was harder and there were no caresses as he did it, but at least it was him. After hit number four, tears sprang from my eyes, and I heard myself sob.

"Well, I think that's enough," Max announced.

I was released and lifted, arranged into a sitting position on the table, like a limp doll without a will of her own.

Softly, he asked, "Liza will be a good girl from now on, won't you, Liza? You'll unbutton your blouse for your favorite professor, won't you?"

"Yes," I replied, my voice barely audible, my gaze fixed only on Max's eyes.

"Go ahead, then," he commanded.

Still sniffling, I ran my fingers over the buttons down my front, which yielded easily to a light pull, exposing my bare breasts.

"Lie back, my dear," Nik said gently, standing beside me. His gaze from above seemed very gentle and kind, and I relaxed, but only slightly.

Slowly, with much hesitation, I lay back attempting to study the expressions on both of their faces in turn. But it was futile—there was nothing to be gleaned from them. Max, as usual, was impassive, while Nick looked almost tender for now, but who knew how to interpret that.

"And now - some additional questions. Liza, take this seriously, you're on the verge of failing the exam," Nik said, furrowing his brows together with visible effort—the role of the stern teacher seemed to be a challenge for him at the moment, and it even made me chuckle a little.

"Yes, professor," I murmured, looking up at him and trying not to smile.

"Five times eight?"

"Forty."

"Six times three?"

"Eight—teen," I stammered—the answer wasn't the problem, though, it was Max. What he had just done almost took away my ability to speak: his strong hands on my inner thighs spread my legs and bent them at the knees. Oh no. Now even my struggling, wet pussy was out on display for everyone to see.

Although, he covered it almost instantly with his palm, inserting three fingers at once—but I couldn't say that made me any more able to speak or even think.

"Nine times seven?"

Nik bent over me, catching a hardened nipple between his lips, and I opened my mouth wide, gasping for air. This was impossible. Impossible to have a single coherent thought while being tortured in this way.

"Mmm..."

"Liza?" Max asked, taking his hand away. "Did you hear the question?"

"Um..."

"Seven times nine?"

"I don't--"

A sharp slap to the pussy startled and made me jump in shock. My knees slammed together reflexively, but Max was vigilant, and immediately caught one, pulling it to the side.

"Very bad, Liza. Try again. Seven times nine?"

Nik's mouth was scalding as his tongue made circles around one aching nipple, and his hand caressed the other. It was unbearable.

"Forty... seven...?"

Another slap with a closed palm, harsh, merciless, stinging. And right behind that, another one, even harder. Oh, no. I felt so vulnerable that I was ready to howl. What kind of person makes it a habit to hit a woman *there*? It felt like being whacked directly on exposed nerve endings.

"Cane?" Max asked suddenly, and I screamed out a desperate no, before realizing he wasn't actually asking me.

"Why not?" Nik replied laconically.

Strong hands gripped my shoulders, turning me over; Max helped from below, and before I knew it, I was face down on the desk, completely defenseless and exposed, my ass out again, this time almost completely bare—the skirt had ridden up to somewhere around my waist.

"Max... master, please don't..." I whimpered, turning towards him.

"Liza?" He came a little closer and crouched, putting his hand on the back of my neck, but not to restrain–to provide comfort. "Are you all right?"

"Master, I don't want this. I can't handle any more..."

"Liza, do you remember your safe words?"

"Yes, but..."

"You can use them. Say them in your head and think about it."

I obeyed him, going still, repeating the words in my head, listening to my body. Once I fully grasped that this was a possibility—complete cessation of the game—and also that this was, despite everything, still just a game, my panic receded. I was able to swallow back any rising tears and shake my head with certainty when Max asked, "Do you want to use your safe words?"

"No. No, I'm sorry. I'm okay. I can continue."

"Okay, then."

Max gathered a bunch of switches in his hand and circled me, positioning himself to shield me from the audience.

"Liza, you've been a very bad student," he said sternly. "You'll receive five strokes, and then we'll discuss a potential make-up exam. Count the strikes out loud. Hopefully, you'll learn at least a few simple numbers."

Nik placed his palm on the back of my head, gently stroking it, but in the next moment, I stopped feeling his touch as the sharp strike bit into both buttocks at once, and I involuntarily cried out.

"Count," Max barked loudly enough for the whole room to hear, "otherwise, we start all over."

"One," I choked out through tears. This punishment was truly painful, yet, at the same time, it stirred up a morbid curiosity—I wanted to know what would happen next, how much more I could take.

Two strikes. Three. On the fourth, I sobbed loudly, and Max stopped.

"Alright. I see, that's enough for you. Or do you need to count higher to boost your motivation?" he asked.

"No! No, Professor," I rushed to answer.

"Fine. In that case, for our next exercise, we're just counting to two."

"Two?"

"Two orgasms, my dear,"Max said tenderly, and his lips curved in a devilish smirk once again.

Chapter Twenty

Oh, *no. Oh, no-no-no.* I could never have an orgasm while being watched by an entire crowd of people. This time, Max was clearly overestimating my abilities. *I am not—*

"Flip over," Nik commanded softly, giving my hair a gentle pull.

Hesitating, I turned onto my back, acutely aware of every single one of the spectators who stood around me, about to witness my demise. Just a moment ago, I didn't care about their existence, but now, it was like I'd taken a plunge into the stifling heat generated by the dense crowd. And even though no one made a sound, I could still feel it, the lascivious, insatiable energy coming off these people, the vibration of their eager excitement, their sticky, smarmy stares, as they thirsted for more—more of the spectacle of my humiliation.

My entire body was wracked by tremors, and only one phrase spun non-stop in my head: "I can't, I won't; I can't, I won't..."

But it wasn't my fear of the audience or the shame of

exposure and vulnerability that bothered me most in that moment. It was the fear of disappointing Max. That would kill me. A perfect submissive, of course, could orgasm at any moment, simply at the command of their master—right? I'd read about orgasm control. It sounded like fiction.

I knew I couldn't do that.

I don't understand why my orgasms happen when they do and not a second later or earlier, and why sometimes, they don't happen at all. I have no say over them and don't know how to—

Suddenly, a gust of warm breath ruffled the hairs on my neck near my ear, and right away a hot whisper reached my consciousness.

"Stop thinking, sub. Otherwise, I'll take the belt right now and replace all thoughts in your head with pain until you scream and beg for mercy. Do you wish to scream in pain and beg for mercy?"

A sticky shiver ran down my spine. I twitched. Oh God, was that Max or Nik? Swallowing hard, I realized with horror that I didn't know, couldn't tell—until a second later, when I turned my head and locked eyes with Nik. His lips twisted into a mocking smile.

"Did you get us confused?"

Wide-eyed with astonishment, I froze, unsure what to do or say next, even propping myself up on my elbows, scrutinizing Nik's face. How did he know? How did he read my thoughts? Are all these BDSM masters psychologists?

Meanwhile, looking quite satisfied with himself and the trick he'd played on me, Nik glanced at Max and nodded. Max nodded back and circled the table, approaching me. He reached into his pocket and pulled out a piece of dark fabric, which I initially mistook for a handkerchief, but then realized—it was a blindfold.

"Liza," he said firmly. "Now is the moment when you look me in the eye and tell me that you're ready to put on this blindfold and submit to me completely. This means you entrust yourself completely to me, and accept everything I wish to do with you or allow Master Nik to do with you. If you want to use a safe word, or have any hard limits or taboos for this part of the scene, you should voice them now."

Master Nik... Interesting how that sounded totally different from just Nik. Somehow, it brought more trust but also took away any warmth. I passed my tongue over my chapped lips, holding back an entire deluge of questions. I wanted to know what they had planned, but it was patently clear Max didn't make a habit of revealing his plans. In essence, I had two options: trust him and forge ahead or continue to resist until one of them acted on their promise to pick up the belt and exert a punishment.

Or end it all. That was a third option—but it wasn't really an option.

I began shaking again. He wanted to blindfold me so I couldn't tell which one of them was doing what to me... but if I couldn't tell who it was, then it would be as though they combined into one entity. Nik would then have as much authority over me and my body as Max. And what if Nik decided to exercise his rights and fuck me? Max's features became blurry when my eyes welled up with tears. I was supposed to trust Max not to abuse his authority—that was the whole point, but— I shuddered and let out an involuntary sob.

Max crouched again, tucked a strand of hair behind my ear. "Liza. What are you thinking about? Talk to me."

"Max. I need you to promise me Nik isn't going to fuck me. I don't want it. That's the taboo."

Max's eyebrows crept up for a millisecond, then returned to their rightful place.

"I promise," he said simply. "Neither one of us will fuck you here. Do you allow penetration with fingers?"

I forced out a nearly inaudible "Yes."

"Objects or toys?"

"Oh, Lord."

"Is that a yes?"

"Yes."

"Okay. Good job," he whispered, leaning over me to touch his lips lightly to mine. "Now there is nothing for you to do but relax and breathe. I've got the rest."

At the same time, I heard several suppressed sighs from the audience, and wanted to turn and see what that was about, but Max chose that moment to lower the blindfold over my eyes and secure it at the back of my head.

"We need a little music here."

That was Nik, sounding calm and businesslike, as though he were just sharing a project idea at a meeting.

"Fantastic idea," Max replied, and a few moments later, I heard the first notes of the ever-present Enigma album.

Enigma! I smiled to myself, recalling how a few decades ago, when Enigma was at the peak of its popularity, this album became fuck music for the whole country as people figured out its puzzling aphrodisiac effects. Jokes aside, though, there was something there. Taking a deep breath, I felt my body relaxing by itself, despite the fact that the decibel level was almost too high; it felt like the speaker was somewhere right next to me or right under the desk, by my head. Maybe it was someone's cellphone.

I couldn't see a thing because of the mask and couldn't hear a thing because of the music. All I could do was wait.

My stillness finally broke when something warm

touched my ankle. At the same time, something scalding spilled over my nipple, and jerked, I flinching.

Oh! *Wow.*

How strange and disconcerting it was not to know what exactly was being done to my body, or who it was being done by... It seemed like an eternity, but it must have only been a fraction of a second before I realized one man was flicking my nipple with his tongue, while the other was stroking my calf with a warm palm, gradually traveling upward.

I was keenly aware of every part of my body simultaneously—how my ass, pressed against the hard surface of the desk, smarted from the caning, how my pussy ached from the accumulated effect of arousal and frustration, how my heels pressed into the desk as I arched my back from the rapidly intensifying desire.

I felt the warmth of a man's hand on the inner side of my thigh, and my left nipple throbbed from the vigorous sucking, while the right one throbbed with the desire to feel the same caresses - until finally, someone's fingers squeezed it, twisting slightly.

An unexpected burning sensation around my lower belly jolted me like an electric shock, and it took a moment for to realize no one was burning or shocking me—it was just a hot male palm laid flat across my body.

My left breast was suddenly cold, abruptly abandoned by the warm mouth caressing it, but then someone's fingers tightly squeezed the nipple and I let out a soft squeaking noise, raising my hand instinctively to push the assailant away—which I regretted almost instantly. Both of my hands were grabbed firmly and pulled over my head, and a few moments later, I felt something rigid and cold, like a belt, being fastened around them. Attempts to tug free revealed that I'd been rather securely bound, without room to wiggle or opportunity to free myself.

A sharp blow caught me off guard—a genuine burn now, to my inner thigh. A vulnerable cry erupted from my throat, but it was completely drowned out by the loud music. Instinctively, I tried to close my legs, but instead encountered two more blows, one to my thigh and one to the lower abdomen. They stung terribly but felt small and fast, the pain subsiding almost immediately. Yet, it was still somehow... startling, frightening, to know more could be coming from an unknown direction, aimed to an unknown location on my body. I panicked and began to fight despite myself, intensifying my efforts when I felt someone grip me by the ankles.

My legs were soon forced apart again, and as I thrashed, I was almost sure that both masters were involved in this act of near-violence. They bent my knees up and secured my legs in a way that not only prevented me from closing my legs, but also made it impossible to straighten my knees.

Then the punishment really came crashing down upon me.

First the flogger. Not overly harsh, I felt each strike deeply as it came down on my thighs, lower abdomen, and breasts. I began to cry beneath the blindfold, out of sheer frustration at my defenseless and vulnerability, but oddly, it felt good. It was as though I couldn't cope with that feeling, yet at the same time I relished in my tears, seizing the opportunity to release that emotion.

With the change of melody, the flogger was replaced by something much harder. A paddle? A belt? I couldn't tell. The strikes approached my pussy, I knew that's where they were headed, I knew it was coming, it was inevitable. My whole body trembled in terror. I was spinning out, and even blindfolded, I felt how the room spun out with me. I couldn't take it. I was going to scream, scream from this unbearable sense of fear, tightly intertwined with an impossible anticipation—

—and that was when it came, a massive shock despite being fully predictable.

A hard, forceful blow right there.

Now I did scream, and this time, perhaps my scream even drowned out the music.

The blindfold was damp—not just from tears, but also sweat. I was covered in a sheen of it, my skin cold and clammy, every muscle in my battered body quivering, as I awaited the next blow, feverishly calculating how much longer I could endure before reaching my limit and using a safe word. Perhaps two more. Or even just one, if they suddenly decided to strike harder.

But then, a hand lay on my stomach again, creeping gently downward, fingers sliding between engorged tissues. The penetration coincided with a new, light but biting, blow to my breast.

What was that? A crop?

And how many fingers were inside me?

Whose fingers were they?

I could feel them delving deeper, the impact becoming more intense, and between the back and forth motion and the strikes to my breasts, a regularly irregular rhythm began to emerge.

Suddenly, the music grew louder, and a strange novel sensation detonated within my brain. In addition to the room spinning around me, the table spun as well, and I myself had been ejected from my body and now floated somewhere slightly above it, observing myself. At the same time, I heard a guttural wail and understood on a cognitive level that I was coming before physically appreciating the actual orgasm.

The out of body experience ended as fast as it began, however, and I was back within myself, climaxing so intensely it felt like it had been building up for years, only now finally finding its way out. I moaned and arched so sharply, my shoulders felt like they were about to dislocate, and fortunately, one of my vigilant masters immediately unfastened my binds, releasing me and allowing me to assume a more comfortable position.

But I was allowed no break. A few moments, and I realized I was being spanked again—this time directly on the clitoris. It didn't feel painful, however, more like a caress— pleasant, gentle, rhythmic strikes with something very soft.

"Ohh..." I moaned, and arched, finally allowing my body to relax. The music had quieted somewhat, and the temperature in the room had been turned out, though not unpleasantly; just enough to cool me down.

Excitement surged once more, almost immediately, and even though the first orgasm had just ebbed, I already licked my lips awaiting the next one.

And then, everything stopped.

All I was left with was one finger gently sliding up and down my clitoris, much too softly and much too slowly to result in any sort of release. Whimpering softly, I focused on enduring the torment, working on not squirming, not grinding my hips, now letting the two masters and the whole club along with them bear witness to my extreme lust and frustration.

"Are you enjoying yourself, sweetheart?" Max whispered softly right by my ear, and I swallowed at the realization that it must be Nik, then, caressing me between my legs, right at that moment.

"Yes," I whispered back, barely finding the strength to speak.

"Do you want to come again, pet?"

"Yes, master."

"Then, submit to me."

"How?"

The last word was said without a sound, just with my lips, but somehow, I had no doubt that Max heard me—the music was almost inaudible, and everything else faded away too. The only ones remaining were Max and I...

...and Nik, who continued to caress me with his fingers, so gently and so tenderly, almost lovingly, that after everything they'd done to me tonight, it seemed a surreal madness. My pussy, which should have lost all sensation by now, after being spanked, teased, and pleased within an inch of its life, somehow, magically, appreciated every single barely-there caress sharply, acutely, much more so than the spanking and rough finger-fucking of just a few minutes prior.

"How?"

"Just submit. Surrender, completely, right now," Max whispered, directly into my lips. "Are you ready to give me everything? Everything?"

Oh, God.

Just a second ago, I thought I'd already given him everything-everything. Wasn't I doing everything they said, and letting them do as they wished to me? But now, suddenly and without a doubt, I realized that there was still a powerful force inside me, resisting Max, resisting giving over.

Max touched my temples with the tips of his fingers, sliding under the strap of the blindfold to pull it town. His gaze locked onto mine.

"Are you ready? Ready to submit?"

My eyes watered. A strange sensation spread over my lower half, as though a bubble had burst, spilling something warm over inside me, and it was pleasant, almost invigorating. I exhaled as Nik's fingers came in contact with this warmth, turning it into fire.

"Yes, master."

There was a short pause.

"Yes, pet. You're ready," Max whispered, finally, straightening, and I felt panic coming back. I didn't want him to leave me like this.

"Max. Max, please."

He laid a heavy hand on my breast, and painfully squeezed the nipple, looking at me imperiously from above. "You want to come, but I want to know how bad you want it. I want you to beg."

"I want it. Please. I'm begging you, master. I'm begging you, please."

They'd fulfilled their promise: there were no thoughts left in my head. My words weren't mine; they didn't come from my mind, they came from Max's, as though they were his words, his thoughts. My body wasn't mine, either, it was his, and his orgasm that he had the full right to take and have whenever he wished.

And then the music returned, pounding in my ears. Whoever that sound engineer behind me was, they were close to genius. To feel the moment like that.

"Max!"

Nothing mattered, only his eyes and lips, commanding me, "Beg me. Louder. Scream for me."

"Max... master... Please, I beg you!"

On those last words, I truly screamed. I couldn't bear it anymore. He was so beautiful and ruthless, standing regally, gazing at me from above, covered in sweat, same as me, his hair stuck to his forehead, even his eyelashes damp. It suited him. And there was not a hint of tension on his face, only the light of pure inspiration.

He waited a brief moment before exhaling, "Now. Come, Liza. Come, right now."

If I had any doubts last time, this time I was absolutely not in my body. It sounds like complete madness, but I know I watched my own orgasm from somewhere by the ceiling, or from the side, maybe even from where Max stood, right next to the desk. And I enjoyed it not at all like any other orgasm in my life before this. It was like I could see every cell of my body, from the tips of my toes to the lobes of my ears, and every one of my cells somehow participated in this explosion.

And my lips whispered his name over and over, stuck on repeat.

Chapter Twenty-One

Lori

By midnight, Lori's anxiety was at its limit, and she was about to start climbing walls in frustration. Max gave her a stern talking-to on the phone and disappeared without a verdict or a pardon. That steely edge in his voice... She'd never heard that from him before, not once in the three years of working with him. He had always been supportive, encouraging, his words therapeutic. He'd always been available! Not once had he threatened her or punished her by withdrawal, fully aware that Lori was terrified she wouldn't be able to manage on her own.

When she came to him, she was in ruins. She broke down as soon as she tried to answer his first, very neutral, question. The breakdown occurred because the mere attempt to explain her issue out loud elicited an amount of self-pity and shame that nearly did her in on the spot.

Thinking about that first day now, Lori couldn't wrap her head around the fact that the club didn't even exist then —it didn't open until about a year later—nor around the possibility that Max didn't have a ready solution to her problems in his genius mind. He was just starting out, and

191

she now suspected she'd been his first paying client. But back then, Max's origin story had been the least of her concerns. She badly needed help.

During their first meeting, she sat in that cramped office, with its view of a concrete fence, hunched over, her hands tucked between her knees, trying in vain to get a grip on herself, to ground herself somehow, so she could coherently articulate her complaint. It didn't matter. She fell to pieces anyway.

The problem, as she told it, was as simple as it was unsolvable.

She'd never derived pleasure from sex.

Never. Not once. She didn't like it and didn't know how anyone else could. Other women said they did, and if they were being truthful, then something must be inherently wrong with *her*. She was missing some essential mechanism responsible for arousal.

She held on until she was almost thirty, hoping that she'd find that "special someone" and have that "awakening." It's happened for other people, right?

So they say.

Not for her. Her body remained dormant with no plans of any sort of "awakening," with any of the wonderful men in her life, of which, she told Max, she'd had plenty.

When she turned twenty nine, it suddenly hit her: she would soon enter her fourth decade and no longer be in her prime. She'd inevitably start aging. Not all at once, but gradually. This, today, was the best she'd ever look, feel, and function. And it was the most sensual and responsive she was ever going to get.

In her frantic search for a solution, Lori immediately received a plethora of therapist recommendations from friends. Somewhat gratified, she realized her problem was nowhere near unique—many women, including some of her friends, also had difficulty reaching orgasm, nearly half the women she knew, as it turned out. One of these women recommended Max, assuring that after six months of weekly sessions, all her life-long problems had been resolved—not just orgasms, but also her career and personal life.

Lori was skeptical and obviously couldn't obtain proof of the first claim, but she readily believed the second. Her friend really did just get a sudden promotion to an executive after years of toiling away in middle-management.

All considered, she couldn't say why exactly she chose Max out of all the recommendations she'd received. Perhaps, she had intuited he was different as soon as she saw his professional page.

Though, to be truthful, his outward appearance wouldn't inspire much trust in most people; he looked too severe, too stern. But it was precisely this kind of professional Lori always preferred, and with whom she was accustomed to dealing in business and other aspects of her life. That no nonsense, honest type, who knows what they want, offers only what they can deliver, demands only what they deserve, and holds up their end without deceit or delay.

Their first meeting lasted three hours instead of the two Lori had paid for, and at the end, Max clarified, "So, your goal is to learn to have an orgasm?"

Lori assented and listened incredulously as he explained that yes, it was possible for her to learn to have orgasms, but they had a hefty amount of work to do and he could foresee real orgasms no sooner than a few months from now—and that was provided she followed all his recommendations to a T, without compromises or cheating.

Lori tucked her hands back between her knees and

shaken her head. "Huh? A few months? What are you talking about? Did you even hear a word I said? I have *never-*"

Max interrupted her gently. "Three months is the maximum, I'd say. I think you'll see results sooner, if you work hard."

She burst out laughing. "What if I work hard and nothing happens? Is there a money back guarantee?"

She was about to walk out, not because the sum Max had named was exorbitant—though, his fee was somewhat higher than market—but because she was a master negotiator and could smell a scam a mile away. They always asked for money upfront and promised impossible things that seemed too good to be true. Maybe, if he'd said in three years. Three months? Please. Laughable.

"No money back guarantee, no," Max smiled.

"I knew it!" snapped Lori, sitting up abruptly, ready to leap from her chair and bolt for the door.

"No money back guarantee because there won't be any money to give back. I won't charge any fee until you see results."

"I beg your pardon?"

Now she froze in bewilderment. No fee? What kind of game was he playing? Did he think she was some kind of guinea pig? Or that she was in need of charity? He had to realize she wasn't, from the way she was dressed at least. Plus, her issue wasn't exactly deserving of charity, was it? It wasn't like she had a terminal illness...

Max chuckled. "This isn't charity," he said, as though he read her mind. "It's pure business."

"How's that ?"

"Helping you achieve your first orgasm will be easy, believe it or not, but it's merely a starting point. Your problem runs much, much deeper than that, and I'm certain we'll have to work long and hard to get anywhere. I know you won't commit to a long working relationship because you think I'm full of shit right now—"

Lori made a noise, but he put his hands up in the air in a gesture of surrender.

"—but I also know if you see a result, you'll change your mind. And then, you won't want to work with anyone but me. So, I am willing to work with you, free of charge, for a month, two, three—however long it takes—"

"Three months or first orgasm, whichever comes first, no pun intended?" Lori quipped acerbically.

Max didn't react. "After that, we'll sign a contract for at least several years of systematic therapy, which will certainly help you establish a satisfying sex life, but in addition, will rid you of nightmares, panic attacks, depression, and your unhealthy dependency on intense and dangerous pain for your pleasure."

He said it matter-of-factly, slipping that last item seamlessly into his laundry list of bothersome physical symptoms, leaving Lori in a state of utter shock. For several long moments, she sat perfectly still, her mouth agape. Then, she snapped it shut and leaned aggressively forward.

"How the fuck did you know that? Natalie told you?" she demanded loudly, but immediately flushed bright red, realizing the friend who'd recommended Max couldn't have told him because she didn't know. Maybe they'd talked about nightmares in passing. Certainly not the rest.

"You just told me yourself, Lori," Max replied gently, stippling his fingers and inclining his head. "Look. I understand you might not believe the science of psychology. Maybe you consider me a quack. But even a quack can see when someone's lying. Or even telling a half-truth. And you just told me an elaborate half-truth. You said you've never experienced an orgasm during a sex act but forgot to mention you meant a *pain-free* sex act."

Lori's breath caught, her nostrils flared, and she was numb for a moment, before she was overtaken by a blast of red-hot rage. She wanted to jump up and scream at this mouthy know-it-all: how dare he stick his dirty fingers right into her soul?

Barely forcing herself to recall, through her veil of anger, that this was exactly what she came for, she tampered down the violent urge, looked away, and muttered, hoarsely, "Fine. It's true. I like to have my ass spanked. Happy?"

"Not just your ass spanked, but your entire body beaten and brutalized," Max objected quietly, leaning back in his chair. "Further, you don't just *like* it. You require it."

Lori thought she'd collapse under the weight of her emotion, but gathered all her strength and forced herself to glance at Max's face, expecting—she wasn't sure what.

But their eyes met, and after a few moments, she was finally able to draw a full breath—she didn't detect any judgment.

"How did you figure this out?" she asked softly, and this time, she really wanted to know the answer.

"I'm observant. For one thing, look at how you're sitting." Max ran a hand over his face and explained, "You won't lean back against the chair, you're up on your hip because you can't sit the regular way. I would bet you're bruised all over. Since you're here talking about sex, and not at a police station, I had to infer this wasn't a random assault, and the two are related."

"It was a leap."

"I was right."

His calm gaze was directed right at her but not into her

eyes, bur past them, into the middle distance, as if he were trying not to intrude. Lori liked that and relaxed a bit more, gingerly letting go of the desire to attack him for the crime of uncovering her darkest, most shameful secret.

They sat in silence for a long time, during which Lori mulled things over, making her decision.

Finally, Max gently asked, "Well, what do you think? Are we going to be working together?"

Lori stood.

"Yes. Yes, we are." She nodded confidently, then rose and extended her hand to him, as she always did when she wanted to seal a deal and at the same time emphasize a purely business type of relationship.

———

Now, three years later, Lori couldn't understand the woman she used to be at all. From afar, she saw herself as unbearably weak and horribly stubborn. A woman who didn't know herself and didn't much care to find out. A woman who was willing to offer up her body to the cruel lash of the whip instead of seeking help--for reason unknown.

Max turned out to be good at his job and in possession of the skills and intuition required to teach her to truly listen to her body—and her mind. And to connect the two.

Once they began their work together, within an astonishingly short time, Lori could already tell the fog was slowly lifting, and an understanding emerged around what was happening to her body and inside her brain. She realized that she simply didn't trust men. She couldn't. She was suspicious and terrified of them on a visceral level. She expected too much, expected the worst, didn't expect anything at all--either way, allowing them to commit violent acts on her body was somehow the only way to release that fear, liberating her to experience pleasure. Up until Max, this was only possible with intense pain, and Lori was willing to go dangerous lengths to attain that liberation.

Naturally, Max's professional advice had been abstinence from sex with men. She looked at him when he said this, eyes round with surprise, and asked, "So, no having sex with men ever again?"

"Ever again is a little loud," he'd replied calmly. "I'd say for now, while we're figuring it out,"

"What am I supposed to do until then?"

In a matter of fact voice, like he was asking what kind of coffee she likes, he asked, "Well, how do you feel about women?"

She was stumped and annoyed, at first. Sex wasn't coffee. Sex with women wasn't an exotic dish she could just try. It wasn't normal to go from men to women just like that.

Max had laughed openly at her objections, and asked her to consider whether it was normal to be whipped until you bled in order to get off... just like that.

"Listen, if you're not drawn to women, you're not drawn to women. But..." he shrugged, leaving his question open-ended, and not particularly demanding an answer.

Lori didn't know how to opine on that topic. Her whole life she'd never given it a second thought—she was a straight woman, she had sex with straight men. Sex without a penis wasn't sex at all. That was her conviction—at least right up until that moment.

Since that moment, however...

Yes, the last three years had certainly been a wild ride, a long and surprising journey of earnest self-discovery.

Gradually, day by day, week by week, she worked on lowering her masochistic pain requirements and reducing the frequency of her sessions, reconditioning herself, learning to recognize her own limits. It was like detoxing from a drug.

And then, not too long ago, she felt something novel nascent in her chest, a new pull: toward dominance and... sadism.

But not right now. Right now she was a sub, at her Domme's feet.

Chapter Twenty-Two

Irina

Irina watched as Lori turned and gave her a pitifully pleading look. "Maybe you could talk to him."

"What about, malysh?"

"Tell him I feel terrible and I'm sorry."

"Sweetheart, I'd say if Max hasn't given you the chance to apologize, it means he isn't ready for an apology. Try to relax and accept this as you would any other punishment."

"But Max isn't my Dom. This isn't supposed to be a punishment."

"But you trust him, no less than you trust me? Correct? Maybe even more? Why can't you trust him here too?"

"That's different." Lori sighed, pursing her lips, and rising from the sofa on which they were resting, in the lounge on the second floor.

"Down, sub," Irina snapped. "I didn't say you could get up."

"I'm sorry, mistress." Lori rushed to occupy her rightful position at Irina's feet. "I just don't know what to do with myself."

Irina felt the spark of a Dominant's indignation. Lori

was too much. "You don't have to do anything with yourself because I haven't instructed you to. Now, if you're dying to stay busy, take that massage oil over there and—" She stopped short—a demanding male voice had called her name.

"Irina!"

Lori, too, startled and turned her head at the sound, shrinking into herself like an alarmed deer at the first sight of a hunter. "That's Max," she blurted out, flushing, then immediately turning white. She directed another look full of supplication toward Irina. "Please, mistress—"

Tersely, Irina interrupted. "Quiet, sub."

She stood from the couch. "I'm here, Max. What's going on?"

As he approached them, Max glanced down at Lori so coldly, the oxygen in the air turned to ice. Lori lowered her gaze, and even hunched a little, looking so miserable that a flicker of worry showed in Irina's eyes. Then, just as fast, it disappeared—Irina was an experienced Domme with an excellent poker face, and she believed it wasn't good for the sub to see too much of their dominant's true feelings.

Irina knew that the dominant's true charm was his or her unpredictability. The submissive couldn't know what internal process was underway, shouldn't be able to guess what going to happen next—otherwise, the game turned boring and became a farce.

Of course, not many could keep an impermeable mask on for ever, or even all night—but some could. Some had phenomenal stamina... Irina peered at Max, impressed, almost envious. She still had much to learn from this man.

"Could you take a look at Liza, please? I'd like to make sure she's alright." He nodded toward the second floor by way of explanation. "She went to some other place entirely during and after the scene, still recovering."

"Certainly," agreed Irina, noting, out of the corner of her eye, the way Lori jumped with her entire body at the mention of Liza's name.

She did feel somewhat badly for her worried sub, but she was in no way disposed to bombard Max with questions on her behalf. Having gotten the details on what happened, Irina was convinced that their illustrious leader was angry enough even without any additional probing. She didn't plan on jumping in front of that train, especially not as a favor to her shifty sub.

Especially not when the dynamic was already coming to its natural conclusion.

Chapter Twenty-Three

By the time Irina arrived to examine me, I was completely fine. To see her in Domme's garb—tall leather boots, a black mini-skirt, and blood-red top —while holding a blood pressure monitor and stethoscope was a bit incongruous. I couldn't shake the feeling that this examination was about to turn into a rather authentic medical play scene.

My eyes were irresistibly drawn to Irina's impressive cleavage, offered for viewing above the daring neckline of her top, and to her beautiful hands with their graceful, long fingers. I found myself wondering what it would feel like to be caressed by those fingers?

These thoughts made my breath catch, and Irina smiled faintly, meeting my gaze. She bent a little lower and, clearly trying to keep this interaction clandestine from Max, who stood a mere three feet away, murmured, "Is this turning you on?"

"Yes," I replied back, my voice barely audible, my eyes immediately darting in Max's direction.

That had been a mistake. As soon as he detected my fear, he tensed, giving Irina a sideways glance.

"Irina, I didn't give you permission to scene with my bottom, so don't start," he threw in her direction, his tone of voice so steely I shrank and flushed. Shit. I didn't want to get Irina in trouble, too.

But instead of reacting negatively to his unfriendly comment, Irina raised her eyebrows and grinned. "I never thought I'd live to see the day you become jealous, Max," she noted with an acerbic, deliberately needling tone.

Max's eyes flashed, and I scooted to the back of the sofa, away from his anger, wrapping the blanket tighter around my body. It seemed to me Max had a temper, which meant the Domme's sharp tongue might end up costing me my hide, especially if he truly was jealous—without foundation, I might add. What if he chose retribution by passing me off to someone else?

But before I had the chance to get truly nervous, Max smiled and shook his head, gazing at Irina skeptically. "You haven't lived to see that day. All I want is to finally fuck my sub after an intense, hour-long scene. And I don't need an assistant."

"You poor, poor dear. So overstimulated," Irina sang, rising from the sofa. "Well, if you sought medical clearance before getting your fuck on, now you have it. Liza is ripe for the picking."

"Fantastic," exhaled Max, reaching to grab a furiously flushing me by the elbow. "Move, sub. Upstairs."

"M-max... Where are my clothes?" I asked timidly as I tripped after Max, clutching the edges of the blanket that shielded my body from view.

"Don't know. Don't care," he replied curtly, nudging me toward the stairs. "Move it, malysh, I'm serious."

"I'm going! Are you always this impatient when over-stimulated?"

Judging by the pause that followed, it was hubris to think I could speak to him so brashly while we were still in play. His response proved me right.

"Three strikes with a paddle for calling me Max, three for your disrespectful tone, and eight for your insulting comment," he said through clenched teeth, and accompanied his promise with a sharp slap on my ass, hard enough to make me gasp and trip yet again, this time almost eating the stairs. He caught me by the bicep and immediately used the opportunity to pull me forward.

He was frankly impatient as he worked the lock, and as soon as the door slammed behind us, turned on me, pulling me close.

"You're getting out of hand, sub," he said, huskily. "Last time, I was lenient with you, but tonight, I plan to punish you for every break in protocol. For every instance of improper address, disrespect, or impertinence. Is that clear?"

I lowered my gaze. "Yes, master."

My cheeks were hot, as though he'd slapped them. My body burned with shame and panic that I'd displeased him or disappointed him by being inappropriate instead of offering gratitude for a wonderful scene and his aftercare and tenderness.

"Very good," he said in an unexpectedly soft voice, and when I glanced at him, I found him scrutinizing my face. Evidently, his "very good" referred to the gamut of emotions displayed on it.

"Please forgive me, master," I pleaded, feeling genuinely penitent, and he nodded.

"Very good," he replied with grace. "Considering your

apology, I won't be too harsh, darling, just a little something to help you remember, okay? But first things first." His voice lowered, became thicker. "Get on the bed. Hands and knees."

Every time I thought I knew what to expect out of sex with Max, he did something different. This time, our union was truly instinctual, on an animal level. He didn't say a word and didn't make a single gesture to assert or enforce his dominance: he didn't hold me down, spank or restrain me.

All he did was fuck me as greedily and shamelessly as he wanted to.

When he tore into me, I thought somehow, by some dark magic, his cock became even bigger than before, and some backward self-preservation instinct made the muscles of my cunt clench up to protect me from the attack.

But if that was my body's attempt to defend itself from an intruder, it was as pointless as when I consciously tried to fight him off myself, kicking and screaming. He merely growled, thrusting in all the way, all at once, claiming absolute right of entry, demanding a robust reaction, which he got—I screamed at the top of my lungs. Not from pain. More, from a rush of uncontrollable emotion: the frenzy of this wild attraction between us, the acute pleasure of finally having him inside me after so long, the desperate need to surrender, the delight that when I was with him, my self-preservation instincts gave way to baser, more carnal urges.

This time, it was over very quickly, as we came at the same time, both of us drenched in sweat and trembling with fervor. Max collapsed, crushing me into the bed for a moment, then rolled over, taking me with him, drawing me near and holding me tightly as I caught my breath.

For a while, we lay in silence, and then, he suddenly

pressed me to his chest, as if his arm went into spasm. He pulled my head back by the hair, forcing me to look into his eyes. "So, you like Irina? Want to play with her?"

"Irina?" I repeated, surprised, but that turned out to be the wrong answer and reaction.

His eyes narrowed and darkened. "You don't want to do that, sub. You do not want to lie to me."

"I don't know!" I blurted out, recoiling in fear.

At the same time, a strange, warm thrill ripples over me. Shit! I was getting turned on? Why? Why did I seem to get turned by anything that came from Max? Even when he was all mad and growly?

"I guess you'll find out," he replied drily, with a subtly threatening tone, rising from bed—stark naked and tense, as though angry with me for something.

What was the problem, exactly? Was I not uninhibited enough for him—even after I just stepped way out of my comfort zone and completed a scene with his friend and business associate as a co-Dom? Or maybe, it was the other way around; was I too wanton? Maybe this was all some sort of test and I failed.

You know what...if that's the case, he can just go fuck himself.

In a moment, my post coital languor turned to indignation, and I sat up, intending to tell him everything I thought of his immature behavior at this moment, but he had already disappeared into the bathroom and shut the door. I heard running water.

A few minutes later, he emerged in different spirits, as though he'd washed off his tension and irritation in the shower—calm and confidence embodied.

"Go rinse off, malysh," he suggested mildly, nodding toward the door.

Poisonous replies were on the tip of my tongue, but I remembered that I was due for a spanking even without them, and wisely chose to remain silent. After our little classroom scene, my ass and thighs already throbbed very noticeably.

Standing under the shower, a curtain of melancholy suddenly descended over me. The playful mood evaporated, and I realized had no desire at all to be spanked again. Maybe I should go home? After all, I was not obligated to play until morning if I simply didn't want to anymore.

After drying off, I stepped out of the bathroom, wrapped in a fluffy towel.

"How do you feel?" Max asked, barely deigning to give me a sidelong glance. There was now no more playful enthusiasm on his face than on mine. Seemed like we were both out of steam, and oddly enough, he also seemed saddened or disappointed by something. Something to do with me?

"So-so. I don't know. I think I'm tired," I sighed, looking up at him with a guilty expression, involuntarily.

Max nodded, either confirming my right to be tired or indicating his similar state. "We can grab a snack, if you want. Or would you rather go home?"

This time, he studied my face more attentively, as though trying to discern my true emotional state. Encouraged by his attention, as well as his favorable attitude towards ending the game, I lifted my chin and looked him straight in the eyes. "I want to talk to Lori. Is she here? Right now?"

My stomach twisted into a knot while Max considered his answer, gazing at me with an undefined expression. Then he sighed, closing his eyes and nodded. "Sure. You can talk to her."

"Tell me, why did you forbid it in the first place? I need to know."

Every phrase was a bit more daring than the last and took me a little further into free waters. I expected a reprimand or threat of punishment with a belt or some other torture instrument any second, but Max, it seemed, had disengaged from game mode completely and was out of his dominant persona. His stance was relaxed, and he seemed overall somewhat distracted, as if I were interrupting some internal thought process that was far removed from sex or games at the night club.

Fully dressed and buttoned up, he looked like he was off to work, and I felt like his home-maker wife, still in her bathrobe, who stopped him on his way out to bother him with questions about trivial domestic matters.

"Sorry, what?" he asked, startled, confirming my suspicion that his mind had been elsewhere. Then, as the meaning of my question dawned on him, he furrowed his brow and said, "No, Liza, you misunderstood: I didn't forbid you anything. I forbade Lori, and she knows what that's about. Ask her all the questions, and maybe you'll get some answers."

"Well, thanks for that," I grumbled.

"You're welcome," he replied, unprovoked, and sighed an exhausted sort of sigh, looking me over head to toe. "You can stay here. I'll find Lori and send her up with your clothes. When you are done with her, lock the door and find me at the bar downstairs, sound good?"

I nodded mechanically as I watched him press the cold metallic key into my palm, but as soon as he left, I gaped at the door in disbelief. What on earth was going on with him? It was like he'd become a different person in the time I spent in the shower. Could someone have called

211

him and ruined his mood, or was this about his jealousy over Irina?

The thought made me pause and shudder, and I could feel my face arrange itself into grimace of shock and freeze with a mute question: did I actually just allow the possibility that Max was jealous?

Oh, no. *That is—oh, yes.*

In fact, I was almost certain of it. The way he had interrogated me... Oh, no. Oh, no, no, no, not this. I don't get involved with jealous types. I haven't for years. I swore a solemn oath, like Severus Snape in "Harry Potter," and I couldn't break it. I just couldn't.

Chapter Twenty-Four

Max

Descending the metal steps, he paused for a moment to sweep his gaze across the hall, ensuring everything was in order, even though today technically it wasn't his shift. On Saturdays, Nik was in charge, on Sundays, it was his turn, and they alternated Friday nights. The club wasn't officially open to guests the rest of the week, though space was available for rent to regular members upon request, including the lower hall. Occasionally, outside organizations would rent it for events on weekdays, and then they simply removed the play equipment. But Friday nights and weekends had long been firmly reserved for "Subspace."

It was packed, the public exalted from watching a scene involving a married couple and a timid sub. Max squeezed through the crowd and approached the bar. He felt the press of fatigue and annoyance, without a full understanding of the cause: the scene with Liza went off without a hitch, the sex with her had been fantastic too—it always was. So, why all this tension? And his own doing too—why did he wind himself up over nothing, snapping at his poor

sub? And now, why the hell was he sitting here, exacer-
bating his shitty mood by pounding straight whiskey instead
of putting the brakes on it?

With a look of disgust, Max pushed the drink away and
nodded at Dima. The perceptive bartender promptly
removed the glass and, just in case, removed himself too,
migrating to the other end of the bar, where he immediately
engaged in conversation with a shy new sub. He leaned
forward, she did too, noticeably more relaxed, laughed,
touched the fake little collar around her neck.

The kid was a natural, a true gem: he managed to create
a friendly and calm atmosphere right in the heart of the
club, smoothing over conflicts, helping newcomers relax,
and making the regulars feel at home. At the same time, for
such a young and virile man, he was remarkable self-
possessed and hardly ever allowed himself to get distracted
by eager subs or hot scenes—at least until he received clear
permission to take a break and find some entertainment.
Max absentmindedly noted that the guy deserved a raise.

But thoughts about the bartender's professionalism
didn't distract Max for long. Soon, he found himself
replaying his last conversation with Liza. Deeply dissatisfied with himself, he ruminated bitterly on his bad behavior
that had soured his sub's mood. Lost in intense, silent, self-
reproach, he completely lost track of time. It wasn't until he
noticed movement out of the corner of his eye that he
looked up, spotting his business partner sliding onto the
adjacent stool.

In stark contrast to Max's glumness, Nik was buzzing
with exhilaration, radiating enthusiasm. As he landed on
the bar stool, he energetically waved his hands to catch
Dima's eye, demanding a refreshing drink to cool his
excitement.

"Max, you're a genius. A geee-nius," he exclaimed, starting a slow golf clap, apparently oblivious to his friend's lack of receptiveness to compliments. "I was just walking through the club, and I gotta tell you, only a lazy or maybe blind person failed to comment how amazing that scene was!"

"Some fucking genius," Max muttered, flaring his nostrils. A moment later, he realized with regret he had openly revealed his emotional state yet again, but it was too late—Nik hesitated and even set down his glass of lemonade without taking the first sip.

"What... what's all this? Are you... are you saying you're not satisfied with the scene?"

"No, the scene was okay."

"The scene was *okay*?"

Nik seemed ready to climb onto the bar in indignation at the idea that the genius scene had been just "okay," and Max smirked wryly, letting his ego have this one.

"Fine. It was a good scene. A *great* scene."

Nik scoffed, turning away. "Oh yeah, it's written all over your face: everything's just fantastic. What's the matter with you?"

"Well... I don't know, it's just... I don't—" Max cut himself off, his eyes narrowing, as the red-haired woman currently playing the role of Nik's submissive suddenly materialized next to Nik, visibly agitated, but not in a good way like her Dom. Rather, she was clearly very annoyed about something.

"You left me all alone again!" she accused, slapping her Dom's arm. "Am I some kind of rubber toy to you?"

Nik eyebrows shot up, and Max automatically scooted his seat back, giving his friend space to stand up and deal with his sub on his own. Max found the redhead to be too quarrelsome for his taste, but Nik enjoyed harsh punish-ments, sometimes allowing his subs to cross boundaries for the sake of the game.

A whole separate issue was that, in Max's opinion, this girl didn't quite grasp the essence of the game and often got genuinely angry at fairly routine aspects of it, which was unacceptable. So, he assumed she wouldn't stay in the club for long. A typical "passerby:" comes in for a couple of months of exotic entertainment, and then returns to the safety of vanilla life, satisfying their hypertrophied sense of territorialism toward their partners, not too carefully disguised as romantic love and commitment.

Through half-lowered lashes, Max watched as Nik exerted himself with the bold redhead, bending her over the back of the couch behind the bar. Somewhat detachedly, he noted that her buttocks were beautiful and became even more enticing as they acquired a rich red hue from the slaps—slightly stronger than he would have chosen to give. And then he realized that apart from this intellectual and aesthetic analysis, his body wasn't reacting to the spectacle. Not the way he was used to.

Not a twitch. He was completely indifferent. That was to say—he remained flaccid.

A chill gripped his chest, rolling down his arms to his fingertips before dissipating. Now it was impossible to ignore—he really wasn't responding. Not to any woman, except Liza, and not to any other scene—for two weekends now. Shit. Damn. Fuck.

Nik returned fairly quickly, after cuffing his sub's wrists coffee table. As he settled back down into his seat, he kept watch on the huffing flushed woman out of the corner of his eye, but his main focus of attention was Max.

"Seriously. What's with you?" Nik asked. "You're so out of it."

"I *am* out of it." Max nodded, passing a hand over his face. "Obviously. Because what I am is I'm jealous."

"Of what?" Nik asked carefully, somewhat taken aback, as Max's gaze was still directed at his red-head, but then, in a flash, he understood. "Oh, you mean Liza."

"Yep."

"Um, Max, how should I put this," Nik said with a hint of teasing condescension in his voice. "It's actually kind of normal to feel a teensy bit possessive of your sub. To be honest, I was rather pleasantly surprised by your trust today—"

"I'm not just a teensy bit possessive. I'm I-nearly-lost-my-shit possessive. Almost yelled at her, for real," Max interjected. "You know how I feel about acting out in anger."

Nik fell silent again, giving his friend the side eye and, this time, holding his tongue for longer. Clearly, this was not the moment for facetiousness—though he could have said a few things about Max's *feelings* about acting out in anger and his actual... acting out in anger...

After a while, though, he softly named his concern. "Is it because of me?"

"It doesn't matter because of whom, Nik. What matters is that it's driving me fucking nuts."

"Is it because she's interested in others, or is it about how you're reacting?"

"C, all of the above. I think. I don't know. Everything is driving me fucking nuts right now."

Max gripped his hair and growled.

"Jesus, calm down." Nik cautiously touched his friend's shoulder. "Just take a step back. Don't share her with anyone for a couple of weekends, play in private. It's normal to be exclusive at the beginning of a relationship."

Max recognized Nik's steady, calm tone of voice—because it was *his*. He used it during therapy sessions with borderline and emotional patients, ones who were liable explode at any time, and that was how Nik perceived him at the moment. Realizing this, he became even more incensed.

"I'm not in a relationship," he snapped, tossing off Nik's hand off with a nervous shoulder movement.

"You're in a play relationship with your new sub, and I think you understood perfectly well exactly what I meant," Nik responded a bit colder, straightening up slightly.

"Sorry," Max muttered, signaling to Dima, for a lemonade this time.

For the next ten minutes, the two men sat in silence, staring into their drinks. Finally, Nik stirred again and sighed.

"It's gotta be projection," he said, looking at his friend hopefully, as if expecting him to wake up any moment, smile, and say, *just kidding*... "You're the one who taught me this: you're projecting the qualities of your women from before, where things didn't end well, onto Liza. But she's... well, she... might not be like them."

Nik finished his thought, stumbling slightly under Max's heavy gaze.

Max sighed deeply and shook his head wryly. "It's not that simple. If you're paranoid, it doesn't mean you're not being watched, Nik. I just seem to be a magnet for these women. Or they're magnets for me."

Nik raised his eyebrows in surprise and shook his head abruptly, decisively pushing his glass aside. He turned his whole body toward his friend.

"Max, you do realize you're being fucking ridiculous,

right? You're the master, she's the novice. And what exactly did you expect bringing her here? You're the one who brought her to the buffet, and now she's eating, just like you wanted her to, and you're over here getting pissed off and driving yourself nuts."

"I brought her to the buffet, yeah. What should I be doing, offering her a five-course meal? Chicken soup, mashed potatoes, and pudding for dessert?" Max retorted, also leaning forward.

"Would that be better?" countered Nik. "If she latched on to you and didn't let go? That wouldn't drive you 'fucking nuts?'"

Max didn't seem to hear him. "The *buffet* is the nature of this club. We made the rules, together, remember?

"Exactly, it's our club and our rules. What is it you want, Max, or do you even know?" he demanded, staring directly into Max's eyes. "Figure that out first. Because the rules are bullshit and can be changed if something no longer suits you, and you know that. And Liza can—"

"Everything suits me." Max declared as the world around him suddenly turned red, and he abruptly rose from his barstool. "And Liza can do whatever she wants, too. Today will be the last time I'm playing with her, that's all. Cause I'm sure as fuck not going down that road again."

"Max—"

But he was not longer listening. He was casting a wild glance around the crowd, a simmering impatience burning him on in the inside like hot cayenne pepper.

Ah!

He laid his eyes on the perfect remedy to put out the fire. That waitress—working in exchange for the membership plus a small wage, just like Dima. Didn't he owe her a

219

scene from last weekend, when he accidentally yelled at her? Yes. And he would pay her back right now.

Right after he took a couple of breaths to calm down.

"Kitten, come here," Max called a moment later in the most velvety tone possible, giving her his softest smile.

Out of the corner of his eye, he saw Nik shake his head in disapproval or maybe disappointment, but right at that moment, he didn't give a shit what Nik thought or thought he knew. Fuck him. The imperative thing was to play with another woman immediately. Someone who wasn't Liza. He needed a break from her. He'd only known her for a few days and was, for some reason, obviously, ridiculously, inappropriately fixated on her. This, when he had sworn to himself that he would never get emotionally attached to a woman ever again, even if he played with her for a whole year straight. Granted—it was an easy oath because he had no intention to play with the same someone for a whole year straight. Not even two weeks straight, to be frank—and, well, he failed there, didn't he? And look where that brought him. He was absolutely losing his shit.

This would stop right now, right away.

Katie blushed and approached him, meekly lowering her gaze. Max gently ran his knuckles along her cheek. "Do you want to do a scene up on the stage with me, sunshine?"

"Yes, master," she breathed out in a whisper, almost fainting with joy. She timidly lifted her enchanted eyes to his face.

"Eyes on the floor, malysh," Max gently reminded, and her lashes immediately dropped.

"Sorry, master."

"Forgiven," he said softly, firmly taking her hand and leading her through the hall.

Chapter Twenty-Five

Throughout my history with men, in the beginning of a relationship, I've often felt like I was faced with making a decision, and by sheer willpower could and would delay the moment of making that decision —the decision of whether or not I was in love. I'd test my feelings if I sensed danger, to make sure things didn't get too far, like I was saying to myself, not yet... not just now... I could fall in love, I already feel it, but I could also switch to someone else and be okay. All is well.

Then, there would come a point when a spring would suddenly uncoil all at once, as if a voice inside me said, "Oh! We're here. I've fallen." And after that "oh!" all I could do was hold on for dear life and pray that everything went as it should, that he would reciprocate, and that he would reciprocate before he got to know all my crazy.

Sometimes it happened for a while. More often, it didn't.

I wonder if two people can synchronize the moment at which they make this decision so that no one gets hurt? Will people learn how to do this in the future?

Both decide no. Both decide yes. *Yes? Yes. Oh good, now, press your button inside, fall in love with me right now. Do you feel it already? What about now? I do. Do you? Oh, it feels so good, and all it took is pressing a button. You love me, I love you. Very much.*

But the main thing is to *agree* first.

———

———

Such was the chaotic stream of thoughts swirling in my mind as I watched Max playing with another girl less than an hour after our scene, where he asked if I was ready to "give him everything-everything," and I said I was, and then did—I fucking gave him everything—and after our passionate, mind-altering sex upstairs.

Such was the thread I weaved, random, philosophical, nearly unhinged right off to la-la land.

It was like grabbing something hot, that eternal instant of numbness, during the inevitable ascent of the stimulus as you wait for your brain to register reality. My brain was ready to fill the space with just about anything, if only it could avoid feeling... what I knew I was about to feel.

And when it hit me, what I felt was:

My insides were being sliced, chopped, julienned; they were crumbling, collapsing, and tearing into shreds. It wasn't a knife plunged into my chest. It was my whole body and soul being tossed in a wood-chipper and ripped systematically and inexorably apart.

Max's hands...they were just as gentle, skilled, and attentive with her as they were when he played with me. In a possessive gesture, they covered the woman's breasts.

They were full, probably at least one or two sizes larger than mine. His fingers squeezed her nipples, and the girl cried out, but her glazed eyes and the half-absent expression on her face said that this pain was a good pain. Exactly what she wanted. Then he spanked her with a crop — so gently, and looking at her in such a way that it made it seem like there was some special bond between them.

And his face was just as focused, yet just as relaxed and calm, as it had been when he'd gazed at me from above, covered and sweat and demanding surrender.

I'd been under the impression that we, he and I, had a special bond. At least, it was special to me.

It sounded naive and stupid now. Especially since for him, it apparently didn't matter whether he was with me or with her. Or with any other pretty girl. He enjoyed it just fine all the same. He looked just the same as he did it.

I startled when someone placed a hand on my shoulder —Lori, who'd been standing next to me, watching me as I watched him, the entire time.

Quietly, she said, "Liza, enough of this. Let's get out of here."

Only then did I realize tears were streaming down my face, and people were starting to look at me. I had to wonder how the fuck I ended up here, in this position, at this moment. How?

Just a minute ago, Lori and I were bouncing down the stairs without a care in the world. We'd had a great chat, I felt much better about our friendship, and excited for the future. I was positive Max would be waiting for me at the bar — I didn't doubt it for a second, because that's what he said. He always did as he said.

I was cheerfully on my way to be by his side, or at his feet, wherever his fancy struck. I was ready to submit again, anticipating the five strikes he had promised me — curious about how he would do it now. I even considered teasing him a little to provoke him slightly, attract more attention, and, if possible, improve his mood with a new twist to the game.

God, I was so stupid.

Honestly, I thought I was imagining things when I saw him scening with another girl in the middle of the hall — it had to be someone else, someone dressed like Max, with a similar build. Someone who smiled like him, moved like him, swung a crop like him...and then— *Oh. God.* I froze, my mouth opening, closing, and opening again, when I realized...

I must have had a ridiculous expression on my face. The ultimate fish out of water.

But as soon as it sank in—what I was seeing—all my emotions short-circuited and disconnected, and I just stood there, watching impassively, and pondering how foolish and unfair it was that one person always falls in love first. And how foolish we are to allow ourselves to fall in love without guaranteed reciprocity. Why do we do it? We don't board a plane with one wing; we don't drive a car with faulty brakes; we don't leave the house wearing one shoe...

————

"One shoe?" Lori asked in bewilderment, and I winced, realizing I had mumbled something out loud.

Focusing my gaze on her made me wake up abruptly. I slapped any residual tears off my face with the backs of my hands. "Okay. Well. That's that. And that's my cue."

"Liza!"

My memory seemed to stop recording everything in a

continuous mode, as if someone inside was playing with the "pause" and "play" buttons. Just a few seconds later, I found myself in the locker room, feverishly changing clothes without any recollection of how I got there.

"Liza!"

Lori caught up with me there and stood at the entrance, giving me an anxious stare.

"Lori, please, go back to the club. I'm leaving. I'm never coming back here," I muttered, barely aware of my own words, as if someone else was speaking and I was just hearing them from a distance.

Slamming the locker door shut, I grabbed my bag, my package with the costume, slipped my feet into my shoes, and headed for the exit, with Lori following closely behind.

"You shouldn't be driving all wound up like this," she said outside as I fumbled for my keys in the dark, "Let me at least drive you home."

Exhausted, I shrugged, handed her the keys, and curled up in the passenger seat. I was shivering violently from the cold, my face was tight from dried tears, and every single muscle in my body was tense and stiff.

Lori silently got in the driver's seat, adjusted the mirror, moved the seat forward, and carefully pulled away, quietly asking for my address. I answered, staring ahead at a single point, and we drove in silence all the way home.

When Lori parked near my building, she turned to me and sighed.

"Liza, please, listen. You're a little infatuated, it happens. Half the club is obsessed with Max, almost all the subs," she said gently, touching my hand with genuine concern. "This too shall pass. You'll get through this, don't make any rash decisions now when you're upset,"

I looked up, sighed in unison with her, and gave a crooked smile:

"I'm so stupid, so stupid—I thought I was special. I've never felt anything like this in my life. I've never felt so... extraordinary, brave, you know? With him, these past two weeks, I felt like I could do anything. You'll laugh, but even work has been completely different."

Lori smirked cynically. "Please, Liza. I'm not going to laugh, but don't think for a single moment that you need his majesty Max to be who *you* want to be. He's an excellent psychologist and good Dom, and that's it. But there are other Doms in the club and out in the world who you'll feel good with. Play with Nik next weekend. If only just to spite him."

"This hurts, Lori. So much. This hurts, this hurts, this hurts..."

I doubled over and sobbed loudly, as if something inside had burst, and the tears flowed freely this time—I didn't want to hold them back, and there was no need to.

"I know, malysh. It hurts like a bitch. Shhh... this too shall pass," she said softly but with the utmost confidence, then awkwardly reached over the center console of the car to put her arms around me. She held me for a while, until I stopped crying.

"Let's get drunk!" she finally suggested. "I feel like you need it."

Chapter Twenty-Six

It was strange to consider that just a couple of hours ago I was almost a whole, happy person, and Lori was the emotional one, explaining what happened with a guilty distressed look on her face. She'd fessed up to some things even before we came back downstairs together, before the night split right down the middle into "before" and "after."

She showed up at the door moments after Max took off, nervous anticipation coming out of her pores.

"Liza," she said with obvious relief, then stumbled suddenly and stopped right inside the door, uncharacteristically shy and awkward.

Fighting my initial impulse to jump and throw my arms around here, I replied, "Hello, Lori."

I'd never seen her this way before, embarrassed, unsure, so I studied her face with interest.

"Max's turf," she explained, crossing her arms, and hunching over slightly, rubbing her palms over her triceps like she was cold. "I've never set foot in here without him."

"Have a seat," I suggested, an involuntary blush creeping onto my cheeks too, as memories of our last encounter in this room flooded back. How she buried her face between my legs until I screamed, and then, how under Max's directive, she violated my poor virgin asshole with a plug.

"Do you set foot in here a lot *with* him?" I asked, unable to restrain my curiosity.

Lori looked at me in surprise, raising her eyebrows: "No, actually. Just the one time. He never invited me to play before that time with you."

"Why not?"

"We have a different relationship—he's my therapist. I was content just being invited to his club."

She took a stroll around the room, as if trying to decide where to place herself, finally choosing the wide, high windowsill, where she perched, letting her legs dangle. Her slim, graceful body was encased in a super-short, tight blue dress that barely covered her nipples, leaving her breasts almost fully on display. When she sat down, she had to squeeze her thighs to avoid exposing her bare pink pussy. For a second, I felt a surge of desire in my lower abdomen and had to force the train of thought away from that track.

I sank onto on the edge of the bed, and fixed her with an expectant stare, waiting for her to begin explaining why she ghosted me. But as she was still silent, I couldn't hold back and burst out, "Lori, what happened?"

Lori, almost interrupting me, began to explain hurriedly, "It's all my fault, Liza. I couldn't stop myself because I wanted to be with you so badly, but I put you in danger, and now Max is very angry with me..."

A strange mix of emotion shimmered in my chest — a sort of satisfaction that he cared enough about me to be jealous or concerned, but also a pang of alarm at yet another confirmation of his apparently jealous nature. But Lori doused it when she said, "See, we had an agreement that I wouldn't Domme anyone outside the club— but obviously, I broke it to play with you."

"Okay..." I said, rearranging my ideas. "So, then, why did you? I was coming back here anyway..."

"Because I wouldn't be able to do it at the club either."

"Not allowed?"

"I'm *allowed*... But for some reason, I feel so awkward, embarrassed. I know it sounds dumb—we do all sorts of things here, and as a sub, I... I have almost no limits, no shame. But as a Domme, I'm a total newbie and painfully shy, painfully."

Lori blushed so furiously, that it was obvious she wasn't lying. On the other hand, she wasn't telling the whole truth either. There was something else. She was taking deep breaths and biting her tongue, as if trying to decide whether to reveal something else. Danger? Max was worried she'd put me in danger?

"But how did you put me in danger? I don't understand. We had safe words and why does he get to forbid or allow anything outside club, I don't—"

"I tend to snap," Lori blushed even more and covered her face with her hands.

"Lori..." I tried to get up and approach, but she shrank away from me, pressing herself against the window, and my hands dropped to my sides by themselves. I froze a foot away from her, lost.

"Give me one second," she mumbled through her hands, "wait... let me finish before I lose my nerve. Okay. Max forbade me from playing outside the club for a good reason. He feels responsible for me, and I'm very grateful that he even cares. See, it happened here at the club once, right on the stage, in front of everyone. I lost control."

I silently looked at her, still at arm's length. My breath caught, and I could feel color draining from my face. So, I hadn't imagined it back then at her place when I felt Lori becoming a stranger, a dangerous stranger.

"I hit a sub with a belt after she said her safe word. She said 'yellow,' and I only hit her harder. I heard it but just couldn't stop, as if I wanted to take revenge on her for..."

Lori fell silent, and I almost heard her throat tighten, choked with tears, my own following suit by association.

"Go on," I said softly after a long pause, during which she worked to regain control of herself.

"Then she screamed 'red,' and one of the doms pulled me away. That girl didn't show up at the club for a month. Max went to talk to her, and I felt just like a monster. But he said it wasn't my fault, took all the blame on himself, as the ultimately responsible. But he was still very angry me... though he tried not to show it... He's even angrier now. He actually suggested he might expel me from the club."

"If he were going to do that, you wouldn't be here now," I objected, but Lori didn't reply.

She looked exhausted at the revelation, and I was filled with sympathy, in spite of myself, so didn't press for further information. Plus, I was also tired—it had been long night. Mostly, now, I felt relieved that it hadn't been anything I'd done, and that I wasn't being deliberately ghosted—and by my first woman lover, whom I was realizing liked more and more. That might have killed me.

At that point, neither of us wanted to talk about it anymore, and we decided to come back downstairs.

We shouldn't have. We should have stayed up in the room for another hour, talking, doing anything else, and then, maybe I wouldn't have seen Max with that waitress. I would have found out anyway, of course, but at least I wouldn't have seen it... and people wouldn't have seen me see it...

————

"Liza?"

"I'm here."

"How does getting shitfaced sound?"

I shrugged.

I refused to go to Lori's or a bar, and so, after a visit to an unexpectedly posh twenty-four hour deli, we ended up at my place, loaded with two bags of bottles and snacks.

As she walked in and cast a glance around, I saw my place through her eyes—a cheap cookie-cutter rental with peeling wallpaper, old furniture, and wildly creaking parquet floor—and suddenly felt a pang of humiliation, and not that kind that I enjoyed.

My life is fine day to day, if I don't think about it much. But the truth is, I'm actually merely surviving, hanging on, certainly not thriving. If I don't think about anyone else and keep my head down, I can pretend everyone is in the same boat. Then, someone like Lori comes along, and suddenly, I understand why people tend to cluster with others of the same socio-economic standing because, god, at that moment, did I want the earth to open up and swallow me whole, as my beautiful, successful, elegant and clearly monied friend absorbed her surroundings.

Under other circumstances, I would have been way too embarrassed to ever invite Lori over and let her see my house, but that evening, I felt so awful that I completely forgot how my shabby place might look to her. And sure, being poor isn't a moral failing, but there was no way not to worry about whether she would see me differently now, or if she was judging me. I know I was judging myself.

It's interesting to me... I grew up when we were all still forced into a semblance of equality. You were dirt poor but so was everyone else, and there was nowhere to go, so it didn't matter. Now, you couldn't help but put your self-worth on the chopping block sometimes when it looks like you don't end up having all the things you could have.

Hey—maybe this is why people keep talking about how great the old regime was... censorship, locked borders, repression be damned? Interesting...

Why was I thinking about this again?

"Sorry, it's a bit messy here," I rushed to apologize when, to my further embarrassment, Lori saw the pile of dirty dishes in the kitchen sink.

My grandmother, may she rest in peace, would have died of shame if she'd known what a slob I'd become living on my own. She had been absurdly outraged to see commercials of women preening on TV when they started showing them in the post-Soviet times; she always thought those women's time would have been better spent cleaning crumbs off the kitchen table. *I'm worth it?* How could she be worth anything when there were dishes in the sink? That's what my grandmother would say.

"Relax, you didn't plan on having guests," Lori said. Then, as if she were reading my mind, she added, "Besides, I like cozy kitchens like this. It reminds me of my childhood."

She carefully placed the bag of groceries on one of the stools and began unloading everything onto the table.

I found the kitchen cozy too when I moved in. Decorating it had been fun and I did it with love from the bottom of my heart—bright blue lace curtains, a cheerfully designed clay clock, a couple of kitchen-themed still-life photos. But all of this didn't hold a candle up to the interiors of her luxurious abode, which had filled me with such pure delight, and evoked an involuntary sense of reverence whenever I thought of them.

I never even dreamed that I could have a place that looked like that. And I still don't...

Dejectedly I began moving the dishes into the dishwasher, soaping up a sponge. But instead of washing the plates, I gripped the edge of the sink and closed my eyes.

"This is so stupid, Lori. I keep expecting him to call any second and explain what the fuck happened," I said. "Like there's a perfectly logical explanation to be had."

"That's mental masochism, honey. Don't do engage in it because once you start you can't stop. Better turn off your phone altogether and try to make it through the moment," Lori said firmly. Then she sighed and added in a completely different tone, "You know what, it's a shit day today. I feel like crying too."

I nodded but didn't turn off my phone. I just went back to the dishes while Lori uncorked the first bottle of Baileys, set the table, and searched for glasses in the old cupboard under my direction.

Sitting at the table, I stared at the canapé of fruits the charcuterie board that Lori had bought at the deli for an amount roughly equivalent to a quarter of my salary. I still had no appetite.

"Tell me your story, Lori. Please, tell me. It won't make me feel worse. I think it will help if I can support you."

Lori looked at me appraisingly, took a couple of sips from her glass, then resolutely set it aside, placed her elbows on the table, rubbed her face with her hands, and nodded.

"Alright. I think you're right, it would be good for you to switch focus right now."

"Yeah, it would," I said. "You never really explained why you turned to Max. You... you were more of a masochist back then, right?"

I was instantly genuinely curious. But even though at this point I'd say Lori and I were close, such questions were awkward to ask. Nowadays, it's easier for people to engage in kinky sex on a first date than to be truly open with each other, and Lori and I were no exception.

Her heavy sigh showed how difficult it was for her to answer, just as it had been for me to ask.

"I could only feel sexual pleasure from severe beatings, Liza. Usually with a whip or belt, often to the point of drawing blood," she said quietly, then downed the rest of her glass and refilled it.

My vision blurred a bit, and the flowers on the curtains turned into a blue mush for a few seconds.

"The marks on your back... you wanted them?"

"Yes. Well, except for that one time."

She still wasn't looking at me, so I took her hand to give her some support, which Lori clearly desperately needed.

"I'm so sorry."

"I'm okay, Liza," she smiled, covering my hand with hers. "Thanks to Max, I'm okay now. It's been a long time since any blood play, and now I can even orgasm without pain, as you know."

We fell silent for a while, focusing on the food and Baileys.

"Wait... so, before you went to Max... were your partners men or women?"

"Men. I always thought sex was only sex with men, but at the same time, I feared them all my life. I only ever started thinking about women because Max suggested it. But he has a good sense about these things."

"So you're not a lesbian?" I asked, astonished.

"At this point, I think I'm firmly in the bi camp. It just took exploring. And admitting it."

"Do you still feel attracted to men?" I asked cautiously after a few minutes of silence.

"Sometimes... a little. But I still always get too scared. Once I asked Nik to play and fainted when he touched me between my legs. I felt so sorry for him; he was so upset, blamed himself. Since then, I haven't dared ask anyone else."

As the first bottle emptied and we started the second, it became easier to talk. Somehow, I began telling Lori about my exes. About how I've been going around in a stupid circle for ten years: meeting, falling in love, disappointment, breakup. And then a new meeting, and around we go again.

"Do you always do the breaking up? Has anyone ever left you?" Lori asked, amazed.

"Never. Can you believe it? Never."

I laughed drunkenly and reached for the kitchen drawer where I stashed cigarettes for moments like this. I don't normally smoke but there are times, like right now, when I feel down and but when I my hands tremble the craving, and I always succumb. Even though I know a cigarette wouldn't make the bitterness in my soul go away—it would just add bitterness to my mouth, too.

"I just refuse to get involved with men who could leave," I continued, taking a drag and blowing the smoke out slowly. "I understand you very well because I'm afraid of them too, but in a different way. Because you see what can happen? Just two silly weeks of sex with a god's-gift-to-women like Max, and I'm shredded."

"I used to struggle with something similar," she said, tapping her fingers thoughtfully on the armrest. "But then, you know, business... and I sort of... learned my worth. I'd bet you'd feel more confident with guys if you learned yours, wherever that came from. Find your passion."

"It's obvious that I don't have it, right?" I smiled, embarrassed and a little tipsy. The room wasn't quite steady and I held on to the edge of my chair. "Shit, I think we should stop drinking."

"Me too," Lori agreed. She decisively put our glasses in the sink, found the coffee, and started brewing it while I sat in a daze, unable to direct her to the vanilla sugar and cinnamon. She found everything on her own, navigating the unfamiliar kitchen surprisingly well.

"I feel so awkward," I mumbled, watching her. "This place is so shabby compared to your fancy apartment."

"Don't worry about it. I was born into wealth, I have nothing to be proud of. Anyway, earning money is a learned skill. I can teach you," Lori smiled, filling two cups with rich, fragrant coffee.

I inhaled the divine aroma, took a small sip, and smiled.

"Teach me to be rich? Seriously?"

"Sure. It's just a different mindset about money and relationships," she smiled again, taking a sip from her cup and squinting contentedly. "Many people think there's some magic to it. But it's just a matter of mindset and patience." She pointed to her head, though I thought she should have pointed to mine.

Lori continued her passionate speech, seemingly unable to stop.

"Just like with sex. Three years ago, I thought my orgasm would always be at the end of a whip. And last year, I came from vanilla sex for the first time. Yes, I'd like to be as free with men as I am with women, but not everything at once. It just takes—like I said—patience."

I took a deep breath, as if waking up. What she was saying made sense.

"I feel a bit better, Lori," I nodded slowly.

"That's good," she nodded in sync, visibly happy about my improved state. "It feels like my suffering has value if this story can inspire someone."

"I never thought of it that way."

We fell silent again, savoring the coffee and the quiet, each lost in our own thoughts.

"Can I hug you?" she suddenly blurted, as if bitten by a bizarre urge.

"Sure. Yes," I breathed out eagerly, feeling an spark of instant response. "I want to!"

We reached for each other, and a few seconds later, we were tangled in a passionate kiss, mouths pressed together, matching each other's aggressiveness.

We rose suddenly as if on cue, and then our hands were roaming all over each other's bodies, too. I couldn't get enough of her lithe body, her languid curves. Lori seemed to feel the same about me.

"I'll bottom if you want," she whispered. "Just relax and tell me what you want."

"That feels weird."

"You don't have to top. Just relax and do what you feel like."

"Okay," I replied uncertainly, swallowing quickly, still unsure I could be that with Lori.

But once we got to the bedroom, all the tension somehow evaporated. Whether it was the alcohol helping me relax or my heartache over Max leaving no room for any other worries. I just let go and did what I felt like, just as Lori said.

The resulting sex was intense, delicious, and quick, culminating in a simultaneous orgasm that seemed to go on longer than the sex it self. Afterward, we fell asleep almost immediately in each other's arms, too lazy even to shower.

Chapter Twenty-Seven

Max showed up without warning on Sunday night.

I'd been lying on the couch all day, watching movies. Lori took off after breakfast, leaving me to languish for the rest of the day. I tried distracting myself by cleaning the apartment, but burst into tears as soon as I picked up the sponge, and decided to screw it, pouring what was left of last night's Bailey's into a glass and collapsing onto the sofa.

His phone call caught me gloomily having my lonely dinner in front of the TV, in the middle of a marathon of all the woe-is-me rom coms I could think of. When the phone rang, I was just starting to receive dubious comfort from Bridget Jones. Her character was obviously created specifically to make miserable women like me feel better about themselves—knowing that there is someone else out there even more awkward and ridiculous than we are...

Bridget's mishaps soothed me somewhat, and also, I liked that each of the awkward, shy, hapless, or otherwise unfortunate heroines in these movies did eventually find her happiness. That gave me a little hope.

On the other hand, the heroes in these stories weren't the kind to engage in kink and sex with two heroines in one night, but who's counting... details...

Regardless, I really wasn't expecting a call from Max any longer, more than twenty four hours after everything happened, so I answered my phone automatically, without thinking or looking at the screen, and when I heard a curt, "Hello, malysh," I was instantly tasered into silence.

"Thank you for taking my call. Could you come down, please, I'd like to talk to you, I'm here, parked right outside your building," Max rattled off quickly, like he was practicing a tongue twister, while I held the phone to my ear stunned, still pondering whether to hang up or give him a chance, since I'd already picked up.

Wait, he was *here*?

Yep.

I looked out the window and silently stared at his car, idling just underneath. It was getting dark, and a light rain was falling, fine droplets illuminated to look glorious by the headlights. The joy with which my foolish heart began beating at the sight of his car was so intense, it scared me even more than yesterday's despair. Was that all it took? All he had to do was show up—and I already forgave him? Was I that easy?

Yes. I was that easy. And pathetic, my inner skeptic noted.

But I simply couldn't help myself.

"Fine," I managed drily, and disconnecting the call, leisurely went into the bedroom to get dressed.

Well—leisurely is being very generous. I *attempted* to do it leisurely, but in reality, my hands shook with the urge to fly down the stairs and jump into his car. I was all aflutter. He was here. That meant he knew he'd hurt my feelings. That meant my feelings were important to him. That meant—

Idiot, my inner skeptic reminded me. *It means nothing.*

I took a deep breath and forced myself to take my time before leaving my apartment. I brushed and braided my hair, spent some time staring at myself in the mirror, unbraided and braided it again...

Fuck it.

I grabbed my coat and keys.

———

He stood right at the entrance—as soon as I opened the door, I startled and found myself immobilized, enveloped in his warm, strong embrace.

"I'm sorry," he whispered into my hair, holding on to me for dear life.

My body became completely stiff, as if seized by a convulsion before finally relaxing, going limp in his arms, allowing itself to be held.

"Are you?"

"Yes."

In the elevator, I had made brave plans to maintain a proud silence, make him squirm as he attempted to explain himself. It was no use. Two words from him, and the dam broke, my stream of consciousness bursting forth, wishing to tell him everything, make him see... and if he couldn't see, I didn't want to know anymore from him. I'd just go.

"You have no idea how much you hurt me, Max. I know, the club and the rules, and I thought I could handle it, but I can't. I can't watch you with other women, and if..."

A lump formed in my throat, making it impossible to continue. I fell silent, pressing my face into his shoulder—still not hugging him back.

"I know. I fucked up majorly, and I just... please forgive me, malysh. I'm sorry. Truly. Please, let's go talk in the car."

With a jagged sigh, I gave a slow nod of assent. Max guided me from the shelter of the building's awning into the nasty drizzle that immediately sent me into an attack of violent shivers, but he rushed to fling the car door open for me, allowing to slide into the comforting warmth of the car interior. However, even after the door slammed shut behind me, I found myself burrowing deeper into my coat, not so much as an attempt to escape the chill, more as the futile effort to shield myself from the raw emotion and bewilderment wreaking havoc within me.

What was I supposed to do now? What was the best, rightest way to respond? Do I express my anger or hear him out and try to empathize? Do I demand respect or take him as he is and just be grateful that he even showed up?

Meanwhile, Max circled the car and got into the driver's seat, then turned to me.

"Liza. Again, I'm very sorry. I realize I didn't act in the best way, and I'd like a chance to make it right."

"Make what right, exact, Max? I'm not sure I understand."

I really wanted to be angry at him, and the words sounded so much firmer in my head. Out loud, they came out sort of plaintive and sad, but it was the truth—I was confused; I didn't understand what had gone wrong, why I was so upset. He never promised me exclusivity...

On the other hand, I never promised I wouldn't get upset.

"I should have had a discussion with you before starting

a scene with someone else. You weren't ready, and I knew that."

"You hurt me on purpose, didn't you?"

My accusation was barely audible, but Max's response was immediate and impassioned: "No. Not on purpose, no."

He shook his head, his voice low but resolute, the kind of tone that made it impossible to doubt him. My breath caught in my throat as I finally raised my eyes to meet his. "Then why? Why did you do it, Max?"

We made eye contact, and when Max saw the tears clinging to my lashes, his expression twisted with pain. "Oh, no, malysh... please... Shit." He swallowed hard, his gaze shifting away as his breath quickened. For a moment, I felt something strange—relief, maybe even satisfaction—seeing him vulnerable for the first time.

"I was jealous, Liza. I was just *insanely* jealous."

His confession hit me like an electric shock, a jolt so intense I couldn't even find the words to ask who or what he'd been jealous of. My body trembled involuntarily, a reaction that seemed to alarm even me.

Max noticed right away. "Hey, what's the matter?"

From the way Max was watching my face, I realized I'd completely frozen—sitting there, silent, motionless, and expressionless for several long seconds. It wasn't the response he was expecting to his confession, and I imagined the shift in my demeanor must have caught him off guard.

Still, I couldn't move. The shock of hearing him admit something so raw and unexpected had my thoughts spinning. All I could do was stare, the weight of the moment pressing down on me like a tidal wave, holding me in place.

"I have some experience with jealous types," I finally managed, looking off to the side. My throat was so tight with suppressed tears that I could barely draw a breath.

It was terror—I was terrified by his confession. Hearing it laid out so plainly, even though it was exactly what I'd suspected before everything went to hell, was still a shock. Suspecting something is one thing. Having it confirmed is something else entirely.

"Did he raise his voice at you?" Max asked after a pause.

I closed my eyes, sighing heavily. I needed a moment to get past the lump in my throat before I could speak.

"Raise his voice is an understatement," I said finally. "Yelled and raged is more accurate. Once, he grabbed my arm and squeezed until I had a massive bruise. I was really scared. I thought he was going to hit me."

As I spoke, my voice became flat and steady. I'd kept these memories at a distance for so long that I could talk about them now as though they weren't even mine. "He begged for forgiveness afterward, swore it would never happen again."

"And you forgave him," Max said, his tone just as neutral, as if we were reading from the same script. "And then it happened again."

"Yes," I said quietly.

"He hit you," Max guessed grimly, a muscle tightening in his jaw.

"Yes," I admitted. "The next time he felt jealous, he skipped the yelling and just smacked me across the face, as if there was nothing weird about that. I doubt I was the first one he did that to."

"I doubt it too," Max replied, his voice even gloomier. "I'm sorry that happened to you, Liza."

"Yeah, well. I am too."

He nodded.

Neither of us spoke again for a while. The car was

submerged in complete silence as Max gathered his thoughts, and I waited for his words. I had no idea what kind of impression my sad tale of woe made on him, but I did realize that where we went from here depended on his reaction and what he would say next. I also realized that he knew this, too, and that he was taking his time for that reason.

The hot air from the blasting heater was becoming overwhelming, and I had to unbutton my coat, pulling off my scarf.

"Okay, I want you to listen to me carefully," Max said, at last, startling me. He turned towards me with his whole body, locking is gaze with mine. His hand, almost as if acting independently of his will, tucked a strand of hair behind my ear and caressed my cheek. "I need you to know that I am not that guy. Do you understand? What we do is not the same. I will never hurt you outside the game. Consent is everything to me. Scolding, yelling, hitting—I can do all that and more, but it all stops immediately, as soon as you say the word. That's the major difference. Do you see?"

"Yes," I whispered, running my tongue over my chapped lips. Even in the dark, Max's eyes were burning, black and deep, drawing me in like a riptide.

"We can redline face-slaps if you think it would trigger you," he added, thoughtfully.

"I don't know," I said thoughtfully. "With you, I... I almost think I might like it..."

"I'd hope so," he noted drily, caressing my cheek again. "It's all for the sub anyway."

I felt the sudden urge to move toward him, lean into him, ask to be held, but something inside me rebelled as a very clear mental image of Max, devouring that girl with his eyes as the tip of his leather crop tenderly strokes her reddened flesh played before my eyes.

A shudder rocked my body.

"Are you always going to punish me with revenge when you get jealous?"

Max's hand dropped from my face as he leaned back and closed his eyes. "Well. I suppose I deserved that," he murmured, then drew a sharp breath. "No. Obviously, this has more to do with me than it does with you. I see the harm I caused, and next time, I'll be more aware and more prepared. I'll work harder to control myself. I see how this might feel like the same pattern as—"

"Do you think I can help you in some way?" I interrupted softly.

It felt awkward to look at Max now, so I gazed at the road, and the dim reflection of headlights on the rain-damp asphalt.

"I think so," Max replied just as softly, turning to me. "Can we try this another way?"

"Try what another way?"

"Us. Our game. Be mine, only mine, submit to me, for real, don't make me fight for it. I need that, Liza, and I think you do too."

"Me submit to you... But you'll still get to play with others?" I asked, still thinking of that other girl, the twinge of pain in my chest sharp like a dagger. If that was what Max wanted, I couldn't give it to him, and it killed me to realize I would have to end this right here.

But Max gave a furious shake of his head and cracked his knuckles decisively before insisting, "No. I don't want to play with others at all right now. Truth be told, Liza, what I want is to lock myself in a room with you and toss the key out the window, then try everything I have on you. All the paddles, floggers, crops, canes. Tie you up and make you come over and over and over as I listen to you moan and cry, until you beg me for mercy. Does this sound like a good plan to you?"

His voice was down to a whisper by the time he got to the end of his passionate tirade, while the ringing in my ears got only louder and louder. My face was in flames, as was the area between my legs, and I had to apply serious willpower to take myself in hand and focus on the conversation.

"If I'm honest..." I whispered, feeling suddenly embarrassed. "I don't really want to play with anyone else either."

It felt so good to say, as if my breath had been released, or even more appropriate—as if someone finally pulled out the stake that had been driven through my heart, and it was free to beat again. The relief was nearly overwhelming.

Max's face came alight too as he absorbed my answer.

Shyly, I added, "Maybe just Lori... Once in a while."

"I'm not jealous of Lori. If needed, I will cuff her to your bed myself so she can make you come over and over too," he mumbled, then looked up, raising his voice. "But I swear to fucking God, if that little minx attempts to play the Domme with you one more time, I will personally—"

"Stop that. Don't touch her. You know how scared she is," I snapped instinctively.

He waved me off. "I'll fix her eventually. We've come this far..."

"Right." I gave him a sidelong glance. "You're a good therapist, Max. But let me ask you something. When was the last time you went for some help yourself?"

I gave him a careful smile, aware that my question could be impudent, but and he gave a smile back, a slightly shy and uncharacteristically unsure one.

"Oh, a long time ago. We are our own worst patients, I know that. I try to help myself when I can, not always doing a great job, obviously."

Suddenly losing all desire to keep up my barriers, I whispered, "I really, really want to trust you."

"Come over here," he exhaled, and finally took my face between his palms and kissed me.

———

That evening, nothing more happened between us than that kiss, as if we both, without saying a word, decided to hold back a bit. We went for a walk along the Moscow River embankment and talked for a long time about nothing in particular, just observing what we saw around us, as if we were playing tourists.

In a sense, we were tourists—two typical Muscovites who almost never ventured into the center for a walk. And I really did notice a lot of new things, and for the first time in many years, I admired the illuminated Kremlin towers, the dark surface of the water, and the clouds, which were rushing across the sky that night as if someone was playing a video in fast forward.

"Max," I called when we were standing on the Bolshoy Moskvoretsky Bridge, silently looking at the sky and water, or rather, at ourselves.

"Yes, baby?"

He moved even closer, hugging me from behind, and I took a deep breath, instantly calming down.

"No, nothing."

"Ask what you wanted."

He wrapped a strand of my hair around his finger, and I closed my eyes.

"Okay. Have you ever gotten too attached to someone?"

"It's happened," he answered softly, releasing my hair and wrapping his arms around my waist.

"And what did you do then?"

"Nothing special. First, I suffered, then I grossly over-intellectualized and went to study to become a psychologist."

"Because you wanted to help yourself?" I guessed, slightly turning my head.

"Yes," he replied curtly and bit my ear. "You're very tasty."

I tired to dodge him. "Don't distract me when I'm prying into your deepest. darkest secrets. Did I here correctly that you don't like asking for help?"

"Hmm... did I hear correctly, or did a cheeky sub decide to take charge?"

"You heard correctly. And I still have more questions."
"Uh-huh."

Max suddenly turned me by the waist, cupped my face with his hands, and looked at me so sternly that I found it hysterical and burst into laughter. He followed.

We both doubled over, and I finally gave in, snuggling up to him, burying my nose in his neck. I no longer wanted to spoil the evening with serious conversations if Max wanted to be silly.

"There's one more important thing," he said into the crown of my head, smoothing my hair with both hands. "You must give me the keys to your car for a week."

"What do you mean?" I was astonished. A whole spectrum of emotions probably flashed across my face as I tried to understand what was going on because Max laughed again.

He said, "This isn't a Dominant's trial. Or a robbery. I

want to take it to the shop, malysh. I hit your car, it's how we met, remember?"

————

By the end of that week, I felt that we had become a couple. I got a good morning text every day when I woke up, and something funny from him in the afternoons. I sent him updates on my day. On Tuesday, he asked to come over, but didn't come up and we went for another walk. On Thursday, he asked me out for a lunch date, and we had spaghetti together at a cafe outside my work.

It was then that he randomly asked what I did for a living.

"Boring shit. Corporate analytics, reports."

"Hm."

"I'd love to quit," I suddenly confessed, surprising myself.

"So why don't you?"

"I don't know where to go from here."

"That's okay," he said gently and smiled. "What do you like doing most in the world?"

"Good question. I don't know... eating and sleeping?"

"That's good! What do you do when you're full and well-rested?" he asked, without looking up as he slowly twirled long strands of spaghetti around his fork.

"I...um... draw sometimes. I took a class last summer, and I liked it. But it's not like I'm a real artist."

"How do you know?"

"I don't have a formal education."

"So what? Get one."

"Get one?"

"Sure. Start right now."

"Right now?"

My fork hovered in the air. Even though I understood that this "right now" was hypothetical meant more like make a plan right now, I suddenly imagined dropping everything that second, leaving my spaghetti unfinished, and without even notifying my job, heading back to that place where I took the three-week course in the summer. I'd sign up for a year-long professional course, then proceed to quit my boring job and spend my days studying and doing nothing but what I love best: drawing and making art...

————

Max silently watched the changes in my face and smiled. "Interesting."

This vision of my future made my eyes well up with tears when I whispered, "God, how I wish that were possible."

"Yeah, too bad your boss drags you out of your house every morning and handcuffs you to the office radiator," he smiled again, even wider this time, brought the spaghetti to his mouth, and chewed with gusto. "Oh, wait. That would be my job."

"But... how do you envision this happening?" I asked, awkwardly smiling in response to his sarcasm. "I mean, I still need to live somewhere, pay for my apartment and food and car..."

"Let me tell you a little story," Max nodded as if he had been waiting for this question. "Once upon a time, there was a boy, he was in his early twenties and worked... let's say, at a bank, as a programmer. He was doing okay, but mostly, he was really bored, sometimes even sort of sad. Also, he really wanted girls to like him and become a Big

Boss. But the girls he liked didn't like him back for some reason. And even when they did, the boy suddenly started to worry so much and became so wildly jealous that he almost turned into a monster. The girls then got scared and ran away in all directions. And no one seemed in a rush to make him even a small boss."

Max waved his fork, and I laughed. He told his life story so enthusiastically and inspiringly that I saw it all as if in a movie and actually imagined a fairytale atmosphere.

"I think I understand them a little," I quipped acerbically, but judging by Max's expression, he wasn't bothered.

"Pay attention, now," he admonished and continued calmly. "The boy became even more sad and distracted, did a poor job, and his life went downhill. One day, he suddenly realized that things couldn't get much worse. And if he was going to take a risk, there wouldn't be a better moment because he didn't have much to lose. So, one fine day, the boy decided to quit his job."

"One fine day? Seriously?" I asked skeptically.

"Absolutely," he nodded. "I wrote a resignation letter in one day and signed up for a psychology course. After that, I spent three years doing odd jobs, wearing worn-out jeans and getting by on Ramen and cereal."

"You still wear worn-out jeans," I snorted, demonstratively glancing under the table.

"Keep talking, see how well I can spank you jeans or no jeans," Max promised good-naturedly.

"So, what happened next? You opened a club?"

"First, a practice," he clarified. "That's my main income. But now the club as well."

I swallowed, suddenly imagining that in five or ten years, I could quite possibly become an artist and earn a living from my art. What if it's really possible for me too? Can I learn in five years if I start right now? Can I or can't I?

"You definitely can," Max smiled, reading my thoughts.

I laughed and shivered a little. "It scares me when you read my mind like that," I admitted in a strained voice.

"I like it when you're a little scared," Max said, and his eyes became such that I felt my whole body tremble and awaken, responding to his call.

"Max," I whispered, dropping my fork into the plate with a clatter.

"About tomorrow," he said in a completely different tone, "are you coming to the club?"

"Yes," I said quietly, involuntarily nodding.

"Good. I'll leave a package for you at reception. You'll put on what's inside and come in. I'll be at the bar at ten sharp. If you're late, I'll spank you right there," he said softly, without taking his eyes off my face. "I promise."

"Yes, master," I replied barely audibly, immediately falling into a kind of stupor, as if hypnotized.

"No shoes. No panties. No attitude."

"Yes, master."

Still in that trance, I silently watched as Max paid the bill and stood up. I only came to my senses when he leaned in to kiss me on the lips, but I didn't have time to say anything or ask anything before he swiftly left the café.

Chapter Twenty-Eight

The next morning, I inexplicably began to feel restless. There was nothing particularly significant on my mind, except for the following two things: one, it seemed as though I had skipped ahead mentally to the point in time when I'd already quit my job, and so, was annoyed that I had to go to work and couldn't understand why. Two, for some odd reason, amusing even to myself, I was very concerned about the outfit Max promised to pick for me. What if it was something really risqué, something that would be make me uncomfortable, like one of those transparent mesh dresses I'd seen on other women there, or some sort of leather strap contraption that would cover nothing and accentuate everything?

Max's threatening voice played on a loop in my head almost all day: "No shoes, no panties, no attitude."

I could handle the first two points. But what if I accidentally said "you" instead of "Sir" or called him by his name? Would that be considered attitude or not? And what would happen to me if it was?

The possibilities of what might happen to me were

broad and thinking about them hit me with a heady sense of panic mixed with intense arousal. By the end of the day, there was no talking about panties. They were long off before I ever left work—hopelessly soaked. No one knew under my conservative work suit, of course, but going commando made it all even worse. My excitement, impatience and anticipation only grew more powerful, until, unable to take it anymore, I escaped an hour and a half early without any explanation.

At home, I attempted to regain composure with a random selection of relaxing music.

It was pretty fruitless.

I resorted to cardiovascular exercise in the form of intensive dancing, but then, I got so into it that I forgot the time. An accidental glance at the clock showed time to be half past eight and, shocked, I began to rush around the apartment. A shower, makeup, a drop of perfume, and... what to wear? Physically feeling how time was slipping away, I cursed myself while standing in front of the closet in a stupor, but I couldn't just throw on jeans and a T-shirt, could I, even though I knew I'd be changing — what if Max saw me walking in? I wanted to look nice for him, regardless.

Finally choosing a long woolen skirt and a tight turtle-neck, I began to pull on the clothes with trembling hands, when suddenly his voice sounded in my ears again: "If you're late — I'll spank you right there." Damn it. I didn't want to be spanked at the bar. The public aspect still made me uneasy, even after my big scene. I didn't feel safe in front of everyone. I didn't like it. But Max was unlikely to cut me any slack this time. Shit, shit, shit.

Running out of the house, I dashed to the car in front of a surprised neighbor who was returning home from walking her dog. I didn't even manage to say hello, and she stared after me, dismayed and judgy, which was unpleasant, but still not as unpleasant as getting my ass spanked in the middle of the whole club as a punishment.

I barely let my little clunker warm up before gunning it to the club.

In the club parking lot, I finally took a free breath with relief—I had fifteen minutes to spare, more than enough time to change and get ready.

When I entered, the security guard silently handed me a package. It was the guy Max called Misha — and learning his name that first night felt like a million years ago...

This time, I met him in the foyer; he was quite gloomy, his eyes glued to his phone. He looked at me just long enough to recognize me, handed me the package, and nodded toward the changing room without taking his eyes off the screen.

Entering, I froze for a moment — there were so many girls inside, about ten or fifteen, changing, doing their hair and makeup, talking, and laughing. It reminded me of a stripper dressing room... Almost immediately, I locked eyes with the cunty red-head from last time, and jerked my gaze away as if scalded. Fortunately, I soon spotted Lori, who smiled at me immediately. The tension eased a bit, and we greeted each other with cheek kisses under the strict gaze of Irina standing nearby.

"Hi. How are you?" asked the domme in a calm, almost patronizing tone, looking me over from head to toe.

"Everything's fine," I beamed, smiling wider than usual because with every second the redhead's gaze burned hotter into the back of my neck.

"I'm glad," Irina softened and winked at me, giving Lori

a gentle pat on the shoulder. "Hurry up, sub. I'm not in the mood to wait for you today."

Hastily, Lori resumed pulling on the bedazzled robe hanging off her shoulders, and I snapped back to reality, remembering that time was running out. I wasn't allowed to be late.

Rushing to one of the empty lockers, I yanked my turtleneck over my head, unzipped the skirt, stuffed the clothes carelessly into the locker, and opened Max's package. My heart trilled with fear for a moment, but then I exhaled in relief, finding nothing more terrifying inside than a tight red crop top and a semi-transparent black wrap skirt. I wouldn't be able to bend over in this, but at the very least, while standing, all my intimate parts would be covered.

"What? Not a schoolgirl this time? Didn't quite measure up, huh?" came a hissing whisper right behind me.

I flinched in surprise and froze with the skirt in my hands.

"How are you doing tonight?" Anastasia asked when I slowly turned, looking at her with astonished bewilderment. "Anyone manage to take you down a notch, or are you still as full of shit as you were before?

The girl's face, twisted with malice and barely concealed ill-intent, was too close, and I involuntarily recoiled, hitting my back against the locker door, which, in turn, slammed loudly, drawing instant attention to our quarrel. The quiet conversations and laughter in the locker room died down. Out of the corner of my eye, I saw Lori tense up and Irina turn her head.

"Leave her alone," the domme commanded in such an authoritative voice that I instantly felt at ease. But my existence seemed to irritate Anastasia too much for her to calm down so easily.

"Her? What would I want with her?"

Her cold gray eyes scanned me from head to toe, and for a moment, I felt my legs turn to jelly and my ears ring. My gaze involuntarily traveled over her almost naked painted body — her nipples outlined in red, the lower part of her belly adorned with rhinestones, and some weird decorative fringe hanging from her leather collar. Looking at the stringy fringe and the bright red painted nipples, I was suddenly overcome by nausea.

"Mousy little weirdos are not my type at all," Anastasia sang, smirking crookedly.

"Shut up, bitch, and mind your own business!"

"Sub!"

Lori's aggressive defense and Irina's sharp rebuke came almost at the same time, and were both loud enough to end all conversations in the dressing room. Silence now reigned, and everyone was lookin in our direction. After a moment, two girls I didn't recognize, walked out with deliberately stony expressions, and another flung the door open on her way in and stopped short, seeing that there was some sort of scene unfolding.

My heart racing, I raised my chin and took a step toward the rabid Anastasia. I could feel my own gaze turn icy and hard, and the redhead seemed to have finally realized that she had enough eyes on her now that open provocation wouldn't be wise. She also raised her chin and smirked once more, turning to leave without saying a word.

"Let's go," Irina said to Lori, her tone precluding any objections, and they also walked out.

———

My hands trembled as I began pulling on the skirt and top. The changing room quickly emptied out, and soon, I was completely alone. Glancing at the clock— five more minutes—I finally caught my breath. I had just enough time to fix my hair, touch up my lipstick, and gather myself, though not completely. Indignation still raged in my chest — what was wrong with that redhead? Why so much hatred? Had I somehow provoked her into that torrent of abuse, or was that just her delightful personality?

Finding no answers to my largely philosophical questions, I slammed and locked my locker door, exited into the anteroom, and stepped towards the door leading to the club's main area, but suddenly, the security guard, Misha, loomed before me.

"Shoes," he said quietly but sternly.

"Wh—" oh no... my heart plummeted. Damn. How could I forget?

"No shoes... no panties..." But, wound up by the crazy redhead's insults, I had completely forgotten, and now I had both on.

Misha must have understood something from my face because his thick dark eyebrow arched, and he crossed his arms over his chest. "Let's see under the skirt."

"No!"

I backed away, color instantly rising up my neck to the tips of my ears, but the guard just smirked and shook his head. "Just take off what you're supposed to take off, and you'll get five spanks. Or you can leave it on and get the fifteen I owe you."

"I'll take it off. Please... Misha... your name is Misha, right?"

"That's Mikhail to you, sub."

"Okay. Mikhail, please, I just forgot... I'll go back to the changing room and take everything off, okay?"

"Nah." His lips were trembling in a smile he was trying to hold in. "It's not your first time here, you know the rules."

"It's a dumb rule!"

"And yet." He shrugged. "Go on. Bend over."

"Mikhail, please. If I'm late, Max will kill me."

"Oh, I know. That's why it's in your best interest to do this quickly," he smirked, looking straight at me.

I closed my eyes. There were only two options — either comply or call Max. If I did the latter, he would surely be angry. Plus, I'd be acting like the hateful redhead, who thought she was special because she was friends with the owner. No, I didn't want to be like Anastasia at all.

So, comply it was.

"Fine!"

Resolutely kicking off my shoes, I turned away, pulling off my panties and, clutching them in my hand, I faced Mikhail again. I couldn't bear to look him in the face, my own face already crimson, and he took pity, taking a couple of steps towards me. Silently taking the panties from my hand, he tossed them onto the table.

"Relax, I'm not a sadist," he said mockingly as I bent over.

The silky fabric of the skirt parted, exposing my fully bare bottom, which his warm hand immediately slapped with a loud sound. I cried out instinctively, but then frowned. Misha spanked me very quickly and rather gently — it was nothing like the scorching blows Max usually delivered. It was over before I knew it, but just as relief that I had gotten off lightly began to fill me, the door leading into the club opened slightly from the inside, and my Dom's formidable figure appeared on the threshold.

By that time, Misha's hands were no longer holding or spanking me, but I didn't have time to straighten up, and Max's eyes immediately narrowed, taking in the scene. His gaze slid briefly over my panties on the table, then over me, and finally settled on Misha.

"How many did she get?"

"Five."

Max's eyes stopped on my shoes, discarded near the table.

"And why so few?" he asked coldly, looking at me with a murderous glare.

"First offense. She agreed to take everything off, so..."

"I see. Thanks, Misha. Liza, follow me, quickly," he snapped, and I realized with horror that Max was truly angry and barely balancing between play and genuine irritation.

As soon as we entered the club, I understood that an unusually large crowd had gathered that evening, and my head immediately spun from the stuffiness and the unpleasant feeling brought on by the clear understanding that Max was angry at me. I could hardly bear it.

"Master, please, don't be mad at me," I softly pleaded, looking up at him imploringly.

"You,'re better off keeping your mouth shut, sub," he threw over his shoulder, not even looking.

However, after a couple of steps, he slowed, took a visible breath. He placed his hand on my shoulder, gently pulling me closer, and instead of going to a playstation or the bar, led me to the second floor.

Chapter Twenty-Nine

Max maintained an impenetrable expression, as he unlocked the door, but I could almost physically feel the tension vibrating within him. It burst forth as soon as he closed the door behind us.

"On your knees," he barked, quickly moving to the stand with spanking devices.

"Master, let me explain..."

"Quiet."

Everything inside me tightened. I was boiling over with the desire to explain the misunderstanding, to assure him of my well-intent, to complain about unbearable Anastasia, and to ask for forgiveness, but his voice frightened me.

He turned to me, paddle in hand. In a flash, I thought understood what had angered him — Max was displeased to see another man spanking me without his knowledge, and he was almost beside himself.

My stomach clenched as I raised my eyes.

"You're jealous again," I blurted, my voice shaking, nose prickling.

This seemed to stop Max cold for a moment, and I

shrank into myself in serious fear, bracing for the blowback. But after another moment, in a steady yet stern voice, Max addressed me calmly. "Are you using a safe word, Liza?"

Scolding, yelling, hitting—I can do all that and more, but it all stops immediately, as soon as you say the word.

Exactly what Max had said to me when we talked in his car after I fell apart at his admission of jealousy. What separated him from my past. Without leaving the game, he was giving me an out.

Suddenly, I could breathe again. "No, master."

With barely a nod, he continued, "I warned you, Liza. I was more than clear with you on Thursday. I told you exactly what I wanted."

"Master, I remembered your instructions, but—"

"But you disregarded them."

"Not at all, I just—"

"You can't stop arguing even now! Can't you be silent for a second?"

I quieted, echoes of resistance still simmering beneath the surface under my skin. But I finally accepted that I wasn't going to talk my way out of this one.

"Elbows and knees on the bed. Not a word. You'll take this punishment silently, sub, or I'll tape your mouth shut for the entire night, clear?"

Nodding silently, I complied, breathing heavily. And I closed my eyes when the skirt parted over my bottom, and my buttocks felt the chill. My stomach clenched in fear again, but damn, the anticipation of seeing him above me—silent, imposing, strong with the paddle in his hand, his gaze imperious as he let me stew in my own guilt and anxiety—was exhilarating. Arousal took my body over almost completely. Somewhere in the distance, I wondered how many blows...

"Ahh!" I screamed when he gave a good spank across both buttocks at once.

Then the blows began to really rain down. Five, seven, ten... Suffering in silence was a big ask when he clearly wasn't holding back his strength. I moaned and yelped, but somehow, in my desire to please, to finally do something right, managed not to utter a single word. This earned me a few short breaks, where he stroked my pussy, teasing carelessly, a dubious respite, because each time thereafter, he returned, even harder. By the twelfth strike, tears had started to well up, and by the fifteenth, I was whimpering and biting my lips.

He stopped at twenty and flipped me onto my back. He lay on top of me and looked into my tear-streaked face.

"I never want to see you punished by security again, sub," he said. "Not when I didn't sanction it. It is humiliating—for me. Do you understand? If it happens again — I won't be responsible for my actions, clear?"

"Yes, master," I whispered, reaching for his lips, but he abruptly pulled away and moved up, unzipping his pants:

"I want your mouth. Now."

The next half hour, he played harshly, throwing out order after order, as if he wanted to make sure I was capable of following them at all, or perhaps, to replace the thoughts in my head only with his admonishments. He'd been successful replacing my thoughts before, after all...

He had me complete the blowjob, then give him a massage, then serve him in the shower, washing his hair and drying it...

...and only after all that did he deign to fuck my yearning, shamelessly wet pussy.

I lost my senses the moment he entered me — the penetration was so desired, so long-awaited. I was already electrified, my nerve endings throwing sparks, and shocks spread through my body as he thrust — from my core to the tips of my toes, up my spine to the top of my head, and down my arms from shoulders to hands.

"You're mine, Liza. Remember that. Mine," he growled into my face at the peak of my orgasm, and I sensed something maniacal in his behavior, but it no longer scared me. I liked it.

———

———

However, to my dismay, Max continued to behave strangely even after sex, without returning to a peaceful mood, as if he was harboring a grudge.

We took turns in the shower and almost in silence, went down to the bar, where Nik suddenly pulled him aside on apparent business matters, leaving me alone with Dima the bartender. I sat on a barstool with disappointed sigh, and asked for a virgin mojito. Dima, who obviously felt it was his responsibility to entertain me, grinned broadly. "Mint or super mint?"

"And super mint is when there's twice as much mint or just really big mint?" I asked, forcing myself to keep up the banter without much enthusiasm.

"Well, there are super ingredients on order for super subs," he said mysteriously, making a circle with his eyes, "Have you been a super sub today?"

It was impossible not to respond to his boyishly open smile.

"Maybe," I smirked. "You'd have to ask Max. So, what's

the super ingredient? It wouldn't happen to be rum, by any chance?"

"Mmm, maybe, why, do you want a little bit of some-thing-something?"

"Maybe just a squirt."

"Did you ask Max for permission?"

I scoffed, my mouth dropping open. "I don't need permission from daddy to have a drink!" I fumed, and Dima laughed, pleased he had finally managed to get a rise out of me.

"Are you sure?" he teased, raising an eyebrow.

"Pour the damn rum," I ordered.

"Yes, ma'am!"

At that very moment, just as Dima turned to get the bottle of rum, a voice came from my right. "Uh oh! She's taken to the drink. Things must be real bad, sweetheart, huh."

The smile brought on by the bartender's gentle teasing instantly vanished from my lips.

Anastasia. Of course.

"Fuck off," I gritted over my shoulder, all the anger accumulated in the locker room flooding back and bursting out.

"Ooh, ooh," she crooned in a nasty, theatrical tone, "Don't be mad about being jilted here at the bar all alone. You didn't think Max was going to actually keep you, did you?" She made a sickening pout. "Aw. Oh no. You did. That's so cute. Well, maybe if you weren't such a stuck up bitch, you'd have realized you need a lot more than a medi-ocre little scene wearing a cheap ugly outfit from Temu to win Max, darling."

"Hey, little sub, take it easy," Dima interjected peacefully from behind the bar. "We make love, not war, here at Club Subspace."

He slid a glass toward me and raised an eyebrow at the redhead waiting for her to order, but she shook her head and once she was sure he was out of earshot, she turned back to me.

"Fuck off," I said again. I couldn't hold back, giving her the harshest look I could muster. Out of the corner of my eye, I noticed Lori appearing out of nowhere on the other side of me, and within moments she was sitting next to me, stroking my arm.

"If you're looking for trouble, we can arrange that," she coldly informed my foe. "Easily."

But the redhead seemed impervious to threats.

"Oh, and who do we have here?" Anastasia asked, batting her eyelashes theatrically. "Isn't that the sub who amazed the whole club with her hysterical attempts to play at being domme? And what are you threatening me with, exactly? A covert belt attack? I hear you're good with a belt. Weren't belts your specialty?"

Feeling Lori's arm tense, I turned to eye her with concern. Anastasia seemed to have a talent for getting under people's skin. Lori's face darkened, her thin nostrils flared, and even the jasmine scent of her perfume grew heavier in an instant. She started to rise from her stool, and the redhead, sensing something, stepped back. But when Lori, obviously deciding to be the bigger person, took a deep breath, composed herself, and sat back down, Anastasia was back in her element, leaning on the counter with her cheek propped on her hands.

"I have to say, what a lovely couple you two make," she drawled again, "one wannabe domme, the other a sub without a top. It's so sweet how pathetic people always find each other. Just like a movie. Everyone deserves a chance at happiness, even the underdogs."

"Let's go," Lori whispered in my ear, pulling at my elbow, but it was too late. I've always been the kind of person who could endure insults directed at me—but not at my friends, and now, a switch had been flipped and something uncontrollable and hot flared up inside me.

My hand instinctively clenched around my sweating glass of mojito, and the next moment, I seemed to watch from outside myself as my cocktail, along with a healthy handful of ice-cubes flew right into Anastasia's perfectly groomed face.

Judging by her momentary lack of reaction, my outburst caught her completely off guard. In a delayed reaction, she jumped up, her hair now icicles, muddled mint leaves hanging from the locks, syrupy drink dripping down her face and from the tip of her nose. Wet, red paint running down her nipples made it look like she was bleeding, and some dark evil part of me almost wished she were.

"Lori will be whatever she wants to be," I screamed over the music. "And Max is mine, got it?"

Her laugh was malicious and absolutely maniacal, like the crazy lady in the attic, and it went on until she snorted, tossing her wet hair back like a horse at a watering hole, and straightened to her full height, planting her hands on her hips. "You ain't shit, you know that right? No one knows who the fuck you are. Not wearing a collar, are you? Max hasn't claimed you. That means you. Ain't. Shit."

The words circled around me like birds of prey and just as they were starting to register, and my breath was beginning to get icy with shock, a roar came seemingly from above somewhere. "What the hell do you think you're doing, sub?"

Nik.

Where he came from, I couldn't say, but he was there, materialized next to his sub, and by all indicators, enraged to the limit, which made Lori and myself flinch—I, for one, always thought Nik was a softer character than Max, goofy and fun, and incapable of showing such anger.

But even in the face of her Dom's ire, Anastasia was unstoppable. She was on a roll, her brakes failing her completely this evening. Either that, or she was purposely trying to provoke her Dom, as a bratty masochist, not a sub. It was almost sad.

Almost.

Then again, it was also almost funny.

"You're only a superstar in your own imagination, you dumb freak!" she yelled at me, a caricature of herself, as Nik dragged her by the scruff of her neck toward the lounge area. Judging by his face, nothing good was in store for her.

Chapter Thirty

For a moment, Lori and I just stood there, frozen in shock, unable to tear our eyes away from the indelible sight of Nik dragging his insane submissive kicking and screaming away from the bar. It wasn't just us—after a few moments, I noticed Dima was standing stock still with a cocktail shaker raised halfway up, and several people around the play area had turned to crane their necks to stare at us in amazement with their mouths wide open.

I realized I had barely been breathing when my own mouth suddenly dropped open and I sucked in a noisy, desperate gulp of air. My knees buckled, and I collapsed back onto my seat, suddenly completely out of juice. Lori silently sank into the next seat and gently stroked my back. This comforting gesture brought me back to reality, and I looked up at her. "Lori? What the hell was she talking about, claiming or whatever she said?"

"Come on, that's nonsense," Lori said, but at the same time, she glanced away in a gesture that made my heart sink. You don't need to be a psychologist to interpret such body language.

271

"Lori?"

I geared up for an argument. determined to get an answer out of her, but then Dima widened his eyes, clearly warning us about something, and at that very moment, I felt warm fingers squeeze the back of my neck. There was no need to guess who it was laying his hands on me in this proprietary way. Swiveling the chair so I faced him, Max bent his face close enough for our noses to touch and whispered, "Sub, have you lost your entire mind? Why the hell are you yelling to the whole club that I'm yours?"

"I —I thought you were."

"I think you've got that backwards. I don't remember switching roles."

There was a short circuit in my brain. Whatever Anastasia, and even Lori, thought, wasn't Max literally saying I was his, plain and simple? Yet, he seemed upset at me again. Clearly, I'd broken some kind of protocol—but I was ruthlessly provoked. "If you'd just let me explain—"

"I'm not interested in explanations. I gave you three rules for tonight, and you managed to break every single one of them. You're not a newbie anymore, Liza. And I have to punish you." Max turned his head and found Dima with his eyes: "Clear the bar counter."

I felt my face go long in shock at the injustice of it all. Bullied. Antagonized. Humiliated—and about to be punished for my trouble. And my so-called master, who hadn't even laid claim on me, as it seemed, despite insisting I was his and not the other way around, wasn't reasonable enough to hear about any extenuating circumstances. Were we even still playing? Either way, I didn't think I could take much more.

I instinctively looked around, seeking protection, but

found only about a dozen curious gazes and a very frightened look from Lori.

"Master, please—"

"Start by shutting your mouth."

An icy wave of helpless impotence and disappointment
washed down my back as I thought that this would be it,
this would be when I safe worded.

But the next moment, Lori suddenly composed herself,
stepped towards Max. I closed my eyes, anxious, but, just as
anxious, immediately opened them again, to see Lori
whisper something in Max's ear. Then he turned his gaze to
Dima and beckoned him over. The men exchanged a few
words, nodded to each other, and only then did Max turn to
me. "Liza, look at me."

Even before he spoke, I knew he had switched out of
game mode. He looked at me with a calm, affectionate gaze,
clearly wanting to reassure me. Something let go inside me
in response, and I felt myself open up again. If he wanted to
reassure me, I wanted to let him.

"Sweetheart, I see you," he said softly, slipping his arms
around my waist. "This is not revenge. I'm not angry. This is
a scene, like any other. You can handle it."

"Forgive me, master. I don't mean to keep getting into
situations—"

"I will definitely forgive you, malysh, after the scene. Do
you trust me?"

"Yes."

Looking him in the eyes, I couldn't say anything else. Of
course, I did.

"Good girl. Get on the counter," he ordered and, grabbing me by the hips, lifted me up.

"A scene here?" I mumbled, lost.

"Yes."

"I—"

The sudden view of the club from above made my head spin. I noticed a bunch of curious onlookers gathering around the bar, and my heart started beating twice as fast.

"Liza," Max called out, clearly sensing my hesitation and nerves. His hand was warm on my knee. "Look at me."

I shifted my gaze to my Dom and nodded, fixing him with an anxious stare.

"I want you to keep looking at me and only me," Max repeated, calmly stroking my leg. "There is no one else here. Just us. Do you understand?"

"Yes."

"Good. You can do this. Now, kneel before me," he ordered in a tone so soft it was barely an order.

Exhaling, I tucked my legs under me and sat as upright as possible, so the slit in my skirt wouldn't spread.

I watched as Max signaled to Dima with a quick glance to the ceiling, and instinctively followed his eyes. Chains hung from the ceiling right above the bar, which I had noticed long ago. I had assumed they were just part of the club's decor... right up until this moment, when Dima climbed onto the counter and fastened my hands into the cuffs above my head.

My mouth opened, and I gasped for air, especially when Max stood up, reached for the other end of the chain, and pulled, forcing me to kneel up. Now I was kneeling with my arms stretched upward, exposed to everyone's view and completely helpless.

"M... master."

"Sshh, sub. You're okay. You're doing great."

He placed his hot hand on my knee and slid it upward, lifting my skirt, and then, to my horror, secured the edge to my waistband, exposing my thigh. And he did the same on the other side.

"Liza, I'd like to do this scene together with two other masters," he said softly, looking up at me.

He let a pause go by waiting for me to object. I waited too, but somehow, the objection didn't come. Max wanted to do a scene with two other masters, and as I looked into his dark eyes, it seemed that now I wanted to do it too.

Still looking up at me, Max slowly gestured to the man who had appeared on a barstool to his right. "This is Master Alex; you've seen him before."

Max took his time, giving me a chance to meet the eyes... damn, of that huge guy who loved walking his partner on a leash around the club and then, driving her to the brink, publicly humiliating her on the bar. Tearing my gaze away from his indifferent and, as it seemed to me, cold face, I felt color drain away from my face. "And this is Master Dave," Max noted in the same soft, unhurried tone, shifting his gaze to the left.

"Dave?" I repeated.

My eyes met the curious and amused gaze of a very young, slender blond man with bright green eyes.

"Yes," he purred softly in a velvet voice and winked, his gaze trailing over my chest, lifted due to my hands being bound above.

Following his gaze, I realized in despair that my top had started to slip. Just a few more good breaths, and it would fall off. Trying to breathe shallower, I froze, looking at Max again. Questions were bursting from my lips, but I realized it must be true, I must not be a newbie anymore, because I instinctively understood that in my current position, it was best for a sub to keep her mouth shut.

"So," Max said softly, his eyes trailing over my body

again, "Relax. Nothing you don't want is going to happen. Each master will take turns approaching you and talking to you, that's it. You still have your safe words. It's in your best interest, sub, to respond respectfully. This is a test of your ability to remain respectful under challenging circumstances. I want you to make me proud and show off your best qualities as a sub. Show me you can be obedient and respectful. I know you have it in you."

Max shot a brief glance up at my hands, already going cold in their binds, and then it dawned on me. Oh God. I wouldn't last long in this position. In just a minute, it would really start to hurt as my shoulders strained and my hands went numb...

I flared my nostrils, and swaying my hips, shifted from numb knee to numb knee. There was nothing erotic about this. It was designed to be plain torture. I would have liked to see Max strung up like this.

"Mmhm," Max agreed, looking into my eyes, watching the realization sink in. "This is bondage, and it's uncomfortable. Show me you can resist being cheeky, arguing, and contradicting a master. Resist making inappropriate remarks. And the quicker you convince us that you can be obedient, the sooner this scene will end."

"And how will I know which remarks are inappropriate, master?" I asked through my teeth.

"Well, that one was a great example," Max responded, amused, and ran his hand over the back of my thigh, tucking my skirt into the waistband there, too, exposing my ass.

"Oh, what a lovely view from here," Dima's voice came from behind, and I blushed deeply, jerking in the chains—not so much out of shame this time, but out of anger.

"You look beautiful, Liza," Max confirmed, encouragingly, as though he could sense my shyness. "I want everyone to see how beautiful."

I had a lot to say to Max about this, but my arms were really starting to go numb, and I gritted my teeth, holding back.

Max stepped aside to make room for Master Alex, and I instantly felt the cold grip of panic. He seemed cruel. What would he do to me now, vulnerable and stretched out like this?

A foreign hand landed on my thigh—almost as hot as my Dom's, but not his. I didn't want to look at this strange man, but he was staring at me intently, and I realized I had no choice.

"I want to touch your breasts, sub," he said, waiting for our eyes to meet.

"No!" The word slipped out, and Max frowned, cocking his head at me from behind this Alex.

"What did you say?" Master Alex. "Are you using your safe word?"

It was strange to look down at the men commanding me, but I realized that even now, when his head barely reached my chest, being near this ruthless Dom was not easy.

I took a deep breath, gathering my willpower for a better answer, as Alex's eyes trailed my curves with a carnivorous look, and, suddenly, in a flash, I became hyper aware of every inch of my body, the way it was burning up, vibrating, hot.

"No, master," I murmured, before I realized I was speaking, to address his last question. "No safe word."

"Good girl," he said softly, "That was very polite. We're not here to force anyone into anything, are we? Now. I want to touch your breasts."

It wasn't a question, but I gathered all my willpower, and whispered, "Yes, master."

In the next second, with an incredibly swift, graceful move for such a big man, he hopped up on the counter beside me. He was still for a few seconds, waiting until he caught my eyes, and only when I finally glanced over at him, did he place a gentle, hot palm over my breast. A soft but very real groan escaped when slightly rough fingers snuck under thin fabric and squeezed my nipple, and a louder groan ripped from my chest when, in a swift motion, he yanked my top down until it was completely off.

I squeezed my eyes shut, not wanting to see who else was getting an eyeful of my naked chest. Alex was enough.

But now, with a soft chuckle, he disappeared, and master Dave called from below.

"Liza?"

"Yes, master," I answered quietly, afraid to open my eyes.

God. Half the club must have been staring at my bare chest, and for some reason, this was much, much worse than when I had been almost naked on the table during the scene with the two "professors." Of course, it was clear why: now I wasn't lying down, and I would have to face all those thirsty, gawking people the moment I opened my eyes.

"Sub, look at me," the insistent voice of the blond Dom called from below. I exhaled slowly and raised my eyelids, trying not to look at anyone but master Dave.

"Say hello."

He sounded almost amused, and I wasn't as afraid of this one as I was of the cruel Master Alex, so the answer came easily. "Hello, master."

As a reward, I received a warm smile.

He moved closer and peered into my eyes, squinting like he was trying to read me.

"Is that pussy wet?" he asked, so quietly that the music drowned out his question for everyone, even for Max and the other master standing nearby, except me.

Until that moment, I hadn't concerned myself with whether or not I was *wet*. The brief flash of awareness from before barely registered as arousal at all. The scene was too awkward and strange, and I was too nervous to even consider any sort of sexual aspect.

But now, falsely shielded by music and under the illusion of a strange privacy and connection with this young master, looking at me so closely, I realized that yes, I was most definitely wet. *Fuck.*

I blurted, "Yes, master."

Dave didn't flinch. He said, "I want to touch you."

"Okay."

"Okay?" His eyebrow rose.

"Yes. Yes, master."

Master Dave's hand slid up and touched the inside of my thigh. "You have such soft skin," he murmured.

"Thank you, master."

"Do you want me to pet you a little more? In some other places?"

"Um..."

"Don't lie to me." His inflection changed just barely, but my body responded to his sudden sternness with a pang of desire, and there was no way I could lie even if I wanted to.

"I—Yes, master. Thank you."

"Good sub."

Dave ran the back of his hand along my leg, up my thigh, and caressed my ass, squeezing burning flesh for a couple of moments, before removing himself. The absence of his touch tingled and went on forever until I let out a hot breath and opened my eyes—to look right into Max's.

A strange sensation bubbled up inside me as I pondered how Max would react to seeing another man touch me so sensually, especially after his violent reaction to seeing me spanked by someone else.

But his behavior just didn't add up—when he strolled over, all he asked was, "Do you want to be untied?"

It was like trying to solve a puzzle with missing pieces. I gave up. In my best submissive voice, I replied, "Yes, master," and gave him a pleading look that should have made even the toughest Dom melt.

"Certainly—in exchange for ten extra minutes of service. Each," he declared with a wicked grin.

I was too overwhelmed to get mad or question him. "Of course, master," I blurted out, eager to get down, unsure if I could survive another minute with my arms stretched above my head.

Max nodded at Dima, who climbed onto the counter again to free me. As soon as my arms dropped down, I let out a groan of relief and rubbed my sore wrists, eyeing each of the masters in turn. And then I couldn't help but wonder what Max meant by "serving."

The answer didn't take long.

"I'll have a Long Island and a hand massage," master Dave announced with a smirk, leaving me momentarily speechless and motionless.

For the next thirty minutes, I assumed the role of bar-wench. A trembling mess of a bar-wench.

It took me a moment to catch on to the game.

Tending bar was something I'd never tried my hand at even in the best of circumstances. Silly me, I thought I could get away with just making the drinks and being polite, even officious. But here, in addition to fumbling with ingredients and shakers and ice cubes, I was subjected to constant physical and verbal teasing. It took me a moment to catch on to the game.

Dima stood beside me, holding out bottles and explaining the steps for making cocktails, but his instructions were constantly interrupted by the masters' lewd commentary and quips centered around my lack of bartending acumen, and when one of the masters "accidentally" grazed my exposed breast for the third time, making me flinch and spill the measure of rum I was pouring out all over the bar, it dawned on me that much like my math exam, this trial was designed specifically for me to fail. There was no point in getting mad, no point in looking for the moment where I went wrong. I would go wrong somewhere eventually. I just had to accept and obey.

A lesson in humility indeed.

"Aw, look at that," Max said with faux sympathy, eyeing the expanding puddle of liquid on the bar. "You ruined it. Looks like you have to start all over. Can you at least try this time?"

He slapped me on the ass, which m didn't hurt but somehow managed to make an impressive sound, and elicited merry laughter out of everyone, and quiet indignation out of me.

Quiet, because although at that point, I wanted nothing more than to pour a drink over each of their heads in retaliation, I knew doing so would turn the scene in a direction I wouldn't like. So I swallowed my pride and started over again, determined to get it right this time, despite their best efforts to derail me.

It never stopped. Even when I got the drink right, they were unhappy with the way I garnished the glass with the paper umbrella, with the number of ice cubes or squirts of simple syrup. There came a point where I didn't have a single thought of my own anymore, sure of nothing, able only to watch my fingers as I squeezed the limes and stirred the drinks.

I'd forgotten that I still had the massage portion of the task, but by the time it came to it, I fell into some sort of meditative state—it reminded me of the way I felt when taking care of Lori in her bathroom. The Doms seemed to sense the change in me and quieted down, making no further nasty remarks and allowing me to finish my job. They even showed signs of enjoyment and made small gestures of praise. By the time I got to Max, I found I was enjoying the process, grateful for the positive rein-forcement.

When I reached out for his palm, he shook his head. "The scene is over, sweet. I'll take my massage privately."

"Yes, master," I exhaled in relief, reaching out my arms, as he took me by the waist and lowered me off the bar, gently pressing me to his body, calming me with one of his long warm hugs.

"You did so good," he whispered in my ear. "You worked so hard. Such a good girl for me."

And I closed my eyes trustingly, pressing against him with a quiet helpless moan. That was all it took. All my anger and frustration, all that negative energy were suddenly directed down a whole other channel.

All I wanted was to be with him. All I wanted was him inside me.

My body was aflame.

Chapter Thirty-One

To my surprise, Max didn't drag me straight upstairs like he always did. Instead, he kissed me without saying a word, helped me to my feet, and firmly led me outside by the hand as if he had something important to show me. Then, as if stumbling over his own thoughts, he halted and turned towards me.

At sight of Max, Misha, our security guard, tried to blend into the wall, pretending to be engrossed in his iPhone.

A secret inner struggle flickered across Max's face.

"Will you come over?" he finally asked in an urgent whisper, shielding me from Misha's bored yet sharp gaze.

"To your house?" I asked, surprised. Inside my chest, my heart thudded loudly and sped up, while a timid smile trembled on my lips.

"Yes, to my house," Max repeated, watching my face closely.

"Yes," I nodded without hesitation, and his furrowed brow instantly smoothed out.

"Then get changed, malysh. I'll wait here."

Bolting for the changing room, I found myself rushing around like I was late somewhere even though the official part of the night was basically over. I sensed that Max was acting impulsively and trying to do something that would mean a big step for both of us—but also, that he was liable to change his mind if spooked.

If I were honest, I had no idea what was going on. The whole evening had been chaotic and strange—and as I analyzed it, I couldn't help but blame myself. If only I'd reacted more calmly to that red-haired idiot. If only I hadn't forgotten about my underwear and shoes. If only I had...

If only, if only, if only.

What I did gain was a clearer insight into Max's "mysterious" persona, which wasn't really all that mysterious. Once you started paying attention, it became fairly transparent.

Max was akin to a powerful predator—independent, strong, ferocious on the outside. Yet on the inside, he was mostly lonely and vulnerable, and just as in need of love as the rest of us.

Max was in need of love.

His version of receiving love was to have someone gift him total trust and submission. By God, I wanted to be that someone; I wanted to be perfect for him, but, it seemed that as if by some cruel trick of fate, things always went awry. The perfect scene never materialized as with every fumble, I undermined his idea of his own authority.

And yet, he trusted me. I could tell. Slowly but surely, he was opening up. I saw it in the way he expressed his anger today instead of acting out in revenge underhandedly. It was as if he had allowed himself to reveal his true feelings to me and realized they wouldn't scare me away.

Then there was that scene at the bar counter. It made no sense to me. Unless he was once wrestling with his inner conflict, his jealousy and temper, testing how much he trusted me? Because if he was such a jealous man, who was working hard not to be jealous, why else would he involve two other men and let them play with me? What if I liked it?

And of course, I had to contend with my own inner conflict. Because I could blush all I wanted; the plain truth was I did like it. My inner prude put up a good fight, but even she couldn't fail to recognize how excited I'd become, getting attention from three men at once—and from the rest of the spectators. Like Lori said: embarrassed at first, but ultimately... everyone is looking at your body, everyone likes it, everyone wants you... What's not to like?

I was an attention whore and I loved it.

Completely naked, I stood frozen before the mirror, watching myself breathe. Sometimes when I studied my reflection, I thought I was pretty ordinary and plain; other times, I thought I was... well... hot. This was one of the latter times. After all the attention at the bar, my body was pinked, warmed, its contours somehow more lush, more provocative. My areolas darkened around persistently hardened nipples. My cheeks were flushed, my eyes sparkled, and my lips looked perfectly bee-stung. I glowed.

Of course, they all wanted me...

Was I vain? Was it really all that terrible that I'd always enjoyed being admired? It pleased me that all these men and women wanted to look at me, touch me, caress me...

And the best part. Only Max could have me. Oh god— how I wanted to belong to him, and only him. Any time, any way.

And he wanted me too. He was waiting for me.

A sharp zap of arousal almost struck me down to my

knees at the thought, pulsing through my entire body from my eyes to the tips of my fingers.

A soft moan escaped my throat, jolting me back to reality. Why was I wasting time staring at myself when what I wanted was literally right outside that door?

I grinned at myself as I pulled on my clothes, and stepped outside, still grinning.

Max raised his eyebrows as he looked up and glanced at my face. "Someone looks very pleased with herself."

Damn. My cheeks suddenly felt as if they were scalded with boiling water. How could he read my thoughts so easily? Was Max really some sort of magician? A mind reader?

"You're funny, malysh," he laughed, clearly delighted by my reaction to his words. "Your every emotion is written all over that pretty face. Let's go."

———

When we climbed into the car, Max started the engine but didn't immediately pull away. Instead, he turned and reached for my face, eyes glowing with a new light I didn't recognize. It was warm and made my own eyes tear up, as he gently stroked my hot cheek.

"About Anastasia," he began, "I want you to know—she won't be returning to the club."

My mouth fell open in surprise. "Really?"

That was not what I'd expected to hear. All this time, Max had acted as if he hadn't noticed Anastasia's bullying. Even today when he punished me, he wouldn't let me explain. Now it seemed that he had seen everything.

"It's my club," Max affirmed, "And I notice everything that happens. I won't tolerate any abuse. I take personal offense at anyone being mean to *you*, specifically. I just wanted to see how you would handle yourself, and you did great on your own. However, that unfortunate girl has shown us for a while now that she isn't Subspace material. After today's incident, Nik agreed to get rid of her."

Finally regaining my ability to speak, I laughed. "Get rid of her? That sounds like you shot her in the head and dumped her in an alley."

"I know you might wish for that," Max said with a soft smile, "but we limited ourselves with charging her a fine and banning her from club.

"A ban is good enough," I protested. "I'm not that blood-thirsty,"

"Oh, sure you are," Max teased back. "I especially admired your righteous rage when you tossed your drink in her face."

His smile widened as his eyes tenderly studied my expression, fingertips dusting over my forehead, eyebrows, cheeks, and neck.

"During our scene, I wanted to toss my drink in your face, too," I boldly confessed.

"I know," he replied with the same infuriatingly lazy and smug grin. "And for that I'll spank and thoroughly fuck you later."

"How thoroughly?"

"Thoroughly enough that you'll remember who's in charge around here once and for all."

"You sure?

"Absolutely sure," Max said firmly. "Today it will be etched into your memory forever."

"Don't threaten me with a good time, sir."

We both sat there staring at each other so intensely that for a moment I thought he would grab me, drag me into the back seat, and fuck me right there on the spot; my body was melting with acute desire, and it was clear that Max was equally aroused. His nostrils flared, his eyelids were half-closed, a muscle at the angle of his jaw ticked as he gritted his teeth. But he took a deep breath, placed his hands on the wheel and, instead of pulling me into the back as I imagined, said, "Buckle up, buttercup. The good time will begin shortly."

Chapter Thirty-Two

As I watched Max drive, I suddenly felt the tickle of mischief. Where was Max's mind at this very moment? Personally, the way his fingers were authoritatively splayed over the steering wheel sent my mind right for the gutter. Was he in a similar place? I carefully reached out and placed a hand on his crotch, partly to verify my guess that he was hard as a rock for me and partly to—well—to keep him that way.

He shifted in his seat in a most gratifying—for me—way.

"Liza," he warned in a barely audible voice, and I paused, but ultimately interpreted his failure to make a move to stop me as a green light. I stroked him slowly up and down through thick denim, just enough for him to feel something—but not everything—until finally, a dull groan escaped his lips.

"Sweetheart, you're playing with fire," he growled as we turned into a dark courtyard. "You're going to be in so much fucking trouble if you keep going..."

I giggled like a teenager and withdrew my hand only

when he parked the car and killed the engine. At that point, the light in his eyes was so dangerous, my insides quivered in response, unstable and weightless, like dandelions.

The way Max stepped when he got out of the car—slowly, too slowly—he must have been really working to control his urges, because as soon as my car door was open, he reached inside and yanked me out by the hand with enough force to give me whiplash. Both impatient now, we ran towards the entrance so fast it felt like we were fleeing from pursuers.

As soon as we entered the elevator, Max's hands were all over me, pulling at my clothes, and his mouth covered mine, fiercely devouring me with kisses. Desire radiated off of him in waves, scorching hot, urgent, and his need fed mine, making me want him more and more with every second, every one of which felt like an eternity.

By the time we reached the top floor of his building, I was practically naked, with my skirt unzipped and hiked up around my waist, and my prim turtleneck hanging on by one sleeve. The heat between us was intense enough to scorch the earth as we stumbled out of the elevator and towards his apartment door.

Without breaking our kiss, Max fumbled with the keys before finally unlocking the door and pushing us inside. As soon as we were through the threshold, he slammed the door shut behind us and pressed me up against it.

His lips were back on mine, and I moaned into his mouth as he asserted ownership over every inch of my exposed skin, and exposed any skin that wasn't already so he could claim ownership over that too.

"Max," I gasped. "I can't..."

I can't wait is what I wanted to say, but didn't get the

chance before Max pulled me into a dark room and pushed me onto something buttery soft—it took a second but as I found my face pressed down into it, I realized it was the backrest of a leather couch.

Max was somewhere behind me and I committed miracles to stay still and act patient as he pulled off my bothersome skirt, while every inch of my body screamed: "Please hurry!"

He complied without me having to say a word, however, and a desperate scream ripped from my chest as soon as his cock pushed into my wet and desperate cunt. With that scream, all coherent thought left my mind, and I lost all control of what my body was doing. Wild moans and animal grunts filled the room as Max fucked me roughly, hungrily, squeezing my hips with his fingers in a steel grip. He was merciless, right up until the moment I screamed out my climax into the leather. Shortly after, he erupted in an animal growl as he came inside me, letting me feel every iota of the full fury of his possession.

When he was done, he collapsed on top of me, damp skin against damp skin, and we quieted. As though by an unspoken agreement, we remained intertwined and motionless, neither of us wishing to shift or change positions.

Soon, however, even as I was still fluttering with the ebb of my orgasm, I felt Max's cock grow hard again inside me, pressing up against sore, hot tissues, and I moaned as he began moving once more, grinding deeply

"Max," I implored softly, feeling too drained for a second round but he silenced me by threading his fingers through my hair and holding my head down.

"Shh," he said. "Just let me."

This time, he fucked me quick, without even giving me

a chance to get properly aroused again. I barely moved, allowing him use me to get himself off until he shuddered through his second orgasm and stilled.

An eternity later, very softly, his words barely a graze against my earlobe, he asked, "How are you?"

"I'm good," I smiled my eyes still closed. "I like it when... when..."

Words failed me, but, of course, Max knew what I meant. "When you surrender," he whispered against my lips, and I nodded silently pressing myself against him.

We didn't say another word after that; just showered in silence, wrapped ourselves in two large towels and then Max led me into a cool, dark bedroom where we crawled under the blankets, also in silence. I zonked out almost immediately, Max's heavy hand on my breast, and came to only when sunlight streamed through the windows flooded the room, and the delightful aroma of freshly brewed coffee tickled my nostrils.

———

Wait, what on earth? I bolted upright, wide-eyed, taking in my surroundings.

Max's apartment.

God. Never thought I'd see this place. Despite my hopes and aspirations, deep down,I never really believed he saw me as more than a fleeting thing, someone to keep at arm's length. I figured our encounters would stay locked within the club's walls. Yet, here I was.

From my cursory assessment, it was clear that I was alone in this compact bedroom, but evidence of Max's apparent taste for comfort was everywhere: a California King bed, floor-to-ceiling windows, and a carpet that begged to be walked on barefoot. No signs of his BDSM proclivity —if the toys were here, they were cleverly tucked away.

Tossing the blanket aside, I hunted for my clothes, but they were MIA. Shielding myself with my hands, I tiptoed out of the bedroom and breathed a sigh of relief when I spotted the bathroom nearby. I found a fluffy bath towel to wrap around myself and felt somewhat more at ease.

"Liza?"

I jumped like I'd been caught stealing. Max had snuck on me, and now took leaning against the frame in the bathroom doorway. Dressed down in jeans and a rumpled T-shirt, barefoot with bedhead hair, he looked just like a college student. A rush of affection surged at seeing this private version of him, but shock of being caught sneaking around his apartment unawares kept me rooted.

"What are you doing?" I demanded.

"What are you doing?" he shot back, grinning as he eyed me up and down. He nodded at the towel. "Drop that."

"Why?"

"I want to see your body."

"But I don't—"

"Sub. I said, drop it."

That voice... My jaw dropped right along with the towel. I wasn't expecting the game to start this early, but I didn't exactly mind. So, off it went.

"Good girl," Max said, his smile warm. "Now, freshen up. There's a new toothbrush by the sink. Want some coffee?"

"Oh, yeah, for sure."

"Oh, yeah, for sure, master."

"Oh, yeah, master," I responded, unable to suppress my grin. "For sure, master."

"Cream and sugar?

"Two creams, four sugars, master."

"You want some coffee with all that sugar too?"

"I like things sweet, master. Just like you, master."

"Two spanks for sass."

Max's face lit up with amusement and mischief so adorably that I couldn't help but tease him again: "You're the one who kept having me add more sugar to his mojito. Grown man drinking sugar water with a mint leaf."

"Four spanks."

"Master, don't let that door hit you on the way out. Even model subs need to pee sometimes. By themselves."

"Five spanks. Breakfast in fifteen minutes."

I took a detour on my way out from the bathroom to look around. I liked what I saw.

If my apartment was a ramshackle hut and Lori's a palace, then Max's place was a cozy middle ground. Tasteful renovations, nothing too flashy. It was a tidy, modestly sized pad that belonged to someone with a decent bank account who valued comfort over flair. Definitely a bachelor's digs—no frills, no fuss.

Small piles of miscellaneous items—a broken laptop, an assortment of unidentified wires,, other electronic detritus—were strewn about in one corner, while over by the wall a stack of boxes was curiously topped with a pair of ski boots.

Despite these quirks, the place was cleaner than mine. I silently apologized to my grandmother.

The kitchen lacked window curtains and decorative accents but made up for it with charming dishware, including a blue plate laden with enticing cookies and a plump cream-colored mug filled with piping hot coffee awaiting me. But before I could move towards the table, Max shook his head and gestured to the wide windowsill.

"Hands here, spread your fingers wide, and bend over."

"Are you serious?"

The coffee and cookies smelled so good, I was salivating, and not in the mood at all.

"Are you serious, master? And yes, malysh, I am serious."

Grumbling under my breath, I reluctantly complied. Spanks weren't high on my wish list, especially after yesterday and how sore it left me, but the sooner it was done, the sooner I could get to my coffee and—

"Shit! Liza, what's this?" Max suddenly exclaimed from behind me. "Why didn't you say something before?"

Instead of delivering a spanking, his hand gently stroked my bruised buttock before he abruptly left me and bolted to the fridge.

"Say something about what before?" I watched curiously as he frantically rummaged inside the fridge. "What are you looking for?"

"Ointment. Cooling gel, anti bruising cream, arnica... Something... You have a massive bruise on your right buttcheek."

"Oh... I thought that was the norm."

"No, it is not the norm. It's way too much. Must've been the paddle. I'm sorry, malysh, got a little carried away yesterday, didn't realize how sensitive your skin was. Stay put for now."

I couldn't suppress a moan when Max began to slather my buttocks with the chilled ointment. He looked so remorseful and focused that it was almost comical.

"It's okay, Max. It'll be gone by the day after tomorrow."

"I know. But I don't like leaving bruises like that." He straightened and peered into my eyes. "Please tell me this hasn't happened before. With me."

"Well, maybe this one's a bit bigger than usual... but it's fine, really. It doesn't even hurt much."

"Sit down and drink your coffee. Playtime is canceled."

"All right." I took a seat and studied him closely. "That's probably for the best. Especially since I have some questions for you about yesterday, Max."

"I thought you might," he nodded. "I agree—we need to talk."

Chapter Thirty-Three

Lori

This Saturday night had somehow crammed months of drama into just a few hours. It all started with an unexpected, soul-baring conversation—courtesy of Irina, her domme. Their paths were diverging, and the signs had been there for a while. But Irina, heavy with guilt, insisted on dragging out the inevitable with a long-winded talk. Lori gritted her teeth and endured it, even though she felt the same way and didn't see the point in rehashing the obvious.

Their mismatched kinks had always been the elephant in the room. Irina loved role-play and couldn't stand pain, while Lori thrived on it and was a terrible actress. It left them both perpetually unsatisfied. Then, Liza came into the picture. Irina must've noticed Lori's shift in attention right away. For a while, the jealousy reignited Irina's interest, making her want to claim Lori fully—pulling her away from Max and his new sub. But when Irina sensed her grip slipping, she gave up. What was the point?

Lori quietly agreed that it was time to part ways. Afterward, she felt drained, too exhausted to play. She wandered over to the bar, where Liza was mid-argument with fiery-haired Anastasia. Another confrontation, but luckily, it ended well. Nik eventually booted his unruly sub from the club, and Max and Liza slipped out so quietly the other patrons buzzed about it for hours—Max had never left a party early with a sub before.

Now, Lori was left not only exhausted, but also restless and sad.

After drowning her sorrows in a few stiff drinks, she found herself half-asleep in one of the plush chairs in the ground-floor lounge. Master Nik was in the chair beside her, looking just as weary and disconnected as she felt. He puffed on a hookah, his gaze fixed on the wall.

When he noticed her stirring, he silently offered her the pipe. She hesitated, then took a deep drag, collecting her thoughts as they both stared at the same crack in the paint. Lori handed the pipe back, their fingertips brushed, and suddenly, she felt wide awake.

On a whim, she slid off her chair and onto her knees before him. Clasping her hands, she murmured, "May I have your permission to serve you, Master?"

She expected Nik to be surprised, and he didn't disappoint. His eyebrows shot up to his hairline, and he chuckled softly. "Are you sure, there, sweetling?"

"Yes." Lori cast her gaze downward, swallowing a sudden tremor of fear. She trusted Nik—he knew her issues and understood the magnitude of her offer. Besides, now, when he was too tired to search for a more experienced sub, might be her only chance to serve him.

"Alright, sweetling," Nik replied gently. "Could you freshen up my cocktail first, please? Then I'd like a private massage."

Lori blinked at him suddenly regretting her offer, but

Nik's calm gaze didn't waver. "It's just a massage, sub. I promise I won't touch you without your explicit consent."

Nodding, Lori got to her feet and hurried off to the bar, hoping the task of mixing a new drink for Nik would help steady her nerves.

A little while later, they headed up to his room on the second floor. Sensing her anxiety, Nik left the door ajar and silently moved past her to lie face down on the bed. Lori took a deep breath, exhaling slowly. She spotted the massage oil by the bed and cautiously positioned herself beside him. Lifting the hem of his shirt, she shivered when Nik sat up briefly to remove it.

Fortunately, he didn't seem to notice her reaction. He lay back down, eyes shut. Once she had a moment to regain composure, Lori poured oil into her hands, warming it between her palms before gently placing them on his back.

She couldn't remember the last time she'd touched a man like this. Her past was filled with one sadist after another, men who demanded nothing but obedience and gave out nothing but pain, who tied her up and used her. When there was pleasure, it was always mixed with blood and tears. She never caressed them. And then there were no men at all. Even when she last asked Nik to try, it had been all him, his touch, until she blacked out from fear.

The hard muscles beneath her hands felt unfamiliar now—she was used to the soft contours of women's bodies. She spent a few cautious minutes testing Nik's tolerance, adjusting pressure until she heard a quiet groan of pleasure. She recoiled at first, but then relaxed and smiled. Something clicked inside her. The fear was gone, replaced by warmth and a newfound desire to continue.

With gentle precision, Lori started kneading his tight muscles — starting at the shoulders and shoulder blades, moving down along his spine to his hips, before retracing her path up his warm skin back to his shoulders. She moved on to one arm, working her way down to the fingers before repeating the process on the other arm until she felt prepared enough to ask him to roll over.

Her voice wavered as she made the request.

Nik slowly turned over, his eyes meeting hers as he gauged her state of mind. Lori smiled softly, not bothering to hide the slight tremor in her hands or the undeniable arousal in her gaze. She was trying to connect physically with a man without violence, even playful violence, for the first time in forever. He had to understand how important this was.

Overwhelmed by his scrutiny, she was the first to look away. She reached again for the bottle of oil to continue the massage. Her mouth went dry when she had to touch his chest, and her fingers stiffened, especially when it was time to go lower.

"Don't do anything you don't want to, sunshine," Nik said quietly. Lori shot him a sharp, wary look, but he lay still and smiled at her gently.

"I want to," she answered with a twinge of sadness. "It's just that..."

"I know. Relax, you're safe. May I hold your hand?"

Lori burned with an almost unbearable shame at his request. She must be a pathetic sight if Nik had to request formal permission to touch her hand.

"Lori? Your hand?"

"Yes, of course."

As soon as Nik cradled her hand between his, she instinctively closed her eyes and let out a sigh, as if he'd flipped a hidden relaxation switch. Noticing her response, he massaged up her wrist and elbow before placing her hand back on his chest and taking hold of her other one.

"That's it... just like that," he soothed. "Close your eyes and just... relax."

The soothing sound of his voice almost made Lori want to give in, close her eyes, and just drift away. But just as she began to relax, something inside her stirred, like a startled bird suddenly taking flight, and her eyes flung open again as reality hit her. She was sitting there, with a half-naked man, half-naked herself, clad in nothing but a see-through robe that left her hard nipples painfully obvious. He must have noticed—what if he took this sign of arousal as some sort of go-ahead sign?

Nik paused, his gaze searching her face. "Lori? Do you want to stop?"

God, no. No, she didn't want to stop. It was all so sweet, just a moment ago, why was she so convinced it would turn sour? She trusted Nik, didn't she? She'd trust him with her best friend. She'd trust him with Liza—hadn't she suggested Liza play with him just last weekend?

So, what was she so afraid of?

Nik's face tightened with concern, and Lori felt a prickling behind her eyes, a sign of oncoming tears of frustration. She was a mess. He was going to call the scene.

"Please, don't make me leave, master," she pleaded helplessly, looking up at the ceiling to hold back the onslaught of tears.

"Of course not, sweetling." Nik shook his head. "Don't worry. You're fine. I'm fine. Everything is fine. I'll give you a minute, okay?"

He got up from the bed and moved to the window, suddenly fascinated by the view outside. The dawn was breaking, and light was beginning to filter through the blinds. He carefully shut them before turning back to her.

"I want you to undress and lie on the bed, sub. On your back."

"Master..."

"I will stand here, by the window, the whole time. All you need to know is I won't come closer or touch you. Now undress and lie down."

"Yes, master," Lori whispered haltingly, beginning to pull off her robe with trembling hands.

Chapter Thirty-Four

I asked my question and waited. Max's face went flat as he stared straight ahead, clearly deciding whether it was worth the trouble to answer it.

"You actually want me to talk about my feelings," he said, at last.

"Yup."

"That's asking for a lot."

"Is it? You're a psychologist, Max!"

He held up his hands. "Your question is reasonable, and it's only fair I answer it because I am going to ask for a lot."

"I'll give you everything you ask for." I glimpsed the skeptical expression on Max's face as his eyebrow arched, and corrected myself, "I will try very hard... to give you everything you ask for."

Max sighed and smiled feebly. "You drive a hard bargain but... All right. But! At the very least, I'm going to want an answer to the same question. If I tell you about my feelings yesterday during the scene at the bar, you'll tell me about yours. I want details, Liza, deal?"

"Deal, master," I smiled, carefully pushing my coffee cup aside and sitting up unusually straight.

I was acting extra cheeky, now that I was dressed in one of Max's button downs, boxer shorts, and socks. It seemed only fair both of us were dressed as we geared up for what was shaping up to be a Very Important Conversation. Wearing his clothes somehow made me feel more at ease in his company than ever before, feeling self-assured in my right to demand answers even as I stared right at his stern face.

"Fine. The truth is..." He exhaled loudly and closed his eyes before bursting out with, "I was so fucking jealous, Liza! At first, I wanted to rip Alex's arm off when he touched your breast, then punch Dave in the face, the way he tried to whisper at you when he thought I couldn't hear. Then, there was a whole internal battle to suppress the urge to grab you and drag you away from there all together. I really kicked myself for my own bright idea the whole entire time. But I wanted to punish the shit out of *you* for all these feelings that were tearing me apart. Especially because I could tell how much you liked it."

"You put me there!"

"And I didn't punish you, did I? Because it wasn't your fault that you were there, and it wasn't your fault you liked it, and you know something else... it's not a big surprise for anyone, either."

"Wh—what do you mean?"

"I mean I could see right through you, sweetheart, the moment you walked through the doors. So supposedly afraid of public attention, but at the same time, you were just fucking gagging for it, Liza, my god. Like I told you, everything you feel is written all over your pretty face."

"Oh."

"Yeah. I could also tell you liked the idea of multiple partners." He smirked shook his head to the side. "Christ, you should have seen your eyes the first night when you watched that girl with two guys..."

A warm flush crept into my face, but Max didn't seem bothered.

"Don't get me wrong, I get it. Boy, do I get it. Being with two women for me is... something else, too. And I also used to be a bit of an exhibitionist when it came to sex — it just got old after a while. But even now, I have nothing against being watched." Again he smirked. "To be honest, I would have loved to..."

He cut himself off, casting a probing glance at me, and said nothing more while I bounced in my chair with impatience and curiosity.

"What? You would have loved to what?"

"It doesn't matter. The point is, our interests align in many fascinating and promising ways. We seem perfectly matched, even though it's so improbable."

"Max?" My voice came out as a half-growl, laced with both excitement and a hint of threat.

"Yes?"

His smile was so smug, so infuriatingly provocative, that I wanted to strangle him.

"What did you want to say? You would have loved to... what?"

Impatience bubbled up inside me, threatening to spill over, and Max's grin widened. That jerk! He was playing me like a fiddle, knowing exactly how to wind me up, and then, without missing a beat, he locked eyes with me and delivered his words as casually as if he were listing off his favorite snacks.

"I would have loved to fuck you right there on the spot.

I'd actually love to fuck you right in front of everyone anyway, Liza. On the spanking bench, the bar counter, the couch in the lounge area. Anywhere, really. Everyone watching. Satisfied?"

"Uh."

I fidgeted in my chair, stunned and parboiled by the vivid images my imagination conjured, feeling color rising up my chest and neck. Even my eyeballs were hot.

"Your turn, Liza. I want to know," he demanded almost without a pause, and I didn't immediately grasp the meaning of the question.

"What, Max?" My mind was still stuck on the image of him fucking me right on the bar, with everyone watching me writhe, listening to me scream, seeing me come undone under his touch.

"Liza!" Leaning over the table, he lifted my chin, looking directly into my eyes. "Focus! I need to know, did you want any of them? Did you want to get fucked by Alex or Dima or Dave?"

"What?" I blinked, my thoughts crashing into reality like I'd just run headfirst into a wall. Getting fucked by Alex or Dima or Dave? The idea hadn't even crossed my mind. "No. Max, no! I only wanted to get fucked by you."

He released my chin, a shadow of relief flitting across his face. "But you liked how they touched you?"

"Yes."

Pulling away, I instinctively hugged myself and shivered. The way he was interrogating me made this feel like something shameful, and I disliked that feeling. Heatedly, I said, "Yes, imagine that. I liked how they touched me. And that everyone was watching. But I wanted to listen to you, give myself to you, I wanted to hear praise only from you, and I even wanted..."

Suddenly, I couldn't breathe. A lump of emotion lodged itself in my throat, and I had to move, to do something. I shot up from my seat, shaky and overwhelmed, heading toward the bedroom to escape the pressure, but Max was faster. His arms closed around me, his breath warm in my ear as he whispered, "Sorry, love, this isn't meant to trigger you. I'm not angry. I had to ask. It's important for me to know where you're at, so I know what to do, that's all, do you understand?"

"I do. But also, I want to be yours. Do *you* understand?" I melted into his embrace, all the fight draining out of me.

"I do." His voice softened, wrapped in sensuality as he buried his nose in my hair. "So... What were you fantasizing about? I bet I know. In the dressing room, correct? Or right at the bar?"

"Both," I admitted reluctantly, my face pressed against his chest. "I just realized that I want to belong to you in every way possible. To be even closer if that's possible. To follow your every command."

I could hardly believe the words that were coming out of my mouth. By the time I finished, my voice had faded to a shy whisper, but Max clearly heard me loud and clear, and his body responded, his cock growing hard against my stomach. He tangled his fingers in my hair, tugging my head back slightly.

"My every command?"

My voice was gone, but my eyes must have said it all. He murmured, "How about we start right now?"

"Yes," I whispered, and the world around me blurred, narrowing down to just the two of us.

But just as he took my hand and began to pull me toward the bedroom, a sharp sound cut through the moment. Max froze, listening intently. After a beat, I realized—it was the phone.

Max sighed, clearly irritated by the interruption. "Sorry, I have to get this. It's a client," he said with so much quiet annoyance in his voice that I found it oddly amusing.

I knew how he felt—desire had coiled tight inside me, too, making the interruption almost painful. But despite the heat simmering just beneath my skin, I forced a sweet smile and said, "Of course, you should get it."

———

Clutching my coffee cup like a lifeline, I retreated to the kitchen, trying to keep myself grounded. When Max reappeared a few minutes later, his focused expression told me everything I needed to know—sex was off the table for now.

"It's Lori. She needs help, and she'll be here soon. Will you give us some time to talk, malysh?"

"Of course." It suddenly dawned on me that in all the excitement of the night, I sort of just... left Lori in the dust as Max and I rode off into the sunset, even after she came to my defense during and after the whole redhead debacle. "Is Lori okay?"

"I don't know yet; sounds like something might have happened after we left," Max said gently, passing by me and rummaging in the coffee maker to remove the filters and rinse them under water. "She's a bit upset and needs support."

"Damn. I feel so bad that we left her yesterday. It's all because of that crazy bitch!" I exclaimed.

Max smiled faintly, shaking his head as he flipped on the coffee machine. "I'm afraid Lori's main problems lie within herself, malysh. Just like with all of us."

"But you'll help her?"

"Of course. As always," he assured me with a smile, sitting down at the table. His hand reached out to caress my wrist, and as I looked down at his strong, beautiful fingers, I couldn't stop my desperate whisper. "I want you. I want you so badly right now."

His voice, when he responded, was a dark, velvety purr that vibrated through me, down to my bone marrow. "I want you too, very much." He paused, considering. "I could probably fuck you quick and hard before she gets here, but... that's not what I want this morning. You?"

I shook my head.

"Didn't think so." He leaned back in his chair, his eyes never leaving mine. "Let me figure out what's wrong with Lori, and then..."

"Yes," I whispered, licking my lips. "And then..."

My thoughts drifted to Lori, and the memory of our first night together in that club room resurface. I was beside myself at the prospect of Lori and Max in the same close quarters again.

"You want her, too, don't you, you little glutton?" Max teased, his eyes twinkling with amusement as he watched me blush.

"Kinda. You don't mind?"

"No, if Lori were in the mood, I wouldn't mind. But she's afraid of me, as you know. Like she is of any man."

"But you could avoid touching her."

"I could, of course. Although it's hard for me too when we're in bed. When I see you kissing and caressing each other I just want to--"

"I understand. You'd like to fuck her?" I interrupted, meeting his gaze head-on. Max's expression remained neutral, but I could sense him weighing his response. Not that I needed to hear it to know.

"Yes, I would," he replied just as bluntly. "I'd like to fuck you both."

"And you wouldn't spontaneously combust?" I asked teasingly, unable to suppress my smile. "From such over-abundance of good luck?"

"No, I wouldn't combust." Max's tone was serious. "I'd spank the shit out of the two of you, fuck you both until neither of you remembers her name, then help you in the shower and tuck you into bed."

"And a night massage for each girl?"

"Don't push it."

A beat went by.

"As a client though..." I trailed off, wondering aloud.

Max nodded. "There are no official rules as far as I know. But I would terminate our working relationship immediately if this were on the table."

"She'd need to be cured?" I asked, half-joking but also half-serious.

"I suppose."

We sipped our coffee in blissful peace, the quiet stretching between us like a warm blanket. A deep sense of serenity washed over me, a warmth I'd never felt before. I searched within myself for any flicker of possessiveness or jealousy and found... nothing. To my surprise, not only was I not jealous of Lori, but I was eagerly looking forward to the day when her fears might fade, allowing us to explore the possibilities as a trio.

But suddenly, through this state of bliss, a troubling voice broke through, a nasty memory from the previous evening, lodged in my stomach like a rock.

"Max," I abruptly spoke up, "that redhead said I'm not

truly yours because you haven't claimed me. What does that mean?"

Max's eyes rolled slightly, but in a way that made me more at ease, even though I still felt compelled to lower my eyes in a sheepish apology for my stupid question.

"It's just an artificially invented ritual, Liza," he explained slowly, with frustration, pushing his coffee cup away. "It hadn't even occurred to me."

"I mean, all BDSM is just an artificially invented ritual, Max," I blurted out before I could stop myself. "That must have occurred to you?"

His brow twitched in recognition of my point, and also, it seemed, in slight annoyance.

"I was just curious about the specifics. Is it like a scene?"

"Yes, it is," Max stared directly into my eyes with an evaluating look, causing me to look away again. "Yes, it is," Max replied, his eyes narrowing as he evaluated me. Clearly, he didn't think I was ready for this information. And in that moment, I wasn't so sure I was either.

"It's not just a random scene, like a kinky sampler, Liza," Max began. "It's a special ceremony in our club. I didn't come up with it, nor did Nik. There was a couple ready to commit who wanted to do it, then two more couples repeated it. But it had to be something special, extraordinary, so they turned to me for guidance."

"I see," I said, though I wasn't sure I did. Something special? Couples ready to commit? This was getting way too heavy. Max hadn't said anything about love or commitment. Was I getting ahead of myself again?

"Shall I go on?" Max asked, his tone skeptical.

Shyly raising my eyes, I saw a slight wariness in his gaze. What was he expecting as an answer? I had no idea and quietly held my breath to hide my arousal and anxiety. "I'd be interested to know about the process, but I'm not insisting."

"All right. I'll tell you, malysh," Max softened, clearing space on the table with his hands as if preparing to illustrate. "First, I usually talk to the sub, try to figure out their secret limits - not their known hard limits, but something special that they wouldn't want to do with anyone they don't fully trust with all their soul. Everyone has a thing they reserve. It could be a dangerous practice or something they've never done in public before. Or maybe never done at all. It's a sign of trust and their gift to their partner, their master - a symbol that they're special."

"And what was it... with those three couples?" My mouth went dry. Something in my stomach twitched and trembled, and I shrunk in on myself, hoping he wouldn't notice this internal turmoil. But of course, Max noticed everything, and his eyes narrowed.

Despite that, he went on, unaffected. "Fire play, knife play, public sex with a bound partner."

I parted my lips, and my gaze darted to the side. All three of those were absolutely terrifying. I talked a big game and my fantasies were daring, but I was not ready to expose my genitals freely in public and show everyone how unhinged I became when Max fucked me. And fire and knives? Fuck that. I was way too much of a little coward.

"The master must offer something in return," Max continued, his voice quieter now, as if recognizing the internal struggle playing out on my face. "He thanks the submissive for their trust and officially takes on the responsibility of caring for it. Usually, he will perform an act he wouldn't otherwise perform with another submissive or bottom, maybe not in public or maybe not at all. Something that would show everyone that this one is special."

I stared, completely unable to breathe. All I could think of was Max between my legs. Ten minutes of tender Max, for me, in private. I had almost died of pleasure. If he did that in public, I would definitely die--of happiness. From the realization that everyone saw his special treatment of me, and no one could dispute it, as the redheaded witch did yesterday.

But that was something I almost never allowed, and it sounded like Max reserved it, as well. Could I even relax in front of everyone, or did it sound great only in theory?

I took a shaky breath, leaning forward as the intensity of my thoughts overwhelmed me. Max reached out, gently stroking my shoulder.

"There's no need no panic. No need to rush things. We're not in a hurry, baby, right?"

"Right. I... I'd like to, eventually, but..."

"I understand. It has to be a conscious decision. That's why this ritual is considered so special. After it, the whole club will look at us differently, and we ourselves will change. In a sense, these changes will be irreversible."

"Sounds even more serious than a marriage certificate," I laughed nervously.

"It's much more serious, malysh," he nodded without returning my smile, "but everything has a price. And we need to be ready. We don't need any psychological trauma, or unnecessary anxiety, right?"

"No, we don't."

"Good. Please, promise me you won't listen to any silly subs anymore, and if you have questions, you'll come to me right away."

"Yes, master," I replied.

"And no more catfights at the club."

"Yes, master."

"I want to reassure you. You are my sub. You're mine. Officially."

"Yes, master," I repeated for the third time, feeling my face spread into an uncontrollable grin.

And then we both jumped a harsh sound that took a moment to register as what it was: the doorbell.

Chapter Thirty-Five

I spent the next two hours alone in the bedroom, mindlessly alternating browsing social media on Max's laptop and my phone. I couldn't focus enough to read or engage in conversation with friends; my thoughts were entirely consumed by the conversation happening behind the closed kitchen door. When I caught a glimpse of Lori, she seemed unusually focused, not as sad as I had feared, but not entirely relaxed either—as if she was the one about to do some work, not Max. Although, I supposed therapy was work for the client as well, probably even more than for the psychologist. For myself, I'd only had the one experience with a therapist, and found it useless. Meaningless chatter. On the other hand, maybe it was because I simply hadn't realized I also had to do some of the work.

After talking with Max and Lori, I started to think maybe I didn't have the right professional, someone who would ask the truly important questions. Or maybe I wasn't ready or willing to be asked those questions. Questions like: why do I work at a job I don't like and find enjoyment in pain and humiliation during sex? Is there a connection, and is this something that I need to change?

Maybe it was or maybe it wasn't, but I wouldn't know unless I asked myself.

At the very least, I could start by working on becoming an artist, which was what I always wanted, as it turned out —something Max somehow clocked immediately.

My thoughts took my scrolling down unexpected channels: about a half hour later, I found myself in a group of aspiring writers, browsing through their posted work. I was surprised and sort of perversely gratified to find their work cute but simplistic and almost careless. Even my off hand sketches from my notebook would compete with them in quality and depth. Why exactly had I been shy about my work? I could have been eons more advanced had I started earlier. I could have been posting, getting feedback, building a community, a platform for myself as an artist. I'd have a supportive network to boost my confidence and maybe a set of mentors who could teach me something.

Completely caught up in a sudden impulse, I joined the group where I had been browsing through the beginners' drawings, then frantically searched for other communities of brush and pencil enthusiasts and subscribed to everything I could find. Excited, I jumped off the bed, rushing around the room, trying to figure out which finished drawings I could photograph and post immediately. Argh, my notebook with sketches was in another bag! And in this one —only a blank one...

Even better. I could start a new drawing right now.

An image for inspiration came to mind immediately— Lori.

The vulnerable facial expression I loved, the delicate

angle of her jaw, her long neck, and a dangling, vine-shaped earring.

Sketching feverishly, I added a coquettish lock of hair and a low neckline, emphasizing the gentle roundness of her breasts, and—

"Liza?"

"Ah!"

My startled heart racing, I clutched the notebook and pencil to my chest. I hadn't noticed Max approach, absorbed as I was in my creation, and now stared at him, wide-eyed, not sure why I was feeling like I got caught doing something bad.

"Is this how you normally react when someone says your name, or is that delightful look reserved just for me?" He teased, his eyebrow arching.

"No. I... I just—"

"What do you have there, malysh?" he interrupted softly, nodding at the notebook.

"Oh—just a sketch."

"May I?"

Lori's curious nose peeked out from behind Max. She looked flushed and cheerful, and when she saw the drawing, her eyes went round and big as saucers. "Is that me? Holy shit! That's me, Max! Oh my gosh! Liza... Liza, this is so pretty! Look at me!"

Her excitement was contagious, and I found myself grinning sheepishly back at her. "You are just so beautiful. I've wanted to draw you for a long time, but I didn't think I was good enough, so I didn't dare."

"Not good enough, she says! Max, did you see this?"

Lori turned to Max so naturally—mouth open in wonder, eyes wide and trusting—that my heart skipped several beats. How was it possible that this woman was terrified of men? She stood next to this one, slightly touching his shoulder with hers, smiling as one would smile at a close friend.

Or a lover.

And... where was my jealousy? My territorial instinct? I was emotional as I looked at the two of them, that much was certain. I could tell from how my nose pricked and my heart hammered in my chest. But the gamut of emotions I was experiencing pleasantly surprised me with the conspicuous absence of anything even resembling jealousy.

I combed through my feelings anyway, just to see.

This was my man. Here was another woman with him. A woman I now knew he would like to fuck. It would be normal to feel jealous. Where was that basest, most primal reaction, as old as time? Was I normal or not?

Nope, I guess I'm not normal...

Because I was anything but jealous. Excited, nervous, overwhelmed, but not jealous in the least.

I love them both. That's the thing.

And I want to fuck them both. At the same time. That's all there is.

I felt my facial expression shift before I could open my mouth to say anything, but Max already noticed, reading me expertly, and as he scooped me up into his arms, he bent to my ear, his voice hoarse with sensual suggestion. "Ready to play?"

"Um, and Lori?" I shifted my gaze towards her.

"Lori fired me," Max said, almost proudly, straightening and turning to look at her as well.

"Lori?" I whispered once the meaning sank in fully and the ringing in my ears stopped. "You did?"

Lori's mouth twitched just slightly, and she nodded, flushing. She averted her eyes as if she wanted to hide some big emotion from me, but before I could decipher anything, Max put his hand under my chin and turned my face back toward him. "Liza? I asked a question."

"Yes, I'm ready," I agreed with smile, my voice cracking.

"Good. Go take a shower and come back naked and wet."

I opened my mouth to make the obvious joke, but Max saw it coming and constructed his face to look stern. "I mean don't dry off."

What? Why? But who was I to argue. Scrambling off the bed, I murmured, "Yes, master."

Max smiled at me encouragingly and gave me a gentle pat on the back to hurry up. Realizing he purposely avoided slapping me on the ass made me smile. His crocodile tears were almost endearing. Who knew such a rough man could be so sweet and considerate, especially when confronted with the aftermath of his own handiwork?

By the time I returned — wet and nude as per Max's instructions — the atmosphere in the bedroom had completely changed. The blinds were drawn and lights dimmed. Even the silence was somehow more muted. Lori, clad in a barely-there thong, stood with her hands up against the mirrored closet door, with Max behind her. As she watched their mirror image from beneath half-lowered lashes, he slowly traced one finger down the elegant curve of her back. His eyes caressed the reflection of her breasts in the mirror with obvious lust, and Lori, clearly aware, was covered with a dewy flush, her nipples hard.

"On the bed, face up, malysh," he told me without looking away from Lori. My heart pounded as I noticed an enormous bath towel was draped over the bed, and sped up even more when I spotted several bottles of lube and an array of devices on the bedside table, including one notice-ably large new butt plug.

"M...Max? Any way we can skip the plugs today?" I quietly asked, but bit my lip as he sharply turned his head and shot me a piercing look.

I lowered my eyes to the floor. "I'm sorry, master. I forgot myself."

"Bad girl," he replied tersely, his gaze still fixed on Lori's reflection as his pointer finger continued its slow descent down her spine. "Shut your mouth and lie down."

I did as I was told, telling myself he knew what he was doing, but my heart still beat wildly in my chest, and a trickle of something unpleasant discolored my elated mood of only moments before. Why was I relegated to the bed on my own... it was lonely here... But before I had a chance to think any more negative thoughts, Max released Lori, whispering to her, and she dashed toward me, grabbing another towel on the way.

Still dripping wet from my shower, I shivered as Lori knelt next to me. Unhurried and serene, she began by systematically drying every inch of me, almost as though she set out to catch each individual drop of water on my damp skin. Then, I groaned in pleasure as I felt her nimble fingers kneading into my trembling muscles, and the scent of aromatic massage oil reached me. When my eyelids fluttered open for a moment, I noticed Max had moved to stand behind her, observing the process without uttering a word.

I frowned. Something I didn't like was happening to both of them. Lori was so tense she vibrated, and Max looked unusually serious and focused, even for him. Oh no. This wasn't going to work. Lori looked like she was about to bolt, and then Max would get angry at her, and at me too—maybe because of my insolence before, when I'd asked about the plugs. I couldn't believe I'd said that, right after I told him I'd do whatever he wanted...

But as the minutes wore on, neither of them moved. The sensation of Lori's caress was insistent and all-encompassing, as she circled more and more bravely over my breasts and down my stomach, inching gradually toward the apex of my thighs. My nerve endings came alive, heating up, sending signals of desire to replace the useless fears, melting them away.

I must have closed my eyes at some point, but I was unaware of when exactly, realizing I had only when my eyelids flew open again at the sharp sensation of pain on my left nipple.

"Oh, ouch!" I whimpered but another icy metallic clamp ensured an equally painful bite on the right side too.

Fixing my attackers with a surprised glare, I realized it was Lori who had done it but obviously under Max's command.

"Too much?" His question was barely audible, as he tugged lightly at the chain connecting both clamps.

My mouth opened involuntarily... but the pain was already subsiding.

"I don't know..."

"If it was too much, you'd know."

"Then... no."

"Good." He sat on the bed beside me, all steely power, shirtless and ruthless. "Spread your legs." he ordered.

As though a command had been issued to her, Lori scurried closer to the headboard.

Max looked up at her. "You're going to watch, touch her, and kiss her. Your main job is to help her through this."

"What?" I asked, incredulous.

What, pray tell, were they going to do to me? What was

so awful that I would require help to get through? Here I was dumb enough to think we were just going to have a little fun, the three of us. On the other hand, I knew Max well enough by now that even as I thought it, I knew it was an absurd notion.

Neither of them answered, and though I tried to direct my thoughts toward happy sexy venues, like my sketch of Lori for example, I couldn't. Max had scared me.

Which was what he wanted, obviously, because he knew how much that would turn me on... I nearly moaned out loud with the sudden surge of adrenaline that coursed through my body.

"Yes, master," Lori whispered, caressing my forehead and temples.

Her gentleness was lost on me, however, as I watched Max reach for the nightstand, where the lube and implements were laid out. When he leaned toward me, in his hands, he held a pair of hand cuffs.

"Hands over your head, malysh," he murmured.

"Yes, master," I said after a beat of internal struggle, and raised my arms.

Together, Max and Lori secured my wrists to the headboard, and the effect was almost immediate. Molten heat spilled over my entire body, and I writhed on the bed, yearning to be touched, by Max, by Lori, by both of them. I knew it was useless to try; it was too soon, and nothing would happen until Max said so. And what *would* happen, anyway? That question again. The possibilities. My mind scattered in a million directions, and I struggled to find something to focus on to get my thoughts away from recalling the sensation of the full length of Max's cock plunging into me with force.

I was unsuccessful.

Chapter Thirty-Six

Max tugged on the chain connecting my nipples again, making me hiss.

"Today you declared you want to be mine. And that you want everyone at the club to be aware of this fact. Is that correct, Liza?"

I was still struggling with focus, and he was using way too many big words. It took a moment before I could manage, "Yes, master."

"I want the same thing, malysh. But I don't want to fight with you for the privilege of your submission and the right to call myself your master. I need unconditional obedience. I refuse to squabble over every order. Is that going to be a problem?"

"No, master," I exhaled, shutting my eyes.

His final words hung in the air, breaking through the stillness. As I thought about my insistence on challenging him at every turn gave rise to a surprising new burn inside me—the uncomfortable burn of guilt. Real guilt and regret. Max put in a lot of effort on my behalf, but I was often a bad student: I violated the rules all the time, broke scene, and didn't pay attention to how I spoke and acted, something that was important to Max, as Nik had mentioned on our first night at the club. As my Dominant, he'd shown patience with me and worked hard to focus on my needs, to satisfy me make me lose my mind and get to that place I craved, every time we were together. Every time since the day we met—as total strangers.

"Liza," he said, studying my expression. "There is absolutely no need for such biblical guilt. I've been around and I understand. But I will need you to remember this going forward."

Relief colored my cheeks red. "Yes, master," I mumbled, looking up at him.

I felt a slight movement behind me, and suddenly became acutely aware of Lori's calming presence and her gentle touch as she dusted her fingers over my shoulders and chest before moving toward my aching breasts, carefully avoiding my clamped nipples. She leaned closer, and I saw her smiling before our lips met.

Our tongues touched and twisted together gently, and I moaned into her mouth, momentarily forgetting about Max. He was not one to be ignored, however. I felt his fingers open me up and find my clit, pressing down enough for me to break away from Lori's kiss and cry out.

"Ow! Please, master!"

"Shh, okay, okay," he said, touching me again, this time much more gently, drawing small circles around sensitive flesh. "There is something else I want from you."

"What, master?"

"To be more precise, something else I want to do to you, and I think... yeah, I think I'm going to do right now."

"What?"

I might have gasped in surprise, but I knew what he

was hinting at even before he bent over me to reach for the bottle of lube on the night stand. He spoke softly, but what he said reverberated through the whole room, flashing straight into my brain, dripping with sex, desire, dominance. Every word was a new surge of adrenalized desire.

"If you truly belong to me," he declared, "then I want all of you. All of you. I mean every inch. Do you understand?" He didn't wait for an answer. "I mean I want your ass, Liza. I want your pretty ass and your wild eyes and your screams when I fuck you there."

"I don't know if I'm ready!" I blurted. I'd known it was what he'd been about to say, of course, and my body shook uncontrollably as fear tightened its grip on me. I tried to arch my back and free myself from the restraints, but gravity pulled me back down onto the bed. I knew what was coming, and it filled me with dread.

He's going to fuck me in the ass. He's too big. He's too rough. I'll be unpleasant. It'll hurt.

My mind raced with these thoughts, each one more terrifying than the last, each one leaving behind a bright red trail, and when the words disappeared, the only image left was a giant, glowing red flag.

I have to say stop. I have to safe-word. I have to—

"Pet?" His voice broke through my panicked thoughts.

I struggled to catch my breath. "Master—"

"Do you remember your safe words?"

"Yes."

"What are they?"

"R-red to stop, yellow to pause—"

"I know you're scared. Do you want to use a safe word?"

All I could do was breathe heavily as the screen in front of me continued to pulse with each beat of my heart. But with every moment that passed, the intensity lessened, eventually fading into a useless dull backdrop.

"Lori," Max called.

I realized we'd all gone perfectly still, including Lori, whose hands ceased their gentle massage. She looked just as terrified as I felt. Maybe that's why she had been so tense earlier – because she knew what Max had in mind.

Coming out of her trance, she resumed her caresses, bending forward to kiss me, but I turned my head.

"Master, I'm scared, I mean it, I can't," I cried, looking at Max pleadingly, but he only smiled down at me softly.

"Of course, you can. You underestimate yourself. I believe you're scared, but I'll help you." His hand traced a path from my knee up my thigh, goosebumps trailing his touch, his voice dropping by an octave. "Do you know why men want to fuck women in the ass when the pussy is perfect on its own?"

"Why?" Lori and I asked simultaneously.

"Because it's just such a beautifully submissive thing, little one: to do something that scares you, something that might not feel good to you because you know it will feel good to me. So you do it for me, for my pleasure, to fulfill my wishes. And that's how I know—" in one abrupt motion he unbuttoned and dropped his pants, tossing them to the side —"that you're all mine."

His voice was a hungry growl now, and I held my breath, involuntarily shutting my eyes. Normally, the sight of his erect cock would thrill me, but right now, fear over-whelmed everything else. I had no desire to see it in all its formidable glory right now. This was going to hurt – was I ready to take it? For Max? Or...for myself? To prove something?

"Ah!" A sharp pain abruptly cut short my philosophical

deliberations. The immediate impression was that he had tightened the clamp on my nipples, until I realized he had actually removed them entirely, causing blood to rush back into the sensitive buds and making them throb painfully. Despite Lori quickly attempting to soothe the tender flesh with her hands, another cry escaped me. "That fucking hurts!"

"What hurts?" Max whispered.

And then I suddenly realized I didn't care about my nipples. What was actually causing me anguish was the aching emptiness between my thighs, inflamed and swollen, on edge and begging for just one... tiny... little... orgasm.

"Really hurts," I repeated less truculently and more thoughtfully, as I tried to get a grasp on what the hell was happening with my body, and threw a pleading glance in Max's directly, silently asking for... I didn't know what. Some form of relief.

I should have known that looking to him was a mistake because he simply smirked and said, "Oh, really?"And with a swift and efficient movement, spread my legs wide apart and bent them at the knees, draping them over his shoulders.

It all happened swiftly — Max seemed to know that if he dilly-dallied, he'd give a chance for intrusive second thoughts, the time to get up in my head about that I really wanted. Perhaps I would have said a safe word, at least "yellow," or begged him to postpone the experiment for later—in direct opposition of what I'd now promised him, twice. And I wasn't philosophically opposed to letting him have me. I was just scared, like he said. And Max seemed to realize that the more he talked to me, the more scared I was going to get.

As such, everything happened almost instantaneously.

A strong pressure for a second, a in impossible stretch, and then he was inside me, and I was holding my breath waiting for it, waiting for the anguish.

But the aguish never quite materialized. In fact, the sensation of having his huge cock inside me was almost impossible describe. Uncomfortable, alien, and something else...

What a fucking liar he was! I'd been waiting for him to start preparing me, stretching me, lubing me up, but instead he lubed up his own dick over the condom, while I was all about my own sensations instead of keeping watch on his treacherous ass. A liar and a cheater. This was not a fair way to play.

He was lucky. I was too terrified right now to raise any sort of objection. All I could do was whimper frantically, "Wait, wait, Max, please, wait!"

"Okay, you're okay, malysh, just breathe for me. Just like that."

He stayed inside me without moving, and peered into my eyes as if we were the only ones in the room. But Lori was there too, petting me, kissing me, soothing me as best she could while I got used to this new sensation of being split open. At long last, Max's attentive, penetrating eyes and Lori's soft hands seemed to take effect and I began to relax.

Finally, with a deep breath, I closed my eyes giving him the silent signal to continue. He shifted slightly, and began to move. His slow gentle thrusts were still intense enough that each one was a wave of a very specific kind of pain I'd never experienced before, but it was a pain mixed with a pleasure so intense that my breath escaped from my lips in uncontrollable moans.

Max had been telling the truth—I was giving myself to

him completely. This was, for me, the most submissive act so far, and the level of trust and connection between us palpably reached new heights as he gazed into my eyes, taking note of every subtle change on my face. In that moment, concern for his own pleasure seemed to fade as if it wasn't his flesh penetrating me with such intensity, but something more transcendental and powerful, like we were coming together in some sort of symbolic way.

Every movement he made brought discomfort, and release seemed out of reach... until he brought out the vibrator. With a gentle press of the tiny round device to my clitoris, my entire body arched, levitating off the bed, twisting in agonizing pleasure.

"Max!" I cried, and mere moments later, burst into a shuddering, shocking climax. Tears sprang from my eyes, and my mind exploded and went blank. I lost control completely—much like our first time together. It felt as if I were somewhere else, released from my body, my mind, even from Max's physical embrace.

I didn't notice as he intensified his movements and shook with his own orgasm without making a sound, as if this moment required solemnity.

Chapter Thirty-Seven

When Max gently withdrew and lay down beside me, I realized it had all lasted only a few minutes, though it felt like an eternity. Slowly, the earth resumed spinning, and I could measure time retroactively. I licked my lips and relaxed my face.

Lori smiled shyly at both of us, visibly relieved. Her eyes had brightened as if she had shared the experience and felt some release from her fears.

Max stood and left without a word, and soon the sound of running water came from the bathroom. Gradually returning to my senses, I stirred and, realizing I was still handcuffed to the bed, said quietly, "Lori, could you take off the handcuffs?"

She nodded and freed my wrists.

We embraced in silence. Words didn't feel necessary at that moment, even though I knew there would be plenty to discuss, ask, and share later. For now, we simply caressed each other's backs and exchanged gentle kisses, enveloped in a sense of warmth and relaxed comfort.

A loud noise from the door startled us, and we sprang apart as if caught doing something wrong.

The crop—Max's crop—had struck against the door frame.

He glared at Lori, giving us both a moment to feel properly afraid.

"Who gave you permission, sub, to take off her handcuffs?" he asked in a voice that was quiet yet menacing, sending a chill down my spine, though this time, it was Lori who was in trouble.

Max's gaze was frightening enough that I felt compelled to reach out and stroke Lori's forearm, not taking my eyes off him.

No matter how displeased he'd be at me, I wouldn't allow him to hurt her—I promised myself this even as I noticed my own pulse bounding in my ears.

Lori tensed up and slightly opened her mouth, her eyes filled with despair.

"Master, I thought..."

"You're not here to think, sub. You're here to obey," Max interrupted. He didn't raise his voice, but that didn't make it any easier for either of us. In fact, it made it worse: Lori's eyes filled despair and tears, and I felt my own face tingle as blood drained from it.

Quiet, but sinister, Max announced, "Five strikes with the crop, sub."

I sharply shifted my gaze to Lori's. She was gasping for air like a fish, looking at Max as if he had just handed her a death sentence.

He went on, "Stand up, bend over, and place your hands on the bed."

When was the last time Lori got punished by a man? Was it in her extreme masochism era, when she needed to be whipped until she bled to finally give herself over to the predators taking advantage of her? Was that what Lori was thinking about now, as she beheld my Dom with such abject horror? For a second, under the influence of her emotions, I felt genuine anger towards Max—he was being entirely too harsh. For a minor offense.

But then Max looked at me, and his expression completely changed. "Relax, malysh," he said very softly in a soothing tone, "this is mostly symbolic. But she needs you to help her get through this. Isn't that right, Lori?"

"Yes, master," she replied in a flat, emotionless voice, which as someone who knew her, I recognized as a sign of raging panic.

Nevertheless, she found the strength to stand and painfully slowly took the position he demanded, while Max silently walked around the bed, stopping behind her.

I silently touched her hand, which was white from tension—Lori's fingers were splayed so hard, pressing into the bed. She clearly wasn't aware of how tense her muscles were, fully absorbed by the effort of will that allowed her to stay in place instead of running away screaming.

In an effort to diffuse her tension, I put my hands on top of hers.

Max's first strike was not very strong—I realized that later. It didn't leave a mark, barely left a sound. But at that moment, we both jumped and closed our eyes, and Lori even let out a loud cry, as if she was in unbearable pain.

"Sub?" Max called out. "Color?" He seemed too impartial, to indifferent to me, and I was ready to call the whole thing myself, but Lori just obediently nodded, blinked, and, with difficulty parting her dry lips, whispered, "Green."

"Four more strikes," Max responded. "You can do it."

He struck her with the crop again—this time harder,

and I flinched again, but Lori, surprisingly, took the second strike almost without emotion or tension. On the contrary, her hands on the bedspread relaxed slightly, and a shiver ran through her body. Stroking her hand, I calmed down a bit, and for the next three strikes, I just closed my eyes and involuntarily clenched my own buttocks. Unlike a paddle, the slaps of the crop hit a very small and narrow surface and felt like mean little bites—sharp, painful, stinging, when not very harsh, and damn right unbearable if forceful.

However, Max never swung as hard as some of the sadists I'd observed at the club. Their kink was to cause truly intense pain, while Max only aimed to subdue, to achieve obedience, enhance arousal, elicit moans, pretty marks, slight apprehension. He wasn't aiming to torture.

It made sense that the tears in Lori's eyes at the end of the spanking rather indicated relief. She clearly expected more intense pain and couldn't believe until the very end that this was all, five tiny strikes with the crop and no further intensification of the punishment.

With the last slap, she let out a deep sigh, and when he patted her thigh as a sign that she could straighten up, Lori even smiled at me—I responded with the same shy smile, feeling suddenly proud of my Dom. He valued the trust Lori put in him. He wouldn't abuse it. He would play within her limits. I was suddenly flooded with relief myself, and happiness that Lori's foray back into games with men could be with my Dom, who was the best. I was happy to share.

Max commanded, "Play with each other for a little while, girls. But no orgasms, understood?

"Yes, master," we replied in unison and laughed.

"And no giggling," Max added in a dissatisfied tone,

frowning. He reached out and touched Lori's cheek with his knuckles, and she shrank into herself. "Yes, Sir."

"Relax, Lori. Come here, I have a few more words for you."

"Yes, master?"

Her eyelashes instantly fluttered upwards, and her eyes reflected such a pure desire to serve, and please, and be obedient, that I swallowed hard in awe. I wondered if my face looked the same when I was at my most submissive. And if not, if it ever would.

To my amazement, Max turned Lori away from me and leaned over to her ear to whisper something to her, giving me a devilishly sly and provocative look. A momentary outrage rose in my chest—the idea that they had any secrets from me when we were in bed together decisively did not appeal to me. But then he beckoned me over, moving Lori aside, and leaned towards my ear:

"Best not relax, sunshine. If you accidentally come, your pussy will get a spanking."

"Yes, master."

For a second, the memory of how he spanked me between the legs during the math exam scene almost catapulted me over the orgasm wall with just that thought. And now I was in confusion—wasn't it better to let myself go? What's wrong with being gently spanked in that place if it brings so much pleasure?

But as soon as Max saw the lascivious look on my face, Max narrowed his eyes. A dangerous smile played on his lips. "There are ways and ways I could torture your sweet cunt, Liza. For example, I could do it with this nasty little flogger I have, and, believe me, it will be torture."

Feeling a cold shiver run down my spine and the smile slipping off my face, I lowered my eyes. Was it just my imagination, or was Max a little drunk on power? Perhaps he was full of his own importance after I allowed him to fuck my ass? Or was it me, was I angrier than usual because I expected some special treatment after this? Suddenly, I craved tenderness, and no longer wanted any harsh punishments or pain.

Reaching for that tenderness, I turned to Lori when we both moved onto the bed. And if in the first few seconds I still felt Max's gaze, very soon I fell into this sensation of bliss and warmth. Once again, I thought it was impossible to find something like this in a man's arms. How did people live with one but without the other? Lori's Jasmine scent, soft palms, sweet tongue. As soon as I kissed her, I forgot everything that existed in the world outside this bed.

We kissed like crazy, greedily caressing each other, as if it were a competition.

No, that's incorrect. We just missed each other, and it felt good to let go and be together, this time with Max's permission and even under his eye. Suddenly feeling his gaze on me again—hard to tell how many minutes later—I was just sucking and teasing Lori's nipples, while she, lying on top of me, was teasing my clitoris with her fingers.

Feeling that I was on the verge of orgasm, I pushed her hand away, but then she slid down, covering my chest, belly, and then my lower abdomen with kisses.

Opening my eyes, through a haze, I found Max's eyes and felt a real explosion of pleasure when I realized that he was watching and smiling from just a few feet away. And I was pleased that he was watching Lori caress me. Immersed in this new sensation of warmth and a sudden surge of tender feelings towards both of them, I lost track of time again.

Which was probably why I missed the moment Lori

made her way down to my pussy, and her tongue found its way to my clit. She made a few strong insistent movements before I could resist or move away. It felt too good, and I let it happen, mind my clueing in too late to stop the takeoff. A deep moan escaped my throat as I twisted with it, and Max's lips, still in my field of vision, curved into a triumphant smile.

Damn, he wasn't angry. This was the point the entire time: he set me up to fail so he could punish me as promised.

Jerking at the last moment, twisting away as much as I could—which was not at all— I was astounded to realize that Lori was holding my knees apart and down, and wasn't about to let go. Just a few more passes of her hard-working little tongue, and my whole body convulsed with deep spasms that heated my blood sending it steaming right up to my head. Further resistance was already pointless, and I gave in, falling back onto the bed to enjoy the moment. Only one thought remained in my mind: "What a fucking traitor, this one, too."

Chapter Thirty-Eight

The first thing I heard when the ringing in my ears subsided a bit was a soft, velvety voice:

"Good girl, Lori. Well done. Come here."

Lori—well done? What? Judging by his voice, he was as pleased as a cat.

"What?" I exclaimed aloud, propping myself up on my elbows, "Lori, did you do that on purpose? Max... you... you... both—traitors! Lori, you snake! Max, you..."

Max's stern voice clearly contrasted with his gaze—his eyes were laughing when he admonished, "Better stop here, malysh. Don't make it worse on yourself."

"Did you order her to do that to me? On purpose?" I interrupted, not even pretending to be afraid of his feigned severity.

"Of course. And I warned you, baby. So, why don't you close your big mouth and patiently wait for your punishment while Lori receives her reward."

Max's grin was wide, lighting up his whole face with pure delight, and Lori was blushing, but I wasn't angry at her, glaring only at my Dom. What a perfectly evil, mean game he played. Since when did the ever-serious, mature Max utilize such cheap tricks? Just incredible.

While one part of me raged in irritation, the other was giddy right along along with him. Something in me enjoyed this new game and this new Max, who looked more relaxed, happier, than usual, especially when he gently took Lori's hand and turned her to face me, with her back to him, his hands cupping her breasts.

Casting a devilish glance in my direction, he whispered something into her ear, making her shiver in his embrace, and she nodded, closing her eyes. Then he looked at me. He said nothing, but his message might have as well have been shouted through a bullhorn. *Eyes on me.*

Max's dark hands glided over Lori's pale skin, gently, delicately, and patiently, and from the way she softened and melted under his touch, it was clear: he'd been deliberate in setting a pace at which she could accept and enjoy his attention. He cupped her swelling breasts, lightly squeezing her nipples, then ran his hands down her ribcage, over her ass and trembling thighs, then back up her stomach, passing near but not quite over her pussy.

I was eager to see what he did next, but his hands were back on her breasts, then her sides, her thighs, stomach...

And breasts again.

And again, and again... and again... In the same circuit over, and over, and over.

The only sounds in the room were Lori's soft moans and the din of street noise faintly audible from beyond the windows. The beating of my own heart slowly rose in volume, too, as I watched Max's fingers graze nearer and nearer to the neat triangle at the top of Lori's thighs, only to pull back, as if it had been by accident. I could feel the touch of his fingertips vicariously through her, recalling what it had felt like on my own skin just moments ago.

The whole scene, all three of us, balanced on nothing, it seemed, like a house of cards, and I held my breath afraid to disturb the equilibrium. As I watched, I felt myself enter an almost trance-like state, as though I might have been dreaming this, sleeping with my eyes open, hypnotized. Lori also seemed to be in the same type of trance, and didn't flinch as Max gently guided her ankle to the side. Spreading her feet wider, he bent down and ran his fingers over her crotch.

He might as well have done this to me. I felt every impulse, shuddering with pleasure, my pussy clenching desperately.

He did it again.

And then again... and again... and again... until his fingers slipped inside, almost by accident.

Lori's legs buckled, and Max caught her in his arms, laying her on the bed with the utmost care, as if she were made of crystal. I quickly moved aside to stay out of his way, but he beckoned me over and pointed to her lips.

He wanted me to kiss her.

Approaching slowly, so as not to spook the entranced Lori, I bent over her.

We were both somewhat dazed, and Lori shivered slightly when my lips touched hers. I gently moved my tongue, caressing her and watching out of the corner of my eye as Max spread her legs again and played with his fingers, slipping them inside more and more frequently. After some time, he leaned over and softly placed his hand on my shoulder, gently separating me from her.

"Malysh?"

"Yes, master."

"Kiss me."

"Yes, master."

I reached for him, emotions surging through me, and without hesitation, he grabbed hold of the back of my head and pulled me in close. Given the ethereal nature of our the scene, his kiss was unexpectedly fierce, our lips meeting in a passionate and possessive embrace. It was all-consuming and utterly dominant.

Lori remained quiet between us, motionless and breathing rhythmically as if she were in a deep enchanted sleep. The only thing that seemed to ground her to us was Max's hand between her legs, caressing her.

"Is she asleep?" I whispered, glancing down at her, when our lips separated.

"Not quite. Lori?" he softly called, looking at her, and Lori's eyelashes slowly fluttered and then lifted, "Please come back to us."

Her body fasciculated all at once, and she let out a long, quiet sigh, eventually opening her eyes and fixing Max with a long and clear stare.

"Lori, I need explicit consent. Are you willing to submit your body to me? Are you consenting to sex with me?"

The expression in her eyes changed almost impercepti- bly. She glanced at me for a split second, then looked back at him.

"Liza will stay right here. Right, baby?"

"Yes, master," I replied with an eagerness I didn't expect in my voice.

An unspoken longing had stirred inside me, the desperate desire for Lori to give in to Max, like I had. The idea consumed me in that moment, the wish for them to come together in one intense moment and for me to bear witness. It wasn't just about them, it was also about *us*, all three of us - Lori's salvation, Max's healing abilities that had kept her spirit alive, and my love for both of them—yes, both of them—burning bright, unlikely as it seemed.

"Yes, master," Lori said and closed her eyes.

Max nodded and looked at me. He smiled. "Liza, relax, everything will be fine."

"Yes, master," I smiled back and saw a faint smile on Lori's lips too.

"Keep your hands and lips within her reach," Max said.

I bent forward again to kiss her lips as I felt Max slowly pitch forward and the world tilt.

"Yes, master..."

His words drifted to my ears, but my eyes were fixed on Lori. She looked peaceful and soft, the very embodiment of submission as she placed her trust in this man before her.

And in me, too, of course, I hoped, basking in her soft sighs as she and Max were joined in their desire, and mine.

———

Max had started by making love to Lori gently, while I kissed and caressed her, but something was wrong. Lori became restless , flushed, and her face didn't show the signs of pleasure I would have expected.

"I can't..." she whispered.

A flash of worry—she was still affected by her trauma, but then, I understood the problem: she couldn't come this way.

Max stopped, refusing to go on without her, or maybe he couldn't come either, as though they hit some kind of plateau. Lori started to cry. No wonder. Maybe she thought she was regressing in the work she'd done, feeling desperate.

I watched helplessly as Max comforted her with the utmost patience.

Once she was calm, however, Max was quick to switch gears, turning ruthless again.

"In the corner, Liza," he ordered, and as I scrambled out of bed, terrified to see him get feral like that, he flipped Lori roughly onto her stomach, and without any preambles, slammed into her from behind.

The change in him startled me, but her cries belied her ecstasy. It was all part of the game. He wasn't really going feral on Lori; he was giving Lori what she needed. Clearly, Lori wasn't into the gentle, tender-loving care style, at least not once she got comfortable, so he fucked her hard and fast, holding her down by the scruff—and this way, she came almost immediately, screaming into the pillow.

When Lori stilled, Max beckoned me over, joining me on the other side of the bed. "Come here, malysh," he murmured.

I crawled over, convinced this was the time for the promised spanking to my poor pussy, but Max whispered, "Let's see if you naughty little cunt can redeem itself," still trying to sound threatening, but all of us knew perfectly well he was not in the mood to be a big bad domly Dom any more.

Feral with Lori, he'd saved the gentle, tender-loving-care for me.

And as I wrapped my arms around him, timidly, worried I wasn't allowed, relieved to find this time, I was, I realized I was okay with that.

Chapter Thirty-Nine

Lori

Sleep? Yeah, right. After the day she'd had? No chance. This might just be the most pivotal day of her life, and what a grand finale it had!

Lori replayed it all in her mind on an endless loop, starting with that strange little scene at the club. A tiny pang of guilt tugged at her, about Nik. She'd gone to him, offered herself, begged to stay, and in the end, he was the one who essentially ended up serving her. He relaxed her, got her in the right headspace, and delivered one heck of an orgasm without asking for anything in return. It was as if he knew all along that he was only prepping her, so she could go on her way to Max and Liza.

When she called Max, then later walked into his apartment, there were a few heart-pounding moments when she considered bolting right back out the door. What if he rejected her? Or worse, what if he used his status as her sex therapist to politely decline? And the worst fear of all— what if it was Liza who turned her down? Lori didn't think she could bear that.

But then Max had said, "You spent the night alone with

a man, felt relaxed enough to come in his presence. Do you think you still need therapy?"

"I—" she hadn't known what to say, what answer he was looking for.

As Max got up from the kitchen table to brew coffee, he delivered his verdict with the authority of a judge. "My professional opinion is that our work together is done."

"But I still don't know if I can let a man touch me," Lori shot back, indignation flaring. It felt like she was being dismissed. She marched right up to him, not about to let him get rid of her that easily.

Max turned on his heel, suddenly face-to-face with her. They were inches apart—no touching, but close enough that Lori realized she wasn't afraid of him. Not even a little. And from the surprisingly lusty look in Max's eyes, it was clear he had no intention of rejecting her.

"I guess I'm wrong," she muttered.

She nearly took a step back, but Max's arm snaked around her waist, holding her close. "Look, Lori," he began, his voice softening, "This is... highly irregular, do you agree?"

She nodded. It was.

"I can't get involved with a patient and I can't abandon a patient."

She lowered her head, readying herself for what she feared most.

"But it's always up to the patient if they want to...leave therapy. If they want to, say... *fire* me."

The meaning of his words sank in slowly.

"Then...you're fired!" Lori blurted out, a giggle bubbling up as a wave of giddy relief washed over her.

"Oh, no," Max quipped. "Well. What shall we do now that I'm no longer your psychotherapist?"

Lori's smile wavered as she fumbled for an answer.

Max pulled her in a little closer, his voice dropping to a whisper. "If you want, you can stay the night and become something more than a client to me... and Liza." His tone was low, suggestive, leaving no doubt that he wanted this too.

———

Finally, Lori felt herself drifting off, lulled by the sweet replay of the night in her mind. But then a jolt of panic hit her—what if it had all been a dream? Her eyes snapped open to check if Max and Liza were really there beside her, that this night actually happened. Right then, Max's eyes fluttered open, meeting hers over Liza's sleeping form. Usually, when Lori met a man's gaze in an intimate setting, she would look away, but this time she wanted to smile— and Max gave her a gentle smile back.

"How are you?" he mouthed, shifting slightly toward her.

His left hand rested on Liza's hip, while the other was tucked under the pillow. Lori's gaze drifted to the curve of his shoulder, feeling a pleasant hum inside. For the first time, she could admire a man's body—its strength, its form— without any hint of fear or discomfort.

The tart scent of his body, the roughness of his skin, and the warmth of his hand holding her neck when he slowly but determinedly fucked her from behind, making her scream with pleasure... These were sensations that were etched into her memory forever.

"I'm good," she replied honestly, smiling at him.

After a moment, without breaking eye contact, she placed her hand on Liza's thigh next to his.

Max playfully pushed her away. "Mine."

"Ours," Lori corrected, gently stroking the soft rounded buttock. Liza mumbled something in her sleep, and they both smiled, holding their breath to avoid waking her.

Lori's mind began to wander—maybe one day, Max might let her dominate Liza. Maybe it could even be a team effort...

"Don't even think about it," Max whispered, reading her thoughts, though the glint in his eyes suggested that anything was possible.

"Think about what?" Lori teased, trying to provoke him. But it was no use—Max was too content, too calm.

"Good night," he smirked, his voice tender.

"Good night," Lori echoed, closing her eyes with a serene smile.

Epilogue

We slept all day, and waking up after was the last thing I wanted to do, even when the quiet sounds outside clued me in that it was evening. The room had cooled off—Max must've opened the window while we slept. Shivering, I darted out of bed, shut it, and dove back under the covers, wedging myself between Max and Lori. We'd slept like a sandwich, with me as the filling. The main event. Even in this small detail, Max had been thoughtful, making sure I wasn't stuck on the side, feeling left out. Did he know how many conflicting emotions I'd have to deal with when I woke up?

Because I was a mess—afraid to wake up, afraid to face the day. It had been my first threesome, my first time with anal, my first time doing half the things Max did with us until morning. Pushing us to our limits, then pulling us back with his tenderness, his certainty, even when Lori cried and I was scared for her and for myself, until we both calmed down. It was extraordinary.

My favorite was watching Lori's confidence soar by the minute, until she became openly defiant to Max, teasing him, doing the opposite of what he ordered with a mischie-vous glint in her eye.

Max, of course, tried to maintain a serious facade, but eventually gave in to his own amusement. "I'll slap you if you don't behave!" he threatened in his best booming voice, but Lori just covered her mouth with her hand, laughing.

I was giddy.

And it all ended so very explosively, in such delicious manner, even the way we passed out from exhaustion together...

"Malysh? Are you okay?" Max suddenly opened his eyes, and I flinched, realizing I had been moving around and probably talking to myself.

I timidly smiled at him and buried my nose under his arm, and he carefully hugged me, trying not to wake Lori. "Probably," I said as I nuzzled his arm. "Good morning,"

"Good morning," he replied, touching the top of my head with his lips.

We lay quietly for a while, then stealthily moved to the kitchen.

"Sit," Max said. "Naked coffee time."

We lay there for a bit before sneaking off to the kitchen.

"Sit," Max commanded. "Naked coffee time."

I laughed, but he was dead serious. "Your duty in the morning is to adorn my home."

"You're confusing me with a Christmas tree," I retorted, but proudly straightened my back, openly enjoying his greedy gaze on my chest.

We exchanged a few more barbs and jokes before I dared to quietly ask, "Did I imagine it, or were you somehow different, Max? Last night, and... even now?"

"It's possible," he answered, then added matter-of-factly, "I had a therapy session on Friday, paid for a three-month course."

"Good psychologist?"

I swallowed hard. For a moment, I felt uneasy. What if they "cure" him to the point where he doesn't want to be with me anymore?

"Yes, my colleague, we studied together. He's good. What's on your mind, baby?"

"Nothing," I smiled, taking a deep breath. Silly thoughts come and go, no use dwelling on them.

Max's voice dropped to a lower, more serious tone. "Last night was different for me too. I'd like to know how you felt about it."

"You already know," I said, smiling. "You always read my mind."

"I'd still like to hear it from you. For instance, why did my jealousy bother you, and how do you feel now?"

Max pulled up a stool and fixed me with a gaze so intense I almost choked on my coffee.

"Well...I didn't want to fall back into that old trap of feeling like I can't move an inch without a jealous boyfriend breathing down my neck. But last night, it was different—there was this whole other level of trust, between me, you, and Lori..."

I threw Max a cautious, slightly nervous glance, but he just nodded in earnest approval.

"A lot of people think BDSM is all about domination or dishing out pain, but for me, it's about trust," he said, gently tucking a strand my hair behind my ear. "You can't let yourself be punished if you don't trust the person doing it. I can't hurt someone unless I trust they're sincere in letting me. You wouldn't let yourself be tied up by someone you don't trust, right? And if you're jealous, you don't trust. I want to do all those things with you—nothing else matters. So, jealousy isn't really an option, is it?"

"Yeah, you're right. I trust both of you so much right now. Especially you."

Max looked into my eyes, his expression serious, but I caught a hint of a smile in his gaze. Just one more second of this overwhelming tenderness, and I'd be declaring this the most romantic moment of my life. But then, a floorboard creaked behind me, breaking the spell. Lori stood in the kitchen doorway, wrapped in a sheet like a sleepy ghost.

"And do you know what I trust the most this early in the morning?" she inquired in a sweet voice, which nonetheless carried an unusual assertiveness.

"It's evening now, Lori," I blinked in astonishment, correcting her automatically.

"Even more important! So many missed hours. I trust in the availability of coffee. Max. Tell me you can be depended on in this way too."

Max silently poured her a huge mug, which she sipped loudly.

"And now," she announced, "Food. It's evening. It's dinner time. Not even an egg in sight!"

She marched to the fridge, muttering under her breath, "Romantics, having a moment, a heart-to-heart... but can't even bother with an omelet. They're quick to screw me, but feeding me? Nah..."

"It seems Lori's got a bit of a different vibe today," Max noted with an amused wink. "I suspect after the omelet, someone's getting a spanking on the kitchen table."

"Max, if you don't tell me right now where the frying pan and cooking oil are, I'm going to eat you," Lori snapped, closing the fridge door with her hip. "And not in a good way."

She stood there, both hands full of eggs, with a hungry look that made me a little uneasy. It was like she was genuinely considering which part of him to bite.

"I think we'd better do what she says," I whispered, leaning towards him. "Smile and wave."

"Probably," Max agreed, carefully circling Lori as he opened the stove and pulled out a large frying pan. After another cautious glance in her direction, he placed a bottle of sunflower oil on the table and grabbed a few more eggs from the fridge. "Make omelets for us too."

"Naturally. You can't survive on romance alone," Lori snorted, as if this was our routine, as if we'd been waking up and having breakfast together as a family for years.

The END.

DID YOU LIKE WHAT YOU JUST READ? ## DO YOU WANT MORE?

Go here ASAP to find the next story being told about the colorful characters who visit Subspace. In *You Asked For It, Malysh,* Irina finds herself the prize in a bet. A proud domme, she can't back down, and her evening turns into something entirely unexpected as she sees her friends in a whole new light.

EXCERPT:

"I'm surprised to see you here. The only thing that would surprise me more would be if you actually bet." He pats me on the shoulder.

Suppressing a flash of anger, I respond to Nik's overly

familiar pat with an equally condescending tap on his muscular bicep. Where does he get off? I'm a Domme too!

"Life sometimes does surprise us," I say, archly.

Nik's no idiot. He's picked up on my not-so-subtle rebuke. He doesn't react negatively, accepts the consequence with grace. I can appreciate that. "Is that so?"

"It is."

Standing next to him in heels, I'm almost his height, and I confidently meet his gaze with the same assured look, certain I've won this round.

A few moments later, Nik proves me wrong. With a crooked smirk, he winks and says, "I respect those who take risks, darling. Glad to see you're one who does. I'll bet against you. I might get to touch you yet."

Read more right now, here! New episode released every other day!

Also by Alexis Rey

DID YOU LIKE WHAT YOU JUST READ?

Read more!

BDSM ROMANCE

Plush

Silk

Leather

Jewel

Ink

Jute

West of Wonderland

Girl Wonder — PREORDER NOW!

DARK MAFIA ROMANCE

Brutal

SERIALS

Master Me Softly

COMING SOON!

Between Desires

A standalone about one woman's quest for what she really needs

You can find it here

The Master's Toy

A dark novella of taboo love and manipulation

About the Author

Alexis Rey, the emerging spicy romance author, is convinced that spicy fictional worlds are far more enticing than our everyday existence, and her readers couldn't agree more. While the rest of us are navigating the drudgeries of reality, Alexis is off fulfilling her calling as the alchemist of escapism. When she's not writing, she's "enjoying" her full-time job, and spends quality time with her husband, two kids, and orange cat.

Sign up for the newsletter and keep up with the latest !
Alexis's Newsletter Signup
Check out the website!
https://www.authoralexisrey.com/

Made in the USA
Monee, IL
08 December 2024